CRITICAL ACCLAIM FOR
Margaret Murphy

GOODNIGHT, MY ANGEL

'Sets new standards in the psychological thriller . . . It's hard to believe something this assured is a first novel. A remarkable debut – threatening, thrilling and thoroughly authentic.' Val McDermid

'Debut crime novels that can be praised unreservedly are rare. Murphy creates terrific menace and tension, well-climaxed.' Marcel Berlins, *The Times*

'An accomplished first novel by Margaret Murphy [who] knows how to wind up the psychological tension as confidently as many more experienced suspense writers.' Susanna Yager, *Sunday Telegraph*

'There is an assurance about the menace that makes this first book welcome.' Tom Deveson, *Sunday Times*

'Will hold the reader from start to finish and is, to coin a cliché, unputdownable.' *Crime Time*

THE DESIRE OF THE MOTH

'A suspenseful thriller.' *Sunday Telegraph*

'Margaret Murphy's first novel was one of last year's most impressive debuts . . . A talented crime writer with the ability to become one of the best.' *The Times*

'The plot is intricately woven and spaced with many mysterious, sinister twists, which keep the reader enthralled right to the end.' *The Leader*

'A thriller that twangs the nerves.' *Peterborough Evening Telegraph*

'The idea is brilliant, with some genuinely frightening scenes.' *Yorkshire Post*

'Thrilling reading.' *Woman's Own*

Caging the Tiger

Margaret Murphy gained a degree in environmental biology in 1980 and has since taught biology and science in schools in Lancashire and Liverpool. She is now head of a department which specializes in teaching children with dyslexia in a school on the Wirral.

Caging the Tiger is Margaret's third novel, following *Goodnight, My Angel* and *The Desire of the Moth*. *Goodnight, My Angel* was shortlisted for the First Blood Award for best first crime novel 1996.

Her fourth novel, *Past Reason*, is published in hardback by Macmillan.

MARGARET MURPHY

Caging the Tiger

PAN BOOKS

First published 1998 by Macmillan

This edition published 1999 by Pan Books
an imprint of Macmillan Publishers Ltd
25 Eccleston Place, London SW1W 9NF
Basingstoke and Oxford
Associated companies throughout the world
www.macmillan.co.uk

ISBN 0 330 36975 X

1 3 5 7 9 8 6 4 2

A CIP catalogue record for this book is available from
the British Library.

Typeset by Intype London Ltd
Printed and bound in Great Britain by
Mackays of Chatham plc, Chatham, Kent

For Barbara Melling, whose optimism bolstered
me throughout the wilderness years.

ACKNOWLEDGEMENTS

I would like to thank Professor Jeff Parker, of Liverpool University, who sacrificed a sizeable chunk of his busy schedule to discuss Behavioural Ecology research methods with me, and who let me look around the Population Biology Research Group Lab and talk to his postgraduate researchers. For their insight into research techniques, I am grateful.

Any malpractice implied in the story is my own invention, and any errors of scientific procedure, I claim wholly for myself.

O tiger's heart, wrapp'd in a woman's hide!

King Henry VI, Part III, I.iv, 137

Chapter One

He looks peaceful in death. It is as she had imagined it so many times before. His eyes are closed. Once so full of censure, so apt to accuse, at times so piercingly contemptuous. Now, mercifully, all of this is shut out from her, or rather within him, and she will never again feel the heat of his stare. There is no surprise, no fear in the strong muscles of his face, now relaxed, expressionless. So, she had remembered to close his eyes, a practised, gentle stroke of her hand over his face, just as she had released from his grip the sheets, straightening them, folding his hands neatly, one over the other.

Frowning, she puts down her briefcase, eases the bag of shopping on to the bare boards. Something is not right. She studies the scene with detached interest. Afternoon sunlight billows in brief shallow bursts through the open curtain. Spring sunshine, chasing clouds. His body, naked beneath the sheets, lies calm, unmoved by the play of light, peaceful, still warm. His face is tranquil, beautiful as it always had been in repose, his hair, almost black against the white crispness of the sheets seems to catch and flare in the boisterous bursts of sunlight, and she glances anxiously at his face, afraid that the quick movement of light will stir him. She is safe, *for his eyes are closed* – she had not forgotten that. Drained by the effort of concentration, she longs almost to go to the bed and lie beside him but, still frowning, forbids herself. *What is it?*

'Something's not right,' she murmurs. Ruth will know. She understands the symbolism of dreams, the arcane language. A slight rush of breath – the blood. So much of it. Too much. It has spilled on to the top sheet, red, glistening, not yet congealed. Sunlight flashes on to it with every passing cloud, its coppery smell weights the air. The smell which of late has banished her from the dissection room, a barrier to her presence and another cause for his ill-concealed contempt.

'Helen? What is it?'

The telephone receiver is in her hand. She can't remember how it got there. She is in the hallway and Ruth's voice comes to her again, more urgently, 'Helen, has something happened?'

Helen focuses on three bright drops of crimson spilling on to the floor as clouds part momentarily and the sun bursts, sudden and hot, through the stained glass of the front door. 'It's not right,' she repeats, as if that explains everything.

Chapter Two

Jack Nelson's amber eyes took in the scene. A little, dark-haired woman sat at the corner of the scrubbed pine kitchen table at the centre of the tableau of three, her head drooping, hair falling on to her face, hiding most of it. She was shaking her head at something the other woman was saying. The second woman bent over her, a tall lean blonde, firmly in control, she seemed to be offering advice. She had noticed him come into the room but ignored him and continued talking in a low murmur to the dark-haired woman. A little off to one side a man stood, apparently trying not to listen to what was being said. He straightened up and stepped towards Nelson, introducing himself as DS Hackett. The new guy. An import from Warrington. Tall enough and beefy, but ginger-haired. In Nelson's estimation that was a serious impediment; to Nelson, ginger hair was an irrefutable mark of weakness. He nodded to Hackett, barely glancing away from the two women, sliding his eyes over them as if searching for something.

'Mrs Wilkinson?' he said at last, and the smaller woman looked up. Nice eyes. Blue. Not showing much at the moment except bewilderment, but eyes that could betray her, given time.

'Doctor Wilkinson.'

For a few seconds Nelson let his eyes rest on the professor's wife, on her pretty, oval face and small, slightly pouting mouth, then her head drooped again and she seemed to have forgotten him. He turned slowly to look at the second woman, raising both eyebrows in an ironical twist.

The blonde woman rose to her full height, poised, pausing to notice his wet raincoat and dripping hair before repeating, 'It's *Doctor* Wilkinson.'

'And you are?' Nelson thought he saw a spark of humour kindle around the heavy-lidded eyes. A shade or two lighter than Dr Wilkinson's, they gave out conflicting signals: impatient intelligence and bored indolence.

'Ruth Marks,' she said. Then, '*Doctor* Marks.'

'Detective Inspector Nelson,' he said, showing his warrant card perfunctorily. 'Now we've got the formalities out of the way, perhaps you could tell us what happened, Dr Wilkinson.'

Her head rose and he caught a glimpse of anxiety in her large blue eyes and a flash of white teeth as she prepared to answer.

'Helen isn't well enough to talk.'

Nelson scowled angrily at Dr Marks. 'You're her GP, are you – *Doctor*?'

'I'm her friend, and it doesn't take a medical degree to see that she's in shock.'

He held Dr Marks's gaze for a full half minute, but it seemed the doctor was insusceptible to the smouldering heat of his stare. The wide, attractive mouth even curved into the beginnings of a smile, as though, having scrutinized his grizzled features, the rainwater dripping into his eyes and irritating his skin, she had conceived some private joke against him, and Nelson, who was unused to such a level return of his most searing glare, was close to being routed. When the doorbell rang, interrupting their silent tussle, Sergeant Hackett, who had watched the exchange with interest, thought he detected a hint of relief in the inspector's eyes.

The visitor was Dr Wilkinson's GP, Indian or Arab, Nelson guessed, with the unlikely name of Patterson. Ruth Marks had telephoned him. He nodded at the two police officers and then, without asking for permission, led Helen Wilkinson to a room off the wide hallway. Dr Marks followed them and Nelson, accepting reluctantly that there was nothing he could do until the GP had finished his examination, rounded on Hackett.

'You've let that ruddy woman run the whole show – letting her phone the GP. Allowing her to twitter on to Wilkinson – I don't suppose you know what she said to her. I don't suppose you got any sense out of the wife.'

Hackett eyed his new boss with cool composure. Jack Nelson – nicknamed Jack the Knife – had a reputation which extended far beyond the small patch of Cheshire he had worked since entering the force twenty-five years ago. Some said he had earned the name because he was sharp, clever. Others, who had been at the receiving end of his irascible intolerance of less than messianic zeal for the job, said he was called 'The Knife' because he was a back-stabbing bastard who wasn't above giving the blade a final twist after he'd stuck it in. Hackett, who had been on the force a good deal longer than his pale, unblemished skin and youthful looks at first indicated, knew that there were reasons for Nelson's behaviour.

'Dr Marks had already made the call when we arrived, sir.' He paused, then added, 'I'm afraid I couldn't get any more sense out of Dr Wilkinson than you did.'

The sergeant's pale green cats' eyes and boy-smooth face showed no outward sign of insolence, but Nelson, who was sensitive to such things, thought he caught a whiff of insubordination. He produced a handkerchief from his pocket and dried his face. 'Talk me through events so far,' he said.

Hackett gave a clear, concise and pointedly unhurried report. 'Dr Marks says she got a call from Dr Wilkinson at four-fifteen. She came straight over. When she found the professor's body, she called us and the GP. We arrived at four forty-five. The police surgeon and the SOCOs got here just before you did.'

'Weapon?'

'A knife—'

'I flaming know that, Hackett! There's a few pints of blood spilled over the sheets in the bedroom, and a ruddy great gash in the poor bastard's chest to account for it.'

Nelson had reached the house less than twenty minutes earlier, shaking the water from his raincoat, ill-tempered and breathless from having to walk from the next street where he had been forced to park his car – tourists unwilling to pay the parking fees in the town centre and more bloody tourists booked into the B&Bs which cluttered this end of Chester.

He had stamped dirt on to the mosaic tiling of the vestibule and had tramped more into the threadbare pile of the green-and-blue runner of the hallway. At the bedroom his progress had been halted by the police surgeon and his team. One stab wound. Fatal. Punctured the heart. Fairly recent – one to two hours old. He had been obliged to view the body from the doorway.

'I was about to say,' Hackett resumed, unruffled, still in that warm, measured tone, 'there's a knife missing from the block in the kitchen. A boning knife.'

'How do you know it was a boning knife?'

'Dr Marks told me. The others have been taken away for forensic exam.'

'What time did Dr Wilkinson arrive home?'

'I haven't been able to question her yet, sir.'

Nelson uttered a grunt of disgust. 'I've had enough of this!' He strode through the hallway to the door opposite, through which he had seen Wilkinson and Marks disappear with the GP, and was reaching for the handle when the door opened. He gasped, surprised, not by the sudden appearance of the dark-skinned GP, but by the marked contrast between this room and the rest of the house. Even in his foul mood Nelson had been struck by the faded complexion of colour. There was a contrived air of refined dilapidation in the worn blocks of herringbone flooring and the carpets that covered the centre portions of the rooms in miserly, washed out squares. The walls of the bedroom were dove-white and there were no paintings. The skirtings were slate-grey − even the curtains were patterned in an indeterminate series of beige and grey stripes. The most vivid colour in the room was the gout of blood splashed immoderately over the fresh white sheets.

The GP stepped back, allowing Nelson into the sitting room. Its colours were vibrant, almost glaring, after the dignified shabbiness of the rest. One wall was hung with a huge abstract in orange, gold and green. Another was decorated with a mural of tropical plants. Bookcases stuffed with books, journals and multicoloured box files ranged from floor to ceiling along one side of the room and a picture window looked out on to a large, walled garden, already thick with primroses and daffodils.

'My patient isn't well enough to answer questions, Inspector,' the doctor said, taking possession of the situation, and with it the woman Nelson needed to interview.

Where have I heard that before? Nelson thought. The doctor looked ill at ease. Nelson guessed this was his first appointment. Young doctor, eager to impress, to establish himself, and since he was already on the university health care listing, he had apparently taken his first few steps up the ladder of professional success. Not a bad placement. He knew about positive discrimination rules and, glancing back at the handsome and athletic GP, wondered if it applied to mixed race. The professor's wife was lying on her side on a sofabed set at an angle, facing the picture window. He couldn't tell if her eyes were open, but he sensed from the tension and the careful control of her breathing that she was awake, waiting for him to leave. Well, he wasn't about to make it so easy for her.

'We need to talk to Dr Wilkinson as a matter of urgency, Dr Patterson,' he said, with as much civility as he could muster, given the circumstances. From the corner of his eye he could see Ruth Marks watching him, that look of indolent amusement masking an intense scrutiny.

'Tomorrow,' said Patterson. 'You can see she isn't up to questioning just now.'

'Her husband has been murdered. We haven't time to observe social niceties.'

Patterson looked into the ravaged face of the inspector. His uneven complexion, a barometer of his feelings, had taken on an angry flush. From habit, Patterson made a rapid diagnosis: chronic alcoholism; some degree of liver cirrhosis judging by the slight jaundice, particularly visible around the whites of the eyes; acne rosacea, caused and then exacerbated by the drinking binges – spirits, rather than beer, judging by the gritty edge to Nelson's voice. A more subjective assessment detected a glimmer of incipient madness in the policeman's amber eyes. Patterson was afraid of the inspector and unsure of his ground, but he would not back down. Helen was relying on him. 'I have my patient's welfare to think of, Inspector, and I cannot allow an interview until I have examined her in the morning.'

Nelson glowered from Patterson to Ruth Marks, and Patterson was struck once again by the wild wolf-like tint of the inspector's amber eyes. Then suddenly and unexpectedly, the inspector turned and left the room.

'Has he gone?'

'We're alone now,' Ruth answered. Patterson had followed shortly after the inspector, leaving a prescription, should Helen consent to taking something to help her sleep. Ruth knelt beside her and stroked her hair. Helen watched her silently for some time, her eyes, a shade of blue that suggested deep water, were troubled; she seemed to struggle with something she wasn't sure she wanted to say or didn't know how to ask. Ruth waited for her to find the words. When they came, they sounded somewhere between fear and hope.

'He really is dead, isn't he?'

'Yes, he really is.'

'Oh.' Helen stared past Ruth at the primroses, flattened like tissue paper by the last heavy downpour. 'I thought—'

'What did you think?'

Helen shrugged. What could she tell Ruth? That she had thought this was another of her fantasies, a stage set – her revenge on Edward? Sometimes, as now, she felt a sapping of her energies, as though her mind had limped away from her body, the dissociation of the one from the other acting as a prophylactic, a barrier to the disease she feared was infecting her mind, anaesthetizing the almost physical pain she felt, acting as a balm. Called back to herself, it was often difficult to reassemble the two, to become one again, whole, entire. It was as if her dislocated selves could never quite realign. As a child she'd had an operation to correct a strabismus. For years her mother had taken her on the long trek from Bolton to the children's hospital in Manchester, grinding along on jerky old buses and all, it seemed to her childish perception, to play a game in which she was required to peer through a viewer at two frames; on the left a tiger, fangs bared, on the right a cage. She had to put the tiger in the cage by twisting the knobs on the side of the apparatus. Helen supposed they could tell by the degree of misalignment how much more work needed to be done on her lazy left eye. What had seemed a perfect capture to her might be out by a few centimetres to the normal eye. Was this how she appeared now to Ruth, struggling to superimpose her two disparate selves one on the other, trying to cage the tiger, and failing?

Chapter Four

The conference room of the department of Zoology and Marine Biology had once been a reading room attached to the chaplaincy. It retained an ecclesiastical aloofness, with its half-panelled walls and mullion windows ornamented by trefoil tracery, but it was not religious respect which curbed the normally confident and assertive spirits of the assembly of academics the morning after Professor Wilkinson's death.

They sat in distinct clusters on the cheap, mustard-yellow foam chairs in the coffee bar. The conference table which occupied the other half of the room, behind fabric-covered screens and potted plants, had been laid with notepads and tumblers; jugs of water had been placed within reach of each setting, but nobody moved to the table or even glanced in its direction. It was as if it were a source of dread. There was no apparent reason why this should be so: this meeting had been scheduled at the last monthly departmental meeting, but there was a palpable air of anxiety in the room.

The Senate had used the planned gathering to call together the junior departmental members, as well as heads of departments, in order to broach the delicate matter of Professor Wilkinson's murder, and the complications it engendered.

David Ainsley had been watching the assembly with the eye of an environmentalist, a role he retreated into when scientific impartiality was less uncomfortable than a more personal involvement. He had seen Tuttle arrive, self-conscious, anxious to hide what was obvious to them all. He had watched the others shuffle from the coffee machine to the chairs, the first establishing a niche for others to colonize. Like attracted like, and warned off unwelcome or incompatible approaches with frowns of territorial ferocity. The room smelled of strong coffee and suppressed fear. Mick Tuttle had placed himself next to the coffee machine; it was the nearest chair to the door and also convenient for refills. He did not like attracting attention to himself by making his laborious way from one side of a crowded room to the other. The squelching leather and clinking metallic joints of his callipers embarrassed him as much as they embarrassed others; the noise and the difficulty with which he moved reminded people that he was a cripple, although 'cripple' was not a word they would ever use – not to his face – nevertheless, it was how many of them saw him, and Tuttle didn't want to remind them of his disabilities. He had been among the first to arrive, finding his safe spot, carefully pulling the cuffs of his trousers over the rods and stays on his legs.

'What the bloody hell's *she* doing here?' said Mallory, loud enough for most of the assembly to hear. Mallory was referring to Helen Wilkinson. She had found a seat at the far end of the coffee bar next to Ruth Marks, unaware that her presence had excited such interest. She sipped her coffee from time to time, distracted, staring at the lattice-work of blurred, buttery-yellow diamonds traced by the play of sunlight through the windows to her left.

Did he speak? I've been trying to remember – it all happened so fast, slickly, like a movie – there should have been atmospheric music. I think – I think – he smiled, no more, smoothed the white linen, laying one hand palm down on the still-warm sheet. The air pregnant with the smell of recent sex: mouth-drying, faintly repugnant. Irrefutable.

No struggle, no panic. Only a push of breath, hands gripping the sheets, twisting them – shock at the unexpectedness of it. But the knife had been well-honed with every ritualized rehearsal of his carefully planned death, and it pierced – dermis, adipose tissue, striated muscle, pericardium, smooth muscle – effortlessly.

Such a small thing, so lightweight, the blade slim, elegant in its way, marked by a thousand tiny striations, sharpened and resharpened in preparation for its work. Strange how one can develop a regard, almost an affection, for one's tools – at least if they give good service.

Like a burst balloon, he seemed to collapse in on himself. A failure of pressure. He was dead in seconds. It was humane, almost painless. The small incision, high in his chest, seeping gouts of bright crimson summoned an image of the crucified Christ.

David Ainsley turned to look at Mallory. He had the grey skin and bad temper of a convalescent. Tufty eyebrows overhung piercing black eyes and his face wore the jowly folds of a fat man thinned by age and poor digestion. His following had been taken in by his blunt irascibility; they hoped that he would say things which they dared not, and that by association they would be considered forthright and fearless in their opinions. But Mallory seldom thought before he spoke and since his opinions were generally based on malice and prejudice they were universally ignored. Ainsley despised him.

His questioning Helen Wilkinson's presence had generated a flurry of whispers among his little cohort of malcontents – four zoologists who were more disgruntled than the rest since it seemed likely that the administrative headquarters of the proposed School of Life Sciences would be housed in their comfortable and newly refurbished eighteenth-century buildings, and that those zoologists who survived the reorganization would be moved to the less architecturally pleasing and far noisier red-brick Victorian street frontage. Ainsley eyed the group with undisguised contempt. The junior lecturers fell silent under his disparaging gaze. John Ellis, a postgraduate researcher in the final throes of his doctoral thesis, continued talking; his gesticulations seemed over-elaborate, stagy, to Ainsley's jaundiced eye. Ellis was nervous, he decided. He always talked too much when he was nervous. Feeney, a senior lecturer nearer Dr Mallory's age, sipped his coffee in apparent unconcern, but Ainsley noted the tremor in Feeney's hand, and heard the clatter of his cup on its saucer.

'She should be asked to leave,' Mallory went on.

'Bilious old tosser,' Ainsley murmured through clenched teeth.

Mallory scowled over at him.

'He's probably nervous that Edward discussed his piss-poor performance on the Research Assessment Exercise with wifey,' Julian Rutherford said to Ainsley, stealing a glance at the dreamy profile of Helen Wilkinson. 'It does seem . . . odd, Helen being present so soon after—'

'She's as much right to be here as anyone,' said Ainsley, surprising himself as much as the group around him by his defence of Wilkinson's widow. 'Well,' he added, realizing he had sounded too vehement, 'I don't see why people have to mind each other's business.'

'When they have trouble minding their own, you mean?'

Ainsley rounded on Rutherford. 'What's that supposed to mean?'

Rutherford took in the sudden angry flush. Ainsley's fists were clenched and his clear grey eyes looked somewhat blood-shot this morning. What *had* he been up to last night? Rutherford wondered. 'Only that there are too many busy-bodies in our caring community,' he said, satisfied that his message had got home. In the main, Rutherford liked Ainsley, but he was prone to a certain smugness which at times he found sickening. He had watched Ainsley analyse the inter-actions of his colleagues during the past half hour, assessing them as they arrived, evaluating their chances of survival in the reorganization, occasionally flicking his pale yellow cowlick from his forehead. It wouldn't occur to Ainsley that he, too, may be observed, that his own personal life could be the subject of speculation.

Interesting, isn't it, Rutherford thought, that Edward, who had all of our lives, or at least our livelihoods in his greasy paw is now gone, the power he wielded so despotically is now meaningless, and what's left of him is already experiencing the destructive force of entropic disorder.

A movement at the periphery of his vision made Rutherford turn from Ainsley. Smolder stalked across to Mallory and heated words were exchanged, none of which he could hear; Smolder was one of the old school who thought raising one's voice an unforgivable vulgarity. Rutherford glanced over at Helen Wilkinson. She seemed unaware of the argument, which was just as well, since Rutherford suspected that Smolder's attentions would be unwelcome to Dr Wilkinson, no matter how well-meant. Others did notice, however, and there was a sudden pall in the conversation which became a definite silence. A polite cough from the opposite end of the room and all eyes turned to the woman who had appeared from behind the screens near the conference area.

'God,' said Ainsley. 'They've brought in Chambers.' *They* being the Senate, who were now in the uncomfortable position of having to take over the selection (or more accurately, *de*selection) of about a third of the biological sciences staff for redundancy, a distasteful task which they had left, until his untimely demise had made it impossible, to the discretion of Professor Wilkinson.

Alice Chambers was a woman of indeterminate age. She wore her brown hair in a careless tangle of curls which bounced slightly as she nodded her head when emphasizing a point – something she did frequently and with considerable vigour.

'Now,' she said, leaning forward and balancing on the balls of her feet. 'I know that you will have heard the distressing news of Prof Wilkinson's death—' She nodded on the words *distressing* and *death*. There was a collective intake of breath and Chambers's glance, as comprehensively inclusive as a fish-eye lens, flicked quickly in Helen's direction and then back to the main body of her audience. She took her time, as if taking a mental roll-call. Her eyes protruded slightly, adding to the disconcerting intensity of her stare, and many had difficulty returning it. 'Unfortunately,' she continued, softening the line she had intended to take in deference to Helen's feelings, 'the Senate has no option but to continue with the schedule as planned. It is by no means an ideal state of affairs, and we would, *of course'* – she nodded once – 'prefer to postpone the selection procedure, but the final staffing matrices *must* be in place before the start of the summer term, so that—' Here she paused and, instead of a nod, gave a little tilt of the head. 'So that everyone is clear as to where they will stand at the new academic year.' She let her eyes rove over the assembly once more. Some became fascinated by the contents of their coffee mugs, others discovered the need to retrieve writing materials from their briefcases. Two people met her gaze directly: Helen Wilkinson, who seemed to be having trouble discerning her meaning, and Ruth Marks, whose expression was a disconcerting mixture of contempt and amusement. 'We have two weeks in which to complete the . . . adjustments,' Chambers concluded.

'If she calls it downsizing or rationalization,' said Ainsley, 'I think I shall do her physical harm.'

Rutherford shot him a look which left him in no doubt that he thought the comment in very bad taste, then Mallory spoke up: 'So you want us to go through with the bloody charade of lectures and seminars?'

Chambers considered. She had not anticipated such a direct involvement so early in the proceedings. She was to have participated directly at the final interview stage, after Professor Wilkinson had made his recommendations. She had left the details to him, and he had told her nothing about lectures and seminars. Would she lose face by openly admitting this, or would openness work in her favour? She chose to repeat the last part of Mallory's question and hope that he would clarify without her really having to admit to her ignorance. 'Lectures and seminars,' she said reflectively.

'If you're worried about time,' said Rutherford, 'we could cut a couple of days by presenting our personal research proposals in a document or paper, to be discussed at the interview stage.'

There was a general murmur of approval.

'Better than having us perform like circus animals for our peers.'

Chambers stared at Mallory, who had made this last statement. She had to admire the man's audacity, drawing attention to himself, after his disastrous showing in the Research Assessment Exercise. Taking her look for disapproval of his criticism of Professor Wilkinson's methods, Mallory stared back with open hostility.

So, Chambers thought, Wilkinson had expected his colleagues to plead their case before their peers. An exercise in pointless humiliation. Pointless, she corrected herself, except for Wilkinson's reputation for vindictiveness. She glanced over at Helen Wilkinson and wondered, not for the first time, what an intelligent woman had seen in such an overbearing and sadistic man. Helen sighed and took another sip of coffee. It must have been cold by then but she seemed not to notice, and appeared to be immersed in some internal debate.

He was flamboyant in his affairs. There was no fun in it without the added piquancy of knowing that those harmed by his casual seductions knew – or at least suspected – what was going on. Edward never passed up an opportunity to humiliate. He went out of his way to engineer encounters, chance meetings, so that he could gloat, fire suspicions, compound the shame.

Well, this was one too many, Edward.

There was a sudden exclamation from the far side of the room and Miss Chambers drew her gaze reluctantly from the pretty, anguished face. John Ellis had jumped to his feet and skittered off to the coffee dispenser, Helen's eyes following him with the intensity of the distracted. Mallory reached up as he passed, but Ellis shrugged him off. He refilled his coffee cup and turned back to the assembly, who were watching him in silence. Ainsley watched, fascinated, as Ellis took two, three steps into the middle of the room and then addressed Helen:

'I don't know why you're looking at *me*,' he hissed. 'Can't you leave me alone?' The academics were divided: the majority were embarrassed by the spectacle, but a few were enjoying themselves hugely and were disappointed when Tuttle stood up from his seat near the machine, and laboured over to Ellis. He spoke in a low voice and Ellis blinked fearfully, then fled the room.

His departure triggered a rustling and shuffling as of a starling roost disturbed by a passing owl, then Miss Chambers had their attention once more.

'A fifteen-hundred-word summary of your work, together with ideas for sponsorship or other funding will be quite sufficient,' she said, nodding emphatically and clasping her hands in front of her. 'Shall we say, by the end of the week? In the meantime, heads of departments should, by now, have their accounts and budget requests ready for inspection, so if there are no questions, the rest of you are free to go. HODs or their representatives will convene at the conference table in' – she glanced at her watch – 'ten minutes.'

She stopped on her way to the screened off area. 'I'm so sorry about Edward, Helen.'

Helen looked up, confused. '*Are* you?' she asked. She seemed displaced from what was happening around her. 'Why?'

Alice Chambers blinked, '*Why?* Well, of course,' she said, floundering for the suitable platitudes. 'He was a great scientific mind. He would have headed the new faculty—'

'Oh, of course,' Helen said.

Chambers was rattled, she wasn't sure if Helen was mocking her, but then Helen went on in a tone which expressed the resolution of a genuine bafflement: 'I *see* – it will be difficult to find a replacement at such short notice.'

'No – I didn't mean—' What she had meant to do was say a few words of comfort to a woman with whom she had no affinity and even less understanding, about a man she had found deeply unpleasant, and then move on to the business of the day, to fulfil her obligations as an administrator and as a colleague. This bizarre reaction was something she had not expected, and did not know how to deal with.

Ruth Marks stepped in to rescue her. 'Helen isn't quite herself this morning, Miss Chambers,' she said. 'She shouldn't really have come.'

'Quite,' said Chambers, with feeling, shaking her curls in disapproval.

'I needed to know what would happen . . . the procedure. If I'm to be made redundant,' Helen said with that dreamy detachment Alice Chambers found so unsettling. 'If I'm to be unemployed I would have to put the house up for sale, look for a new job.'

Miss Chambers's eyebrows shot up. Could the widow really be thinking in terms of her own security of tenure the day after her husband had been murdered? Ruth Marks seemed to read her thoughts. 'You aren't thinking straight, Helen,' she said. 'I'll take you home. Maybe I should call Dr Patterson.'

'Before you do,' Chambers said, remembering the other reason for her detour through to the conference area, 'perhaps you could spare me a few moments.' Her eyes darted around the room.

Ruth was intrigued. She tilted her head to one side, looking down at the administrator. 'OK.' She turned to check on Helen. She was frowning at the back of her hand, lost again to reality. Ruth sighed and followed Miss Chambers through to the screened area.

'I'm asking you this because I know I'll get an objective answer.'

'Good opening gambit,' said Ruth, smiling. 'Flattery, wrapped up in a plea for honesty.'

'No flattery,' said Chambers, unsmiling. 'But, since you are leaving us for pastures new, and would not be involved in the selection procedure, I feel I can rely on you to state things as they are. I assume, from what Dr Mallory said, that Professor Wilkinson had planned to – to *require* – staff who were seeking re-employment within the new faculty to present their case to the *existing* body of academics?'

Ruth didn't answer immediately. 'How like Edward not to tell you,' she said. 'And how like the Senate not to enquire.' She shot a wicked look at Chambers, who at least had the good grace to seem embarrassed. Ruth shrugged. 'For once in his sorry life, Mallory was right. Distasteful idea, isn't it?' The ambiguity was wasted on Miss Chambers whose only interest was a direct answer to her question. Ruth sighed. 'Edward called everyone in yesterday morning, told them they would have to present a lecture to their colleagues and conduct a plenary session. Full attendance compulsory. A secret vote to follow each presentation. So, our distinguished team of academics were expected to plead for re-employment to the very people they would put out of a job if they were to succeed in their persuasion.'

Miss Chambers's thin lips disappeared to almost nothing. 'You, no doubt, were exempt from these . . . proceedings.'

Ruth was gratified that the administrator was finding it hard to suppress her feelings of distaste. She smiled tightly. 'But he did give me the right to vote. Between you and me, I think Ed had already made up his mind exactly what recommendations he would make to the Senate. But Edward liked to rule by division. You'll find few people who actually trust one another in the departments you're seeking to axe, Miss Chambers.' She listened for a few minutes with half an ear to Alice Chambers's explanations of rationalization and projected student numbers, the difficulties of high levels of supervision and equipment costs in practical science subjects, per capita allowances and sponsorship.

'Some of the departments made a very poor showing in the Research Assessment Exercise,' Miss Chambers explained. 'Government funding will be cut by quite significant amounts as a result. We *must* rationalize staff numbers in order to balance the budget as well as looking to the future and ensuring at least a level three ranking at the next assessment.'

'Universities used to be about academic rigour,' Ruth said when she had heard enough. 'Not about balancing budgets. Scientists used to be able to research without having to justify their interests in terms of commercial applications and the need to compile a tick list of recent publications. And what about staff who are excellent teachers? Can't we recognize their contribution?'

Miss Chambers pursed her lips. 'It's heart-warming to see such loyalty, Dr Marks—'

Ruth laughed. 'I hate to disillusion you, Miss Chambers, it's a quaint notion and all that, but I'm not talking about Mallory. He's a lazy, dried up old prune who thought he could wing it for the next five years till retirement. I'm talking about the poor bastards who have to cram in lectures and tutorials and seminars and marking – and with groups three times the size I taught when I first came into university teaching.'

'*Efficiency*' – Miss Chambers nodded emphatically – 'is considered a dirty word in some quarters.'

'This isn't efficiency. Surely you must see that. Driving people to the edge isn't efficiency. We're not machines. We can't be driven to exhaustion and still be expected to have the creative inspiration to provide the research and the papers required by your criteria for grading. I'd like to know how much weighting you'd give to Dr X, brown-nosing for a research grant, compared with Dr Y, say, coming up with a new perspective on a research area. Knowledge used to be considered a worthy goal. It was our job to ask the profound questions. Corny, isn't it? Embarrassing almost. But no more embarrassing, I can assure you, Miss Chambers, than grubbing for sponsorship, cap – or should I say mortarboard? – in hand. We spend more time grovelling to our sponsors than we do on research or – God forbid – teaching.'

Alice Chambers seemed to think hard before she responded to this. 'I have a certain amount of sympathy with your view, Dr Marks, but we live in the real world.'

'Of academic accountancy—' Ruth broke off. Mallory had arrived. He regarded her with the kind of alarmed concentration her first-year students showed on their first experimentation with electro-stimulation. They knew the animal was dead and couldn't hurt them, but the appearance of life was strangely disturbing, and more were made ill by the twitching of a dead vertebrate limb than by the dissection which preceded it. As her boss, Mallory had good reason to be curious about a junior member of his department – worse, one who no longer had anything to lose – deep in conversation with a senior member of the Senate administration. As an academic approaching sixty who had not published any-thing of note in five years nor anything at all in the last two, he had even greater reason for concern. He had nothing to offer, nothing that would convince the Senate that he should be funded until the next Research Assessment, when he could be safely put out to grass. His reliance on Ellis's crackpot ideas producing anything worthy of submission to the scien-tific journals proved only how seriously out of touch the man was.

David Ainsley debated whether to return home and attempt to patch things up with Clara. He had seen Helen Wilkinson leave with the florid, pock-marked policeman and didn't feel up to being questioned himself. He walked out of the zoology buildings and through the gates into the leafy lane at the back. The blustery winds and bursts of sun and showers of the previous day had died down and the morning's brightness had given way to a quiet, sullen greyness. The clouds hung low in opaque folds, unmoving, like fossilized smoke, threat-ening rain. He turned his collar up and looked first left towards home, then right to his own office in the environmental science building. He decided that he didn't want to patch things up with Clara, just now. He wasn't sure he ever would.

He couldn't pretend to be sorry that Edward was dead, he'd deserved it – David was just sorry that the end had been so quick and clean. And now what? The tabloid press would enjoy finding headlines. It seemed to him that there was only one thing they hated more than success, and that was an intellectual. They would find out the sordid details and print them with vulgar relish.

He picked up a few journals and took them to the stacks; they were quiet, most of the first- and second-year students had gone home for the vac, but Ainsley could not concentrate.

He found himself in the Horace Shelby coffee bar, a tray in his hand, and a look of slight puzzlement on his face. Renowned across the campus, better by far than the college refectory although three times as expensive, it served home-baked cakes and biscuits and freshly made sandwiches. Housed in a large basement room of the library, recently refurbished and painted blue and turquoise, it had a light, modern, vaguely Japanese air. The tables were well spaced and most were vacant, so Ainsley was not in danger of being joined by his colleagues, one or two of whom he could see dotted about the room. He focused with a fierce determination on the chalkboard, scowling ostentatiously as he made his choice. He sat at one of the farthest tables, trying to avoid the eye of any of the academics, but he could not keep his attention from Ruth Marks, who sat with one of her third-year tutees. She seemed to be reading over an essay or some notes. Carelessly slopping her coffee and dropping crumbs over them, she would sit in silence for several minutes at a time, then talk in staccato bursts while the student nodded deferentially, and jotted down notes, darting anxious glances at the rapidly degenerating condition of his precious manuscript.

Ruth happened to look up and smiled over at him. Ainsley looked away, picking up a discarded newspaper as a defensive gesture. The front page bore a picture of Edward Wilkinson, smiling, handsome. He tore it out and carefully shredded it, first into thin strips and then into minuscule bits of dark confetti. He tried telling himself that now he was dead, Edward could not hurt anyone else, but there was no reassurance in the constant repetition. Edward, he thought, would seep like poison into an aquifer, tainting all their lives.

Chapter Five

Ruth found Helen in her office. She had spent the last hour looking for her, being sent from one end of the department to the other by various sightings and had even sought her out at home. Helen was sitting at her desk, her arms folded, hugging herself. There was a blue tinge to her lips and she had a greyish pallor. Ruth picked up the telephone and dialled through to Patterson's surgery, then she drew up a chair next to Helen and put both hands on her shoulders. Helen flinched, then, looking up at her friend, smiled apologetically.

'I can't stop shaking,' she said.

'I noticed. Where have you *been?*'

Helen glanced anxiously over her shoulder. 'Inspector Nelson—'

'The bastard!' Ruth yelled. Helen jumped and gave a little yelp. 'It's OK,' Ruth reassured her, stroking her shoulder. 'Jesus, he really spooked you, didn't he?'

'I'm sorry. It isn't the police—' Ruth found it difficult to understand Helen because the shaking was so violent her teeth were chattering. 'It's not their fault. It's me.'

Ruth took Helen's hands in hers and stared into the bruised and hollow sockets of her eyes. She hadn't slept much the previous night. Ruth had insisted that she stay at her flat, since Helen's house was still overrun by police and she had woken at five to find Helen in the kitchen, sitting at the table, ghastly pale in the greenish light of the street lamp outside the window, staring at nothing. 'Helen,' she said, 'you kept to our story, didn't you? That we were together most of the afternoon?'

Helen made an effort of concentration. 'I don't know.' She passed a hand over her eyes, pressing at the temples as though it would help her to think straight. 'He kept asking things I – I didn't know what to tell him, Ruth.'

'Oh, Jesus, *no*, Helen!' Ruth grabbed her shoulders tightly and gave her a shake. 'You've got to stop this. You're making them think you did it. It's crazy! You've come through so much and stayed sane. Why let this get to you?'

Helen looked up. 'Let this get to me?' she said. 'My husband has been *murdered*.' Her total bewilderment affected Ruth with unexpected force, a feeling almost of physical pain. How could she have so badly misjudged Helen? Was there more to her reaction than understandable shock?

'Look,' Ruth went on. 'You did *not* kill Edward.' She bent down, trying to make eye contact, but Helen turned her head away and twisted her hands, trying to free herself. Ruth held her fast.

'Let me go, Ruth.'

'Talk to me,' Ruth said. 'Tell me what you're thinking. Tell me what it is that's got you so scared. Better me than that mad-eyed copper.'

Helen continued struggling, but Ruth was too strong for her. 'All *right*!' she said, breathlessly, still fighting against Ruth, against the apathy which had wrapped around her like a straitjacket since she had found Edward, against the very words she was about to utter. 'Sometimes, I don't just hate Edward for what he did to me. Sometimes I swear I wanted him to suffer like he made me suffer, but not only him—' The effort to control her voice failed entirely and it rose to a scream. 'Sometimes I want to tear the whole *fucking* world apart!'

Ruth moved back, shocked, and Helen gave a short, angry laugh. 'You see it? You see the thing I can't control? It scares you, doesn't it, Ruth? It should do. It should scare you – it scares the shit out of me.' A brief flash of raindrops, frozen in a car's headlights; the face caught in the beams; the slow arrogant smile turning to terror; the terrible, shameful shock of pleasure in his fear. She stopped for a moment, panting. 'It's like I'm two quite different people. One is rational and calm. It takes – took – whatever Edward said or did and barely responded. The other – the other is murderously *furious* with him. And the really scary thing is that I *wanted* to be the murderer. I have fantasized about it and planned it and done it so many times in my head that I didn't want anyone else to get there first.' There were tears in her eyes now, she was pleading for understanding. 'Do you see, Ruth? Do you see what I'm trying to tell you?'

'And I thought *I* hated the bastard,' Ruth said, lightly, but Helen did not return her smile, and she nodded, dipping her head apologetically. 'All right. I watched him use you, brainwash you, indoctrinate you – Pavlovian conditioning – he rang the bell and you came bounding out of your cage drooling guilt. *There goes the bell – oops! Must be my fault.* Your mother started the job, your religion consolidated it, and Edward, good son-in-law that he was, finished it. If you didn't have anything to blame yourself for you'd accuse yourself of the sin of pride. I have to say, Jewish guilt never had much of a hold on me – maybe my mother should have tried Catholicism – maybe I wouldn't have turned out so wicked.'

Inspector Nelson, Helen remembered, had been far less convinced than Ruth of her innocence. He kept asking her questions, many of which she missed or could not remember answering. He and the sergeant – Hackett – had set up in Mallory's office. She didn't know where Mallory was, but became preoccupied with the idea that he may return suddenly and demand to know what they were doing. Such inconsequential thoughts had obsessed her since January, and she had often found herself incapable of directing her thoughts to important matters. She caught herself looking around the room, trying to discover evidence that Mallory had been working on his presentation to the interview panel. She supposed there would have to be a panel, now that Edward . . . Her thoughts had trailed off at this point and she had come round a few minutes later to find that Hackett was trying to persuade the inspector to let her go home. She remembered raised voices, but the argument had rumbled like thunder over her head and she had been content to let it.

Hackett had arranged for a patrol car to drop her home. The police had left and the house was quiet. It seemed somehow bereft in the icy chill of the sullen spring morning. She had stood on the doorstep in the cold, looking up at the window of the bedroom where she had found Edward, and had seen herself, opening the front door, finding him in bed, smelling of another woman's perfume. He had smiled at her and she had gone to him, bent over him, smelling the freshness of the linen she had changed only that morning, and the perfume that was not hers and the spicy smell of his body overlaid with recent sex. She had kissed him, sliding her tongue into his mouth, probing the soft inner surface of his upper lip taking care to avoid his sharp, scrubbed teeth as she slid the knife between his ribs. No more than a flicker, a tease, and then out, and it was done.

She couldn't remember returning to the university, but there, in her own room, she had become aware, gradually, of her surroundings. Of colour and light. A grey, unforgiving light. Rain had begun to spatter the windows and she had watched for some time the random streams of water formed by one droplet merging with another, on and on down the window until it trickled on to the ledge. It was strangely soothing and she discovered a calmness which was quite unlike the numb feeling of the past day. She turned back to the cosy clutter of her books and notes, the laptop computer standing open next to the PC on her desk. She had been working on her own presentation – Edward had made it clear that there would be no special concessions for her. She had picked up her notes, not meaning to read them, not having any clear intention in mind. Perhaps it was a simple attempt to connect with something tangible, something comprehensible and safe. Her submission was to be a development of her work on murine leukaemia. Of course, she could not deal with the mice, with their sometimes unpleasant deaths – death of any kind had become too distressing for her – but her cell cultures had brought in some interesting data and several pharmaceutical firms had shown an interest. She was confident she would get sponsorship. Even Edward wouldn't have been able to argue with that. Abruptly, and with a violence which made her drop the typed sheets, she had begun to shake.

'I stood on the pathway under our bedroom window and I could remember it,' Helen said. 'Exactly how I did it, precisely how I felt.'

'You're in shock, Helen,' Ruth said, getting up to answer a knock at the door. 'Tell her, Sanjay,' she said, not bothering with greetings or explanations. 'Tell her she's in shock.'

Sanjay Patterson crossed the room in three strides and knelt beside Helen. 'I'll give you my opinion when I've examined you,' he said, talking directly to Helen. 'You were supposed to be at home. Sergeant Hackett telephoned me. He said he'd sent you home in a police car. He was worried about you.'

'That man's just too *nice* to be a policeman,' Ruth said,

flopping into a chair. 'Charming, well-bred, a positive paragon of old-fashioned courtesy. Now, what's your opinion, Doc?'

'BP low, pulse rate up. When did the shaking start?'

'Right after that pustular policeman, Nelson, dragged her in for questioning.'

Patterson shot Ruth a look, silencing her at least momentarily, and said, 'Helen?'

Helen closed her eyes. 'I've had it off and on ever since . . . For the last two months . . . But not as bad as this.'

Patterson took her hand. 'Either,' he said gently, 'you go home, take two of the pills I prescribed and get some sleep, or I book you into the Countess overnight.'

It had the desired effect. Helen was horrified. 'I'm not going into hospital,' she said.

'Then go *home*. You have to remember that you've been through a lot. Not just this, but . . .' Helen looked away and he knew there was no need to go on. He turned to Ruth. 'Will you supervise?'

'Sure, I've one or two things to do in the lab, but it'll only take a few minutes, then I'll drive you home,' Ruth said, 'if that's where you want to go.' She raised both hands to quell Dr Patterson's objections. 'I'm simply suggesting my flat as an alternative.'

Helen shrugged. 'I should go home I suppose.' She shook her head to displace the image that was beginning to form of Edward lying on the bed, blood spilling on to the sheets, the knife, made heavy by the weight of guilt, bloody in her hands. 'I don't know what happens next. I mean, will they let me start arranging the funeral?'

Patterson shook his head. 'They're not likely to release the body just yet—'

'Oh God!' Helen's hands flew to her face. 'My parents! If they've heard about this they'll be frantic.'

'I spoke to them last night,' Ruth said. 'They phoned while you were . . . out of it. Your mother wanted to come over.'

'She can't see me like this!' Helen was suddenly tearful. 'You didn't tell her she should come?'

Ruth and Patterson exchanged a look. 'Helen,' said Ruth, 'your mother won't expect you to be on top form when your husband has just been murdered.'

Patterson rolled his eyes at the bluntness of the statement.

Helen didn't reply, but Patterson saw something pass between the two women which he suspected came from a deeper understanding than his of Helen's behaviour during the previous day.

'Yeah, yes. OK,' Ruth said when the moment had passed. 'I put her off, OK? She said she'd wait until she heard from you today.'

Helen slumped in her chair, hugely relieved. 'I'll phone her when I get home,' she said. Then, to placate Patterson: 'And then I'll take your bloody pills and a few hours of oblivion.'

The argument between Nelson and Hackett had continued for some time after Helen had left. What enraged Nelson more than anything was the reason he had given way to the sergeant.

Hackett had been restless from the moment he had called Dr Wilkinson into the office they had requisitioned from the head of the zoology department. He had become increasingly tense, kept glancing from the woman to Nelson, then he stood up and paced from the window to the desk and back. Mallory's office was not large; it reminded Nelson of a film set in a black and white B-movie of the 1950s, cluttered as it was with the kind of artefacts generally used as a visual shorthand for sinister scientific types. An array of rodent skulls of increasing size were lined up along the edge of the shelf opposite the desk, all turned so that the empty eye sockets stared beadily down on the occupant. There were cabinets comprising mahogany trays with glass tops. Nelson had taken a glimpse at the top drawer – a display of different species of a large black beetle; different stages in the life cycle, some with the wing-cases splayed open exposing crinkled wings that reminded Nelson incongruously of plastic rain hats his mother used to wear when he was a child. He found the proximity of the shiny black creatures with their hooked legs and huge antennae unnerving. A live tarantula occupied a glass case next to the computer. No doubt it kept Mallory company as he typed up his reports. A human skull sat on the desk – it looked real – with a cigarette clamped between its teeth: evidence of a heavy-handed humour.

The small, airless room was not made for men of Hackett's size and bulk; he stirred the air with his pacing, and Nelson flared his nostrils at the mixed odour of chemical preservatives and dust, the warm, new, plastic smell of the computer and an older, mustier smell of mouldy books and animal decay.

He had glowered at Hackett, but his sergeant wasn't paying attention, at least not to him. He had asked a few questions of his own, speaking in that imposing bass voice of his. In the confines of this dusty office it seemed to boom even when he spoke quietly. After a while he had passed a note across the big, buff ink blotter. Nelson had glanced at the note, not really believing the sergeant would have anything helpful to suggest, but willing to give the new boy a fair chance.

You have to let her go, it read. Nelson had screwed the slip into a ball and tossed it into the bin. Hackett had then asked to speak with him in private. He had refused. Hackett had insisted. Nelson had stood up, glaring into the sergeant's pallid face. Strange, how he found those eyes disconcerting. He imagined it was similar to the effect his own amber irises had on people, not realizing that whilst Hackett's stare was calm, speculative, his own had a frenetic intensity which was truly frightening. He had warned Hackett that he was interfering in the interrogation of a suspect.

'If she's a suspect, take her in and interview in compliance with PACE regs. She should have an appropriate adult present.' Hackett added in a whisper, 'She's not making *sense*.'

Dr Wilkinson had retreated into her private world. She had seemed unaware of the row going on over her head. 'She's sick or in shock, or mentally unstable. Surely you can see that?' The emphasis on the *you* was almost indiscernible. Nelson wasn't sure, half an hour later, that he hadn't imagined it. *Surely* you – *you of all people* – you *who should be a bloody expert in the diagnosis of mental instability.* He had folded. Crumpled. Given in without another word. All on a probably imagined implication. And having let her go, he was now furious.

He had launched into a face-saving tirade almost as Helen Wilkinson left, but the sergeant was proving remarkably resilient. If Hackett's skin appeared practically translucent, appearances were deceptive: he had the hide of an elephant.

'If you ever interfere with my interviewing a suspect again, I'll have your lily-white arse out of here. I'll have you out on the streets knocking on doors and keeping back the sightseers.' Hackett looked like he was considering the advantages of this proposal. 'You're not indispensable, Sergeant. Get that into your thick skull, will you? I won't be undermined by my officers.'

'No sir.' But the look on Hackett's face said he'd do it again. And again. Those bloody eyes! They reminded Nelson of a ginger tom his wife had taken in as a stray. He had booted it off the settee once when he'd caught it licking its backside and dropping fur and spreading God-alone-knew-what diseases all over the place. He never caught it after that one time, but there were always ginger hairs on the Dralon and the sodding

cat would be staring down at him from the top of the bookcase, tail twitching, out of reach, out of danger. He was
tempted to tell Hackett to piss off back to Warrington or
wherever he'd come from and then find himself a nice, trac-
table DC, preferably female, who wouldn't mind making the
odd brew and typing up his notes for him. Then the dream
shattered. They hadn't made them that way since the '70s.
Nelson grunted in disgust.

'We need to interview some of these lecturers,' he said.
'We're wasting time here.' Everyone not directly involved in
the HOD meeting, which could go on for hours, had scattered
when Alice Chambers had dismissed them.

'I could have a chat with Prof Wilkinson's secretary,' Hackett
suggested. 'She may know the likely bolt-holes. And I could
ask her about this reorganization that's going on.'

'She might also have some background on Wilkinson and
his associates,' said Nelson, conceding to the idea reluctantly.
He didn't like to let Hackett off so easily, but there was
precious little they could do with no one to talk to. 'And
talking of background – how's Wright doing with that check
on Dr Wilkinson?'

'Nothing on the computer, but I've suggested they do a
paper check as well – their computer records only go back as
far as 1988.'

Mrs Roberts's office was an ante-room to Professor Wilkinson's;
a plasterboard wall and a door through to the larger room of
which it had once formed a part. She was a generous woman,
both physically and by disposition, and the cramped quarters
in which she found herself seemed all the more stingy when
measured against the cloth of her unstinting good nature. She
was not tall – five feet seven or so, but her iron-grey hair was
extravagantly coiffed into a creation which gave her a couple

of extra inches, and she had the kind of padding which takes years of maternity to acquire. She was a solid, comfortable, substantial woman whose generosity extended even to Edward Wilkinson, although Hackett had already developed the conviction that the professor was less than deserving of her loyalty.

'The Research Assessment Exercise – RAE,' Mrs Roberts explained to him in her fruity, rather masculine voice, 'was completed at the end of the last academic year; the reorganization of departments into an umbrella faculty is a result of the assessment.'

'How does the RAE work?' Hackett asked.

'Each department sends in a sheet of information for each member of staff, listing the best four papers they've submitted for publication over the previous five years. Also, details of grants or other funding they've brought in – a very important factor in these lean times, Sergeant.'

'They're given some kind of grading, I take it?'

She nodded. 'By an independent body of specialists, eminent in the relevant field. Each academic is given a rating of one to three – three being the highest, and denoting academic work of international importance. The assessors work out an average grade for the department, then compare it across all of the biology departments, so that a ranking may be given, from one to five. Most would feel content with a three.'

'How *content* were the various departments here?' Hackett asked.

Mrs Roberts glanced over his shoulder towards the open door. 'I'd have to check with the Senate before giving out that sort of information,' she said. 'But the result is the proposed merger of several departments and the institution of the parent faculty.'

'Which will mean job losses . . .'

She raised both shoulders. 'Inevitable, I'm afraid.' Hackett asked her to describe Professor Wilkinson's elimination procedure, which she did, but only after he persuaded her that it had now been altered, something they knew from their interviews late that morning.

'I could see that would make him a few enemies,' Hackett commented. He often found oblique comments far more productive in provoking unguarded responses than direct questions, and Mrs Roberts obliged.

'I hope you're not suggesting that any of the staff would have wished him harm, Sergeant,' she said. 'No matter what Prof Wilkinson was, I'm sure nobody here could ever do such a thing.'

'You didn't approve of his methods?' he asked, hoping to surprise an honest answer from her and filing away the use of the term 'what the professor was'. He succeeded only in putting her back on her guard.

'I imagine Prof Wilkinson thought it was the best way. Universities are far more competitive than they used to be.'

'Yes, but from what you say these people have been worrying about job security, grants for research and so on for over a year now; that must have a terrible effect on morale.'

'Certainly this performance didn't help.' Hackett was back on track now, disapproval had returned to her voice, and this time it was not aimed at him.

'They must have been dreadfully upset—'

'Well of course—'

'Angry, even.'

'Wouldn't you be? Asked to justify your job, your funding, your research to members of the fraternity who have a vested interest in depriving you of that position, divesting you of your funding and rubbishing your research? Not because the staff here are mean-spirited, they are not, I assure you.' She paused for breath, held it a moment, then, as if deciding honesty was the best policy, she resumed. 'The professor cultivated a climate of interdepartmental competition so fierce that it made even the mildest people desperate.' She stopped and put a hand over her mouth in a curiously childlike gesture. 'I did *not* mean that the way it sounded, Sergeant Hackett,' she said.

He smiled and she narrowed her eyes at him, angry with herself that she had allowed him to lead her into an indiscreet response.

'I'm sorry, Mrs Roberts,' he said. 'I have to ask these questions.' He hesitated, then decided he couldn't descend any lower in her estimation and asked, 'Was anyone more upset – more angry – than the rest?'

Mrs Roberts's benevolent blue eyes were piercingly cold. 'I do not eavesdrop on the professor's conversations,' she said, letting her tenses slip for the first time.

'I'm not suggesting that you did, but people would have to've made appointments with the professor through you. I suppose they would have to wait in here if they wanted to avoid standing around in the corridor. And you seem to me to be the sort of woman people would confide in.'

'If they did – and I am speaking purely hypothetically – I should certainly not be at liberty to discuss such confidences.'

Hackett sighed. 'Mrs Roberts, I understand your position, really. You are obviously a woman of integrity. But the fact remains that a man has been murdered – your boss, a respected academic – and we need to know anything, *anything at all* which might help us find his killer.'

Mrs Roberts was not a vain woman, she did not respond to his flattery, but he saw doubt flicker over her face and guessed that she was torn between public duty and private allegiance. She fiddled with the notepad on her desk, straightening the coils of the spiral. 'Isn't it more likely that Prof Wilkinson disturbed a burglar or something? One reads of people on drugs, schizophrenics and the like—' She muttered something about care in the community.

Hackett was glad Nelson wasn't around to hear that one. He measured the situation carefully and came to a decision. 'There were no signs of a break-in, no indication of a struggle.' He watched Mrs Roberts's reaction carefully. 'I'm telling you this because I want you to understand how important it is that you tell me what you know. And I think you know a good deal more than you've told me. I think Prof Wilkinson knew his attacker.'

Mrs Roberts was shaken. She did not answer immediately but rearranged the writing materials on her desk as though each represented some aspect of what she was about to reveal to him. Hackett waited, suppressing the excitement he always felt when he had hooked an important witness. But Mrs Roberts was not so easily won over.

'They were all upset, Sergeant,' she said, having organized her thoughts. 'You have to appreciate that Prof Wilkinson was . . .' She hesitated, regretting the appearance of disloyalty, but resolving to be perfectly honest, at least in this. 'Edward was a difficult man. He really rather enjoyed having people at his mercy. If I were to give you a list, I should have to say that fifteen of the twenty people he saw in his office yesterday left in tears or furious – or both.'

'Dr Wilkinson,' said Hackett, trying a different tack, 'Did she have to go through the same process as all the rest?'

Mrs Roberts nodded. 'But even if he had exempted her, I think she would have insisted on taking part. Helen wouldn't like anyone to think she had been guaranteed a place next year just because her husband had been appointed to the chair of the new department.'

'That was confirmed, was it? His new status, I mean.'

She blushed a little. 'Not officially, but Prof Wilkinson

had told me in confidence that it was merely a matter of administrative protocol.'

'Dr Wilkinson is younger than the professor?' Hackett asked, taking advantage even of this slight imbalance in her equilibrium.

'By ten years.'

'How did they meet?'

'What are you implying?'

Hackett shrugged. 'I'm not implying anything. What did you infer?'

Mrs Roberts raised her eyebrows – the snob in her was surprised that a policeman could make the distinction.

'He taught Helen as an undergraduate, but they hadn't seen each other for years. In fact, he didn't recognize her at first. I remember the staff gathering at the start of term—'

'So he had nothing to do with her appointment here?'

Mrs Roberts threw up her plump hands in a gesture of resignation, then let them fall into her lap. 'You're evidently determined to make nepotism an issue here, Sergeant,' she said.

'I'm simply exploring possibilities.'

'Well I don't see what relevance it has to poor Edward's death.'

Hackett raised his eyebrows. *Poor* Edward? What happened to the difficult man who relished the chance to make his subordinates squirm? Was she saying *poor Edward* because she wanted to say poor Helen, but didn't want him to think that Wilkinson's wife had sufficient grievance to murder her husband?

He looked up, startled. Mrs Roberts was standing over him, quivering with rage. 'Helen has been through a lot, and I am not about to add to her problems,' she said, apparently reading his thoughts. 'Now, if you'll excuse me, I have an appointment at the Senate offices to discuss my own security of tenure, and I don't want to be late.'

Hackett didn't move immediately. He wasn't quite sure what had caused this sudden flare of anger. Was it his implication that Wilkinson may have known Helen before she came to the university? If he had, then they would be looking at a relationship between lecturer and student. Very improper. And if he'd done it once, he could do it again.

'What's the matter, Sergeant Hackett?' Mrs Roberts sounded suddenly bitter, too sharp. 'Are you wondering whether I had a motive? Well, if it's of any interest, I'm more likely to be put out to grass now than if Edward had become head of the new faculty.' She laughed, an unattractive, dry rattle, like windswept winter leaves and Hackett was further taken aback. 'Not that he had any special affection for me, but I am used – *was used* – to his little ways, and the idiosyncrasies of his filing system.'

'You should play that to your advantage,' said Hackett, matching her bitterness with sarcasm. 'The new professor will need an interpreter. Someone reliable and sympathetic.'

She stared at him, brimming with dislike, and for a moment her resolve held, then he saw, fleetingly, and with regret, hurt in the crystalline blue of her eyes.

Chapter Six

It's strange how memory works. Ask me to recall an event and my picture of the day is likely to be sketchy; ask me to recall a feeling, and I may be unable to remember even the name of the emotion I might have experienced at a particular time. Emotions are particularly slippery for me . . . they're — I don't know — untrustworthy. Love and hatred have always seemed to me to be so closely allied — it's almost impossible to resolve the two — at least that's what I've found. And memories, like emotions, are so coloured by the mood of the moment. What might have seemed enjoyable, exciting — thrilling perhaps — the day before becomes tedious, boring, irritatingly dull the next morning when the sheen of newness has gone off it, the exhilaration of noise and laughter no more than an echo in the mind and, let's be honest, sobriety exerts its influence. Of course the converse is true — awful events can develop a kind of nostalgic charm given time and if a mellow mood takes me. But once in a while something happens which triggers a flashback that is so close to the real thing it's like time travel — like being transported back through time to the exact moment and setting it has evoked — except in these semi-hallucinations I am the age I was when it first happened. Whatever 'it' happens to be. Maybe only a gang of kids playing tick in the street, their voices rupturing the night air, their shouts making puffs of vapour, like Indian smoke signals, and me in the background, watching, disdainful. The trigger depends on the memory. Sometimes it's a tune, an old song — 10cc, The Police — one of the old bands, or it may be a particular tone or quality of light. More often it's a smell. I can never quite get over the evocative power of smells.

I found a beetle in my bathroom this morning – nothing exotic, only a carabid. It wasn't even a particularly interesting specimen. Rather small and with a dull greenish tinge – commonplace. It was trying to climb up the side of the bath. It would find a scratch in which it could momentarily gain purchase, then it would slip, scrabbling hopelessly back into the well of the bath. I was transfixed for a time, watching it. Struggle, climb, slip, grip. Struggle, climb, slip, grip.

Something about the way the sun dazzled, honeyed, warm through the glass and a faint whiff of new growth which came in through the open window made me recall a day . . . It must have been a holiday, summer maybe, but the way the light sparkled both silver and gold makes me think that it must have been one of those rare spring days which is almost too hot to bear and you begin to believe that the rest of spring and all through summer will be warm, temperate, golden. I can't have been more than nine years old, all gap teeth and scabby knees. I was playing alone, as was my preference, squatting in the dust at the kerbside, winding molten tar on to a stick, building a stock which I planned to hide and burn later, and make believe I was a medieval knight.

I was in the lane that ran across the top of the street. Prospect Street stood alone, fields bordering one end and a pitted, pot-holed lane the other. My mother had sent me out to play because I was getting under her feet – an expression I scorned, for it gave the impression that I was a clingy child and although I liked to watch her, I had no real need of her. She was an interesting behavioural model, no more. So, she sent me to play, not with the other children – she had long given up on that idea – just out. Away from her. So that I couldn't watch her with my clever, observant eyes. I was distracted from my torch-making by a movement on the periphery of my vision – a giant black beetle.

The image in my mind's eye was so sharp it made me gasp. I had forgotten it – not just its appearance, but the very fact of its existence and now, standing in my bathroom so many years later, I see it with such clarity I might almost be there. The edges of its thorax and wing-cases shimmering violet in the heat haze, a multi-layered metallic sheen of green and black and shades of blue — I see it so clearly. It's at least three centimetres long. Its waxy, articulated limbs make tiny scratchy sounds on the ruined tarmac. I bend down, put my ear to the roadway to hear. Scratch, scratch, scratch. The heat from the tarmac is searing but I keep my face close to the ground, testing my endurance while watching the beetle lumbering on like a clockwork toy, its belly raised on its spindly legs, a fraction above the damaging heat. It moves in a straight line, purposefully, as if it has somewhere to go, reminding me of the hard lads who stalked the high street in town, swinging their arms, with their fists clenched. I watch the beetle's meaningless journey from my giant's perspective and it stares back with its blank red multifaceted eyes, as plump as berries.

I will it to see me but it carries on, its ridiculous, inefficient, barbed feet scraping the tarmac. Suddenly I want it to notice me with an urgency that borders on hunger. It continues, clawing forward, as if I don't matter, even though I could do anything I want to it and it couldn't do a thing to stop me.

I purse my lips and blow a sharp puff of wind. It freezes momentarily. Road dust lifts like powder, I can taste the grit on my teeth. The beetle waves its antennae and then the maddening paddling motions begin again. It is too much. I pick it up. It feels like one of those fake insects — joke toys — the kind of plastic they use for spiders and bats and bluebottles in the joke shops. For a moment I wonder whether it is a practical joke. I half expect to hear muffled laughter from the field behind the hedge. I turn it over, looking for the groove where the key fits to wind it up. I look around me while the beetle keeps up its incessant paddling motion, trapped between my thumb and forefinger, a fixed diagonal pattern, like rowers with bad timing. I scream into its mute face:

LOOK AT ME!

It appears to quiver, but then it carries on, as though convinced the pointless movements will eventually set it right. I am close to tears with frustration. I want to crush it, to hear the crack of its outer armour and the wet squelch of its soft inner pulp, but that would be too swift:

With the impotent rage of a child I want it to know the power I have; I want it to feel my presence and I want to make it suffer. I take it to the side of the road and build a ring of stones. Then I put the violet-purple beetle in the centre. The stones are big and for a time it circles, probing with its antennae, then it starts climbing, but I had chosen smooth, pebbly stones, constructed a sheer wall, and it keeps slipping back.

The heat is baking and I sit a small distance away, in the shade of the hawthorn hedge already in leaf and speckled with clustered tumescences of flower buds. It takes half an hour for the beetle to reach the top of the stones.

Do beetles feel triumph?

Smiling, I flicked it lightly with one fingernail and it tumbled on to its back into the centre of the arena.

Do beetles feel despair?

It kept climbing up and I kept flicking it back.

The sun is like a solid mass, battering down, relentless, fierce, pitiless. I feel like the sun, its power is vested in me.

The big black beetle must have been slowly cooking in its own juices. I remember wondering how long it would go on until it collapsed from exhaustion. After an hour or so I got bored. I thought, Why doesn't it just fly away? I knew beetles could fly, so why didn't it just take off? How could I know then that there were beetles as earthbound as humans?

I make an obstacle course for it out of broken bits of hawthorn and blackthorn twigs. The blackthorn I make into a kind of barbed wire perimeter, but the beetle doesn't seem to mind the thorns; in fact it makes the climbing easier. I am hot and thirsty by now and the game hasn't gone as I had planned. I am angry — furious — with the beetle. I hate it for its brutish stupidity, for its barbed black legs, for its inability to fly, and most of all for its refusal to notice me. I pick it up and impale it on a vicious spike of the blackthorn, finding the soft tissue between its thorax and abdomen.

It minded that all right. It noticed that. I felt weak and strong at the same time. I was trembling, breathless, but the punishment of the beetle had given me power; I had broken through a barrier which had, until that point, prevented me from being what I could be. Even as a nine-year-old, I understood the portentousness of that moment. The beetle's legs flailed and its antennae waved blindly in a futile attempt to escape. Avoiding its pincer-like jaws, I broke off each antenna near the head. Strange, I had expected it to scream, but it didn't make a sound. I stuck the twig in the centre of the circle of stones and left the hated creature twitching on its spike, its mechanical legs winding down to eventual stillness.

I went back the next day but it had gone. The arena was still there but the twig and the beetle had vanished.

I don't know how long I stood watching the beetle in the bath, but when I came to the sun had tracked beyond the corner of the house so that the little beetle now toiled ineffectually in the shadow of the bath rim and only a faint gilding of light remained on the naked tips of the shrubs at the back of the house. It was a small creature, unlike the other I had found. Insignificant.

I picked the bleach bottle up from the windowsill, but it was empty. I reached for the hot tap, but something made me pause and, on impulse, I bent and cupped my hands, scooping up the beetle and releasing it through the window, fanning my fingers like a conjurer releasing a dove. At the instant of release its name flashed into my mind: Carabus nemoralis.

Chapter Seven

The smell of food and the noise of conversation hit them like a solid mass. Helen actually took a step back.

'Christ,' Ruth muttered, misinterpreting the action. 'Half the faculty's here.'

Helen stood blinking for a moment. The artificially high pitch of the voices above the clatter of cutlery on plates invoked a vivid recollection of meals in her old high school canteen. 'Cabbage,' she said.

'With custard by the smell,' Ruth said, her nostrils flaring involuntarily. 'Sure you don't want to eat in town?'

'I might be recognized,' said Helen. 'And I've had reporters trailing round after me whenever I set foot outside the house – or the university walls.'

They had come to the college refectory because Helen had developed a sudden ravenous hunger when Ruth had taken her home, and her fridge had been empty. 'A gleaming example of minimalism,' Ruth had commented dryly, lifting the solitary yoghurt tub from its lonely position on the middle shelf and checking the date on the lid suspiciously. 'I can't say I approve of your standard of housekeeping.'

'I haven't felt much like eating recently.' Helen had remembered that she had done some shopping on her way home the previous day but, when Ruth checked, she found the carrier bag of spoiled food on the bedroom floor, where Helen had left it.

'You'd've thought the police would have the sense to pack a few bits of shopping away—' Ruth stopped. 'What?'

Helen was laughing. Real laughter. No hysteria, she just found the whole thing hilariously funny. Ruth was torn between annoyance and relief. 'I'm sorry,' Helen said, making an effort – and failing – to compose herself. 'I just had this image of Inspector Nelson packing away my perishables.' She went back to giggling.

Ruth smirked. She had to admit, the idea of the mad-eyed policeman fussing over Helen's supermarket shopping did create a farcical picture. She reached into the carrier bag, which she still held in her hand. 'Can you account, *Mrs* Wilkinson,' she said, imitating the rasp in Nelson's voice, 'for the bloody kitchen roll in this bag?' She lifted out a dripping twin pack and dropped it into the kitchen bin. The pork joint Helen had bought had thawed and leaked over the entire contents of the bag. Helen paled, but Ruth had found the character of Inspector Nelson, the cadence of his voice, the manner of speech. 'I mean, can you assure me that this pork was outdoor reared? That it was treated with respect, allowed to roam free, to roll in shit – green, naturally. Has it feasted on swill? Organic, of course – and was it humanely *laid to rest?*' She stopped as Helen bolted for the door and tore upstairs to the bathroom. Ruth listened to her retching painfully for some minutes, then she followed her.

'You OK?' she asked, leaning against the door jamb.

Helen pulled herself to her feet, using the sink for support. 'Great,' she said tightly, flushing the toilet, and then running a sinkful of cold water and rinsing her face.

Ruth handed her a towel. 'Sorry,' she mumbled. 'I wasn't thinking. I shouldn't have mentioned the blood.'

Blood and screaming, and later, a feverish memory, vivid, like the

*dreams of delirium – a tiny, lifeless form in her own small hands.
Unbearably perfect.*

'Leave it, will you?' Helen sighed. 'It doesn't help to talk
about it, Ruth.'

'How would you know? You've never tried.'

An itching had started behind Helen's eyes and if she didn't
act quickly it would turn into burning and she would find
herself in another exhausting fit of crying. 'I'll phone Mum
and Dad and then we'll go to the canteen.' Ruth had been
sufficiently chastened to forget to correct Helen. The *refectory* –
for this was the only permissible term amongst the established
members of the faculty – was hot and the combined smells of
boiled mince and over-boiled vegetables, chip fat and sweet
puddings were overpowering. Helen asked for vegetable soup
and a bread roll. Ruth's selection took a little longer, and
consisted of high fat, high carbohydrate, low-fibre fillers. 'I
don't know how you eat so much junk and stay so slim,' Helen
remarked.

'Bulimia.'

It was said with no hesitation and in such a matter-of-fact
tone that Helen turned, slopping a little of her soup on to
the tray. 'You *are* joking?' she asked, unable to read her friend's
expression.

'You don't think it's funny?'

'No, I don't.' For the past three months eating even enough
to sustain herself had been an effort of will for Helen.

Ruth turned down the corners of her mouth and raised her
shoulders. 'Sorry,' she said.

They moved on, edging between tables, looking for a quiet
corner. The college rented out the undergraduate accommodation to foreign students during the vacations, and they
were all here today, practising their English on each other
with an assiduousness that was at once touching and amusing.
A few of Helen's third-year students, in to continue their

honours project work, smiled up at her as she passed, embarrassed, unsure how to greet her, but anxious to convey their sympathy.

They ended up sharing a table with Mallory and his entourage. Ainsley sat at a table for two, looking so morose that even the foreign students didn't venture to ask if the unoccupied seat was free.

'Either DA isn't getting his nooky or his wife is getting hers away from home,' Ruth said, grinning wickedly, as they took their places.

Mallory gave her a sour look, then turned at a forty-five degree angle so that she was presented with his shoulder and half his back. Ruth rolled her eyes at Helen. She reached past Mallory for the salt cellar and began shaking the container intemperately over her plate of chips. Grains fell in a flurry on her food, the plate rim, her tray, the table, a few even dusted the cuff of Mallory's ancient tweed jacket. Mallory glared at her over his shoulder and she smiled back sweetly. She ate rapidly, spearing four or five chips on her fork and jamming them into her mouth. While she chewed, she smeared her bread roll liberally with the contents of several of the tiny tubs she had picked up from the dish by the cash register, then she made a sandwich with the remainder of the chips.

Such anger, Helen thought, as she sipped at her soup, trying not to think of it as food, because any acknowledgement at a conscious level would summon the nausea she had suffered since January. Surely Ruth hadn't meant what she said about being bulimic? But you never could tell with Ruth. Anger and hunger were, in a way, synonymous in Ruth's mind. Anger at being delayed in her inevitable progression to the top of the academic tree – and it was inevitable, for Ruth was one of those rare people who can, without hesitation, be called brilliant – and hunger for the opportunities academic success would provide. Ruth had never been interested in material gain. What she wanted was acclaim, a chance to air her views and expound her theories before an audience of academics who would see her as a scientist, rather than a woman; to research under circumstances of generous funding, using state-of-the-art technology, rather than the five-year-old computer programs and hardware which represented the best St Werburgh's could provide. Helen saw her established as a *grande dame* of science, the sort of woman the media would love to consult because of her unguarded comments, her passion for her subject – and her Oxbridge-sculpted English accent.

Helen admired Ruth for her clearness of purpose, her vision, and was grateful to her as a reliable friend. Although Ruth had despised Edward, he had held a grudging respect for Ruth, a sneaking admiration for her intellectual ability and research skills.

Helen nodded to herself, smiling a little to think that the only friend of whom Edward had approved had been a woman. This was both ironic and predictable: ironic because Edward believed women intellectually inferior to men; predictable, because he routinely flirted with Helen's women friends. Of all of them, Ruth was the only one who had not been taken in by him. 'Passive immunization,' she had said. 'I saw what happened to you and the others when he got bored. They say a standing prick has no conscience, well you could add that a flattered fanny shows no judgement. I've a natural distrust of flattery – and I've never yet been proved wrong.'

Stirring the cooling soup with her spoon, Helen resolved to try another mouthful, but this was a task to be approached crab-wise, and as a distraction she concentrated on her surroundings. The big, low-ceilinged basement room was clad in tongue-and-groove pine, in a style popular in the '60s. It had oxidized to an almost chestnut orange–red and was overlaid with nicotine and vaporized cooking fat. The university had introduced a no smoking policy eighteen months previously and efforts had been made to remove the stench of cigarettes, but it had seeped into the wood, and on warm days it exhaled into the refectory air. The floor – chequered black and white tiles – had its usual grubby tint.

Helen looked around at the faces, familiar and unfamiliar, and felt that strange detachment which had become almost a part of her since the New Year. New Year. Time of hope. New resolutions. She frowned. And what have I resolved? she wondered. Rutherford was there, talking in his studied, courteous manner to a postgraduate researcher – Helen couldn't remember his name – looking like a prep school master instructing an acolyte in the art of conversation. Helen liked Rutherford, but Edward had dismissed him as 'a Cambridge queen'. Mallory and his group buzzed like angry wasps to her left. She studied Mallory's profile for a few minutes, wondering what it was that made a man so embittered with life. She knew he had little chance of retaining his post in the reorganization, Edward had told her as much, dismissing him as 'lax, lazy, incompetent and entirely without ideas'. In this instance, though she hated to admit it, Edward had probably been right: Mallory had not published anything in the past few years, he was pinning everything on John Ellis, and it was unfortunate for both of them that the Ph.D. student had taken Mallory as a role model. She had not examined his research closely, of course, since it was not her field, but Edward had shown an ominous interest in his work in the last month, and she knew they had argued on the day Edward had been murdered. He was a skinny, rangy young man, no match physically for Edward, but Edward himself had proved that strength was not needed to wound the heart, only a sharp blade and a steady hand.

Ellis avoided her eye, as all the others did, and Helen, pitying him in a way that perhaps he did not deserve, turned her attention away from the gathering at the table, to the rest of the room. Ainsley, poor David, sat diagonally opposite, hunched over his food like a dangerous animal, barely concealing his desolation. Edward had taken his scalpel to quite another part of David's anatomy than the heart, and now, Helen knew, the entire community, and even the wider world, would get to hear about his emasculation. Did he know about this before Edward's death? Did *she* know about it? If she was honest, she did. She knew about all of them; there was a stage between ignorance and suspicion, a point on the continuum, and she thought David had reached that some time ago. Would he have done anything about it? That depended very much upon what Edward had said to him on Monday morning.

Edward had made so many people miserable, seemed almost to delight in it, that she had thought that his death would bring, if not happiness, then at least a kind of relief, but the fear that had become so entrenched among the biology staff remained, and if anything seemed heightened by his absence. It was as if they felt safer with Edward because they knew what he would do, and it wasn't always the worst he *could* do, but Alice Chambers and the policemen who had rudely elbowed their way into the academic circle which had until now been a haven for them, these were exotic creatures, capable of objectivity, willing to judge actions and draw conclusions which might prove uncomfortable for some. Edward, on the other hand, was at least predictable in his vindictiveness, and they had known that if they had anything to offer him, then he might be prepared to haggle – though not with money: Edward's was strictly a barter system, based on favours owed and repaid; less traceable than money, but often extremely lucrative. Some staff had appealed directly to her, misunderstanding her influence with her husband, but these individuals were few. Nevertheless, she was tainted by her association with Edward, and generally she felt her colleagues did not trust her.

They were, all of them, aware of her, all strenuously avoiding making their awareness apparent, even to the extent of constraining their vision to parts of the dining hall where she was not. There was a pointedness to their looking away, as one avoids the eyes of a beggar or someone who is disfigured. Helen supposed that was how she must appear to them – disfigured by two tragedies, two bloody deaths. They could not know that the first, the lesser in their minds of the two, had left deeper scars.

Helen returned to the other possibility: that one of these people, these seemingly gentle, unworldly academics could not bring himself to meet her gaze because he had murdered her husband. Helen considered how she felt about this prospect, and decided that she bore the killer no ill-will. Her mother would call this wickedness, and of course she would be right.

Helen sighed and she looked up. An involuntary exclamation escaped her. Isaac Smolder had seated himself a couple of tables away and was staring at her. He let his gaze drop to his plate, which was piled with plain salad, and began cutting the lettuce into thin strips, attaching it with meticulous care to his fork, chewing slowly, as if counting the number of mastications before each swallow, eating without enjoyment, as though it was a task which must be performed, tedious, but necessary. Helen studied him trying to establish some tangible reason for her abhorrence of him. A small man, Smolder did not carry a physical threat. He was neatly dressed, as always, in shirt and bow tie. His hair was carefully combed. His hands, which manipulated his knife and fork as though dissecting an interesting specimen, were clean, and the nails were evenly clipped. It was these hands, and the fastidious precision with which he used them, that Helen noticed most particularly.

The polished nails and smooth, slightly yellow skin, which was barely wrinkled, even at the knuckles, so tightly was it stretched over the bones. She was struck by an overpowering sense of parsimoniousness, as if Smolder rationed out his ectodermis because he couldn't afford to waste it, had nothing to spare.

She looked away sharply when he caught her eye. Ruth was teasing Mallory and she made an effort to listen.

'It must be a bit of a drag, being booted out of your office by the filth,' she drawled, deliberately choosing terms that Mallory would abhor.

'I volunteered the use of my study,' he answered with sniffy dignity.

'Of course,' Ruth said, pursing her lips, 'it's going to hamper your preparations for the written submission—'

Mallory looked at each of his allies, but each, in turn, looked away. He focused on his soup bowl. 'It's all in hand,' he said, stirring the sludgy brownish liquid.

She smirked and muttered, 'Whose?' Then, in mock sympathy she added, 'Even so, the thought of nasty, brutish coppers polluting your air with all those dropped aitches and glottal stops . . .' The smile broadened to a grin, but Mallory, who refused to meet her eye, did not see it. Then, as if a sudden thought had occurred to her: 'Perhaps the Senate will give you an extension, since you're unable to gain access to your notes—'

Mallory flung down his spoon violently and spat into his napkin. 'I bloody knew it!' he shouted, spluttering, red in the face. 'There's ham in this vegetable soup.' He picked up his bowl and stalked off to the cook who stared blandly at him as he blustered and raged. Heads turned.

'That was uncalled for.' John Ellis, the postgraduate student, who had left the meeting so hurriedly the previous day, had spoken. 'I mean, wasn't it?' he added, suddenly appalled at his own audacity in speaking so plainly.

'Let me guess,' said Ruth, leaning on one hand, and using a slightly flaccid chip as a pointer. 'Since he can't do any useful work on his own submission until the police have finished with his room, and since he has such a breadth of experience in these matters and would *really* like to help you out, and anyway, he's your supervisor and there simply *hasn't* been enough time to talk through exactly what it is you've been doing for the past six months, Dr Mallory thought today might be a good time to go through your thesis with you, right?'

Ellis blushed.

'Trust me. Mallory wouldn't give a shit if you couldn't tell a littoral zone from an erogenous zone.'

'I don't know what you're trying to say—'

Ruth smiled slowly and leaned in to whisper, 'I'll give you a clue: the latter gives far more pleasure than the former.'

The flush spread from Ellis's face, down his neck and up to the roots of his hair.

Ruth jerked back in her chair and took a bite out of the chip, grinning. 'But of course, marine biology isn't your *thing*, is it John? *Drosophila melanogaster* is more your line. And what exactly *have* you been doing? I mean we've all heard the hoo-ha about your theory, if you can call it that.' She shrugged. 'It's rather like calling Gaia a hypothesis. Earth as superorganism is a pretty concept, comforting even. But isn't it more an analogy? A metaphor? And analogies aren't testable; metaphors, no matter how beguiling, are, by definition, literally false.'

'There's a growing body of evidence for co-evolution,' Ellis began, but he was not a natural orator and did not have sufficient knowledge of his subject to provide a confident rebuttal to the counter-arguments.

'Co-evolution – that's where the earth is supposed to be evolving to keep us snug in our little niches, isn't it? Well what about global warming, mass extinction, holes in the ozone layer, the depletion of oceanic fish stocks? Are we supposed to let the great god Gaia sort it all out for us? She doesn't seem to be getting very far – no sense of urgency.'

Feeney, caught between sympathy for Ellis and exasperation at his inability to argue his case, chipped in with, 'The Gaian theorists have a lot in common with conventional science. Their ideas and ours do converge at certain points.'

'There you go again,' said Ruth, enjoying the debate, aware from the general hush from the tables around them that they were drawing an audience. 'Calling it a theory. The *convergence* you talk about can be explained in terms of good, old-fashioned, testable science – biological and physiological feedback, physical and chemical fact. Of *course* organisms have an enormous impact on the abiotic environment – climate, soil conditions, recycling of minerals – and, yes, there *are* homeostatic features in the system, but it is not new, Feeney. Gaian protagonists are just tearing off bits of the old ideas which fit their models and Pritt-sticking them to their – their cause – I can't call it a theory, I'm sorry.'

'Lovelock's models—'

Ruth threw back her head and laughed. 'Models!'

Ellis muttered something about the models giving the right answers, and Ruth went on more kindly: 'Look, it's not that I'm against models – they're useful in their place, and I have to say your mathematical model is *elegant*, John, but does it *mean* anything? In terms of actual biological systems, that is.'

Ellis pulled himself together enough to say with pompous self-importance, 'I'll be publishing an interim report in *Nature*, next month, you'll have to read that.'

'Oh, well!' Ruth exclaimed. 'Mallory will be impressed. Or should I say relieved?' She leaned in again and Ellis looked somewhat alarmed. Lowering her voice to a stage whisper, Ruth went on: 'You know they'll want to see some actual stats, a bit of field data, dope, facts and figures – lab work – that sort of thing. Boring details, but even geniuses have to justify their theories.'

'I've got the data,' Ellis said, affronted. 'Dr Mallory thinks—'

Ruth snorted. 'Dr Mallory *thinks* – I'd be surprised,' she said. 'Look, I've got nothing against you, John. You may be shamefully naive, but that in itself is hardly a crime.' Ellis's colour deepened. He really was such a boy. Inoffensive to look at, if rather gawky; filled out, he may even be good-looking, but not in his present sorry state. 'Look, we've all been there,' she said. 'We know all about supervisors who couldn't give a shit about you, who couldn't even tell you the title of your dissertation or thesis, but they want their name right up there on any published material.' She looked for acknowledgement, but Helen was watching the escalating row between the cook and Mallory, and Feeney was rubbing his eyes vigorously. She resisted the temptation to mention displacement behaviour and instead turned her attention back to Ellis, who was blushing so hard his ears had turned red and she could almost feel the heat from him.

'I'm not incapable, you know.'

'Nobody's saying you are. All I'm suggesting is that you be circumspect in what you claim for your research. You have to get a sense of proportion – you have to adopt a realistic perspective. There's nothing worse than being routed by academics. I know. It's happened to me more than once.' Ellis was looking at her as though seeing her for the first time. Some of the colour had begun to fade from his face and he was listening intently. The others around the table had fallen silent and were listening too, and even Helen watched her with close attention.

Perspective. Now you may have something there. I dreamed, once, of giants crossing a causeway – huge, tilt-legged monsters striding jerkily across a vast expanse of sand and silty water. Blue sky above, mud and puddles of captured sky below.

As I awoke, I remember thinking 'It's all a question of perspective.' It was one of those rare revelatory moments in which a small but significant piece of the jigsaw fits into place with a satisfying click, and it's as if you had always possessed this little bit of wisdom.

Just as figures on the horizon seem taller, elongated by mirage and their relative position in the landscape, my rank must seem vast, monumental to those of lower status, so Edward must have seen me, from his vantage point, as bearer of an important title, his accepted superiority magnifying his tiny intellect fooling even Edward himself into thinking that he held monstrous power in his hands. Looking down, he considered me small, insignificant, dispensable.

Smolder stood up and carried his tray back to the trolley. 'Your cynicism does you no credit,' he told Ruth quietly, then, without allowing her a chance to reply, he left the refectory.

Feeney coughed. 'Yes?' Ruth waited, but Feeney fell to picking up crumbs from the Formica table top with the pads of his fingers and rubbing them on to his plate.

'A lot of people are going to be seriously pissed off if you don't deliver, John,' she told Ellis. 'Not just Mallory, not just the Dean of Faculty – there's a whole raft of New Age potheads desperate to make your results fit their faith. Publishing contracts hang in the balance, waiting for your results before they can be signed and advances paid. You hold entire *careers* in your sweaty palm.' She eyed him thoughtfully. 'But you already knew that, didn't you?'

'I think,' said Ellis, 'my results will satisfy the academic community and the Gaians.'

Ruth laughed. 'Naivety, I can tolerate, but pomposity,' she shook her head, 'that's unforgivable.'

Chapter Eight

'Are you here for the night, or is this a fleeting visit?' Sheila was standing at the kitchen table, peeling potatoes. Her tone was strained, her blonde hair tousled and windblown, and she looked flushed and out of sorts.

'Somewhere between the two.' Terry Hackett knew better than to rush in.

'Well, if you've time, you can pick Lisa up from her rehearsal. I've only just got started on dinner. Your mother phoned – she said it was urgent. Thought someone was following her after she'd picked up her pension from the post office.'

Hackett felt a sudden stab of fear. 'I'll fetch Lisa and call in on my way back.'

'No need. I went round. I think she was just lonely.'

Before his father's death, six months earlier, Hackett's mother had been an independent, bossy, argumentative, infuriating and loveable woman; now, she was lonely, depressed and anxious, a burden to her family and herself. Without Terry Sr to argue with and order about, she seemed to lose interest in life, beyond a morbid taste for real-life crime programmes and a belief that, as a widow, she had become a natural target for every type of villain: burglar, confidence trickster, rapist, drug fiend (she called them this, in preference to the more vulgar expression, 'druggy'), mugger, it didn't matter, she was afraid of them all.

'I'm sorry, love.'

'She can't help it. But you'll have to get something sorted, Terry. At least she could have her money paid directly into her bank account. We can't go on like this.' She moved her head sharply as he reached to touch her hair. It was unlike Sheila to be so irritable. What she meant was *I* can't go on like this, since it generally was Sheila who ended up doing the looking after, the running around, the calming down and setting right.

He moved closer and kissed her gently on the forehead. 'It's this bloody murder investigation, else I'd be home more.'

She lifted her shoulder and bent her head, capturing his hand briefly and pressing it to her cheek. 'We haven't even had chance to talk about your new job,' she said. 'What's your new boss like?'

'Angry.'

Sheila smiled. Terry was fond of summing people up in a word, on short acquaintance. He wasn't often wrong. 'Best watch him, then.'

'Eyes in the back of my head.' He kissed her on the lips this time, and she returned it, holding her arms wide to protect his clothing from the potato she had been peeling.

'Good-looking bloke, that professor,' she said, gently extricating herself and continuing with the work.

'My boss has taken a dislike to his wife. Thinks she had a hand in it.'

'She wouldn't be the first.'

'No.' Hackett picked up the kettle and shook it, then carried it to the sink and added enough water for a brew. 'There's a lad – a DC – bit of a whiz on the computer: Jem Tact. Peculiar name. Funny bloke, come to think of it. But he knows his stuff, does Jem. He was sifting through the junk in Prof Wilkinson's office and decided to check the files on his networked PC. Took a bit of doing, but the computer services department eventually came up with the right passwords and such. He started with the most recently updated files. Wilkinson had one called Apocalypse.'

Sheila raised her eyebrows in question.

'There's a lot of staff expected to lose their jobs in some sort of reshuffle. The file lists everyone he interviewed on the morning before he was killed.'

'Religious, was he?'

'Not as far as I know, but it looks like he fancied himself for the god-slot. Apocalypse is the one where everyone gets their come-uppance, right?'

'Day of Reckoning. Four Horsemen. That sort of thing.'

Hackett threw a couple of teabags into the pot and filled it with boiling water, then stirred the brew thoughtfully.

'So who's for the chop?' Sheila asked, with her usual perspicacity.

'Suspiciously few,' Terry said dryly. 'There are fifteen entries and it reads like a fairy tale – everyone lives happily ever after.' Rutherford and Ainsley, whom they had already interviewed, both safe. The faithful Mrs Roberts confirmed to continue as his secretary. Mick Tuttle to have his contract renewed. Helen Wilkinson was listed as 'query promotion', Feeney recommended to continue until retirement in a year and a half, two lab technicians cleared for renewal of contract, ditto the departmental librarian, a group of junior lecturers and a couple of researchers.

'Looks like he was a benign sort of deity, then.'

'Inquiries so far suggest Prof Wilkinson was not a philanthropist.'

'Not *all* inquiries, surely, love,' Sheila corrected.

'Excluding the computer files,' Terry conceded. He poured them both a mug of tea and sipped from his own, dunking a biscuit into it before continuing. 'The only two we had any doubts about were a Dr Mallory who is definitely out on his ear, and a Ph.D. student called Ellis. There was just one word written under his entry—'

'Which was?'

'SHOP.'

'Oh, dear.'

'That's what we thought, until someone told us it stands for Senate House Overview of Progress. It's a panel the Ph.D. students are referred to periodically. A matter of routine.'

'So Mr Ellis can breathe a sigh of relief. But what about this other chap?'

'Dr Mallory. Bit embarrassing, really. He's loaned us his office for interviews. Then young Jem discovered the file had last been modified on Tuesday at 2 p.m., the day *after* Wilkinson was murdered.'

'So you need to find out either who changed the file, or what the original entry was, so anyone who gets a better deal on the new version is suspect. Be interesting to see if Dr Mallory's entry had been changed.'

Hackett grinned. Sheila had been a CID officer before she had retired to bring up the kids.

'Don't you give me that indulgent smile, Terence Hackett, I'm not one of your trainees. I take it you've checked his office for back-ups of the original file?'

Terry made an attempt at seriousness, but he could see that the strain of Sheila's afternoon was wearing off with the intellectual challenge of the puzzle he had set her. 'There weren't any,' he said.

'What about home?'

The smile returned, but only briefly as Sheila threatened him with the wet end of a peeled potato. 'DC Tact has been despatched to search the professor's study. I'm meeting him back at HQ at seven.'

Lisa took a few steps at a run when she saw him, then stopped, throwing a furtive glance at her school friends. She turned her back on him and stood in a huddle for a few minutes, engaged in excited chatter and over-loud laughter with the three other girls. Lisa was twelve years old and couldn't wait to be grown up. She had coerced her mother into letting her have her ears pierced on her twelfth birthday, and insisted on wearing large, brightly coloured earrings which flashed in her hair. She had inherited his hair colour and she let it cascade gloriously over her shoulders. She fiddled with it constantly, a kind of preening gesture, and Hackett was uncomfortably aware of the attention it drew from boys her own age and older.

She finished her conversation and sauntered up to him. 'Hi, Dad.'

He bent swiftly and kissed her on the cheek before she had time to react and she scowled up at him. 'You did that deliberately.'

He grinned back. 'It was an accident, your *honour*.'

'Very funny.' She sulked for a minute or two in the car, but soon forgot that she was supposed to be cross with him when he asked her how the rehearsals were going. 'Miss Armitage said the boys'll have to overcome their self-consciousness if they're to be at all convincing. Chris was practically *monotonal* in the balcony scene.' 'Monotonal' was a new word she had learned from her drama teacher, and she had been desperate for an opportunity to try it out. 'I mean *totally* crap!'

'There's no need for language like that, young lady.'

Lisa rolled her eyes. 'Oh, Dad, crap isn't a swear word.'

'It's not very nice, either.'

'Not *ladylike* enough for you?'

This was an old theme: expectations of girls and boys being different, double standards. 'It's not a question of you being a girl, I just don't like my children using bad language.'

'You should hear what Daniel says.' She slid him a sideways glance.

Hackett realized suddenly that he hadn't seen Daniel at home. 'Where is he tonight?' he asked.

'How should I know? Miss Armitage said I was a natural. She said I carried the scene, but Chris couldn't rely on that on the night. Everyone's got to pull their weight. She said Gita's the best Nurse she's seen in years – a real comic talent, she said. Dad, can Gita stay over tomorrow night, after the rehearsal?'

'No.' He knew Gita and liked her. A big, robust, slightly blowsy girl who was inclined to raucousness and insomnia. 'Not during the week, Lisa. You've homework to do.'

'You let Daniel do whatever he wants, but I can't even invite my friends over.' From ennui to enthusiasm, poise to petulance in seconds, this had become the pattern for Lisa since reaching her twelfth birthday.

'Daniel does not have friends over during the week. You know that.'

'Yeah,' she said. 'But you don't know where he is, do you?'

This was said out of spite, he knew, but it made him uneasy. Daniel had become secretive of late. Normal, he told himself. Entirely normal. The majority of boys Daniel's age went through a phase of not wanting their parents to interfere, but in a way, he preferred the blatant flouting of his authority that had been the norm for a time, the succession of trendy causes on the periphery of what Hackett was willing to allow as 'normal', or even legal. Just after his fifteenth birthday, they had had to fetch Daniel from a demo against a new housing estate which was due to be constructed on green belt land near their home. It hadn't got as far as an arrest, and Daniel hadn't even got his picture in the local rag; it was embarrassing, but at least they had known where to find him. The more subtle bending of rules, the evasiveness of recent weeks had been more difficult to deal with; he had warned himself against overreaction, but could not help running through a mental checklist of Signs and Symptoms.

'Do you know where he is?'

'Per-*lease*, Dad, don't do the Detective Sergeant on me.' She looked out of the passenger window and started humming to herself, a sure sign she was hiding something.

It was almost a relief to return to work. Hackett couldn't take Sheila's easy-going approach to their children's bids for independence, and he thought it was probably just as well that she dealt with them more often than he did. Coward's way out, his conscience told him, but at least this way they got some peace at home, uneasy though it might be at times.

Jem Tact was a curious combination of intense, nervous energy and other-worldly dreaminess. He had a sensitive, kindly face and was softly spoken, and Hackett suspected that if it weren't for his basketball player height and rugby player breadth, he would have been a target for canteen barracking.

He wasn't strong on details, so Hackett had spent the first five minutes of their meeting bombarding him with questions which Tact seemed to view as a minor irritation, and a diversion from the main item on the agenda, namely, the results of his search. Hackett's questions drew out the following facts: Dr Wilkinson hadn't been keen on a second invasion by the police; she was even less keen on the removal of the disks, but had accepted Tact's properly made out receipt with bad grace, and only after an argument. Tact had offered to make a copy of the disks for the good doctor, but she had refused.

'Odd thing, to make all that fuss and then refuse a copy.'

'Mm.' Tact was loading the disk files into the computer on Hackett's desk, and was not really attending to the sergeant's questions.

'Have you seen this already?'

Tact gave him a sideways grin; his eyes remained fixed on the monitor. 'Had to,' he said, then, adopting the manner of a man explaining quantum physics to a two-year-old: 'That disk represents about .001 per cent of the total bank of floppies Prof W had at home. That's about a thousand disks,' he added helpfully.

'Thank you, Jem.'

'That's OK.' In his intense mode, Jem was immune to irony. 'Luckily, he had a good filing system.'

'Did—' Hackett found himself talking over Tact's lecture. 'Sorry to interrupt, but did Dr Wilkinson see what's on the disk?'

'Of *course* not. I shut the door.'

Consider yourself dismissed, Hackett thought. 'I hope you were, um, subtle about it,' he said, floundering for the appropriate adjective.

'By name and nature,' Tact had apparently learned, even at his tender age, that it was always best to get the name jokes in yourself. Hackett chuckled obligingly. He'd had enough of 'Terry looks a bit *Hackett* off,' type jibes in the early days to sympathize with the lad.

'These're the alterations,' Tact said, indicating the screen. He'd highlighted the changed items of information in blue font.

Mrs Roberts had been mistaken – or perhaps she had lied to them – Prof Wilkinson had intended to offer her early retirement. David Ainsley's contract was recommended not to be renewed. Mick Tuttle was to be referred to the equal opportunities panel – the recommendation being non-renewal of contract. Feeney was down for early retirement. Rutherford was a borderline case.

'When was this file last updated?'

Tact grabbed the mouse and clicked in the file menu, too fast for Hackett to follow exactly what he did. A grey box opened on the screen. Hackett skipped down the list: File name . . . Created . . . Last saved . . .

'That's last Sunday, isn't it?' He leaned over Tact's shoulder, a feat which was only possible because Tact habitually slumped in his chair with his size thirteens sticking out the other side of the desk for people to trip over, then tapped the line indicating when the file was created.

'At 9.30 p.m. Last saved at 9.45 p.m. Sunday. No revisions. He really wasn't a very nice man, was he Sarge?'

Hackett looked hard at the constable, then deciding that this was Tact's brand of irony, replied, 'He'd already made up his mind what he was going to do – who he'd recommend to keep and who to sack, and he was going to put them through the interviews, the presentations, the seminars, all that crap – I'd say he was an out and out bastard, Jem.'

Helen looked out, through the pupil of her right eye and beyond it, saw the slightly blurred aureole of iris and pupil of another, distinct eye. Unexceptional, but for the fact that she was viewing it from within, the spokes of radial muscle curved outward, concave, rather than convex, and their colour was the mud-brown of muscles, fibres, blood vessels.

She remembered, as clearly as only dreamers can, of that other time when the tiger had slipped free of its prison and her other self had sought out the man under the street light. A flash of silver, orange light reflected on tarry black. His look of terror; his mouth opening to scream, the impact that stopped it.

She woke with a start, and lay still for some moments. Had she killed Edward? She had wanted to, though she realized that didn't necessarily amount to the same thing – and she couldn't always remember what her other self had done in those moments when despair or blind rage took over.

Helen screamed. There was a face at the window. A man peering in, his hands cupped to the glass. She leapt from the sofa and drew the curtains, shouting at the man to go away. Her scream, or the subsequent shouting seemed to trigger a burst of noise at the front of the house and Helen whirled, disorientated by the furious knocking and rattling at the letterbox. Half a dozen, maybe more voices raised, calling for her to come to the door, cajoling, asking questions, wheedling for just one picture. She had returned home after lunch and fallen asleep, the pills Sanjay Patterson had given her were still working their sluggish way through her system and she felt adrift, out of touch.

Alone in the house, her instinct was to call Ruth. She edged slowly to the doorway of her sitting room and slipped silently into the hallway, keeping close to the wall, inching towards the telephone. She had slept at home the previous night and Ruth had asked:

'You're not afraid?'

'What's there to be afraid of?'

She had sensed Ruth's smile rather than seen it. 'Nothing,' Ruth had said. 'Nothing at all.'

But they had reckoned without the Press.

Ruth arrived ten minutes later, striding up the path as though it were empty. She rang the bell, then whirled suddenly on the unruly flock of reporters crowding behind her. They took a joint step back, cameras still ready, pocket-sized tape recorders thrust forward. She scanned the group and picked on a fresh-faced youth with red hair – a photographer, by the look of his gear – he had the dishevelled look of a student, first time away from home. She hooked a finger through the strap of his satchel which hung from his shoulder, and drew him closer.

'Now, you know you're getting old,' she said, inviting the collusion of the others, 'when they start sending schoolboys to cover murders.' She gave the lad a friendly shove and turned away from them, enjoying their good-humoured laughter.

Helen let her in, hiding behind the front door from the curious faces. The babble of shouting followed them through the kitchen, where Helen had pulled down the blind. 'What the hell started all of this up again?' she asked.

Ruth dragged a folded copy of the *Chester Recorder* from her coat pocket. A black smudge marked the tan wool of her jacket. 'This,' she said, opening the paper and holding it up for Helen to read.

It was a good picture, almost contemplative in its detached serenity. At first Helen did not recognize the subject: a small woman, bundled up in a dark overcoat, evidently slight; there was an ethereal, almost fey quality about her. Her head was tilted upwards and she seemed to be staring at one of the upstairs windows of the house which formed the backdrop of the photograph. Her hair fell away in one silky sheet from her face, revealing a pretty, rather pale young woman. She seemed to see something beyond the glass, beyond the closed curtains of the upper room.

Jeff Townley, editor of the *Chester Recorder*, had been more than pleased with the photograph. He had previously been agonizing over a choice between using a blurry snapshot of Helen Wilkinson on a field trip with some students, taken several years previously, her face practically obscured by mizzly rain and the hood of her waterproof jacket, and a formal portrait of her in cap and gown after receiving her doctorate.

'What you got there?' Dermot Molyneux had arrived from Dublin nine months ago and had been on the staff of the *Chester Recorder* for three weeks. He had freelanced for the paper for six months prior to that and Townley still couldn't work out how Molyneux had talked him into signing him up and paying him a salary.

Townley squinted aggressively at the photographer – a habit he'd developed when smoking was the norm, and the norm for him was to have one fag permanently in his mouth and another burning to nothing in the ashtray in his office.

Molyneux edged between Townley and Rick Lazenby, his news editor, a practised, insinuating movement, born of years of filching pictures that his elders and betters had spent hours setting up, and Townley found himself nose to curls with Dermot's auburn mop. 'I know her,' Molyneux said, picking up the studio photograph of Helen in cap and gown.

'You damn well ought to – you were sent to get a picture of her yesterday. Oh – but I'm forgetting myself,' Townley said, ladling on the sarcasm. 'An artist such as yourself needs the right lighting, the ambience, the setting.'

'Well you're right about the ambience,' Molyneux said, refusing to be ruffled. 'But finding the subject was the hard bit, in this case. No – what I mean is I've *seen* her – in the flesh, so to speak. Only I didn't know it was her at the time. She's not much like these shots, you know.' He stopped, listening to the silence, relishing it.

For a few seconds the only sound in the room was the gentle rasp of Townley's breathing, then, bracing himself for disappointment he said, 'Tell me you got a picture.'

Dermot Molyneux suppressed a sigh of pleasure, allowing himself – just – the tiniest of smirks. 'I'll tell you anything you like, boss' he said, 'just so long as it makes you happy.'

Townley looked ready to do murder and Molyneux decided it would be safer to play straight. 'Didn't I look everywhere for the good doctor yesterday, and wasn't she nowhere to be found?'

'Do me a favour and cut the professional Paddy crap,' Townley said. 'What's the bottom line?'

'To tell you the truth, boss, I didn't know it was her. I'd given up on finding her at the university and I was too shit-scared to come back with nothing, so I thought I'd do a few spooky shots of the house—'

'I saw them,' Townley interrupted. 'Hackneyed.'

Molyneux shrugged. 'Yeah, well.' His ego didn't bruise easily. 'Wait till you see what else I got.' He rummaged in a battered, brown leather satchel which looked like it had seen service during his school days. He placed three A5-sized black and white photographs side by side on the desk.

'Fuck me,' Townley said softly, his tone so caressingly gentle that Molyneux couldn't stop the reply tumbling out of his mouth:

'Well that's an interestin' suggestion. Perhaps some other time. And what do you think of the photos?' Townley's stare put him in a spin. He'd gone too far. Blushing, he added, 'I mean, sir, Mr Townley, boss. Oh, shit.'

Lazenby laughed, setting the room reverberating with his barrel-chested ho-ho-hos, and Townley, startled by this sudden reminder that he and Molyneux were not the only people in his office, forgot his annoyance with the Irishman.

'It's a pearl of a picture,' he said, picking up the centre photograph as Molyneux had hoped he would. 'Haunting.'

'Now that's what I thought,' Molyneux said, swivelling his eyes in Townley's direction to gauge his reaction. 'I thought she was just another ghoul, come to see the house, but there was . . . I don't know, there was something about her. That face – it – it's . . . What would you call it?'

Townley laughed. 'Let your camera do the talking, Dermot, lad. You're no orator. Practically inarticulate, if you don't mind my saying, but your pictures could persuade the simians from the arboretum.'

'I'll have you know I've kissed the Blarney stone,' said Dermot.

'Well it's done your mouth no good, but what an eye!' Townley examined the picture at close quarters. 'It's like one of those holograms – look at it from a different angle and you see something else. What the hell is she thinking?'

Dermot grinned. It was just the impression he'd had when he'd taken the shot. It was the very expressionlessness of her face that made it so compelling; was it sadness, or fear, or a dull rage, or cold contempt? It all depended upon the perspective of the observer.

'We'll have to choose the caption carefully,' Townley said, the same thought having occurred to him.

Helen took the paper from Ruth and read the caption: *'Dr Wilkinson returns to House of Death.'*

'I didn't even notice him – the photographer,' she said.

'You've been pretty much out of it since it happened,' said Ruth. 'Nice to have you back.'

'Oh, no!' Helen had begun to read the article under her picture. There were names, details, more than she had known herself. 'Who gave them this? Can they say these things and get away with it?'

Ruth shrugged. 'Don't they say you can't libel the dead? Anyway, it's true, isn't it? I'd say they've a fairly restrained and dignified style – wait till the tabloids really get their teeth into it – the *Herald* is running a story on *Don* Juan, the Casanova of St Werburgh's. I think they've rather mixed their analogies, but that's the *Herald* for you. And as for who, take your pick

– Edward made enemies like I make jam sandwiches: with flair, with panache, and with the compulsiveness of an addict.'

Helen read on. 'Poor David!'

Ruth snorted. 'David Ainsley can take care of himself. The good thing is it's given the police a few more suspects to keep them busy. Don't look at me like that, Helen. You were out of your skull for a couple of days. You more or less confessed to the murder of your husband. If it weren't for that nice Sergeant Hackett, Inspector Nelson would have you banged up by now. You should be grateful the Press have given him a few more names to think about.'

'And what if I did do it?' Helen asked, thinking uneasily of her dream.

Ruth groaned. 'What if? What if? What if Gazza becomes cultural attaché to the European Community? What if I'm awarded the Nobel Prize for my contributions to scientific advancement? Hey, anything's possible – it might happen.'

'Now you're being preposterous,' Helen said angrily.

'Because it is preposterous, Helen. The notion of you killing is beyond serious contemplation. You can't bring yourself to cross the threshold into the dissection room because the sight and smell of death appals you. You can't even do the research you used to because you can't face the corpses. You haven't eaten properly in months. You're nauseated by the smell of animal flesh – and you're asking me to believe you stuck a knife in him? Watched him bleed to death?' She shook her head. 'You haven't got it in you. Whoops!' She caught Helen as she buckled at the knees and helped her to a chair.

'I'm sick of this,' said Helen, pale, but rallying. 'I'm sick of feeling so weak. So—'

'So eat!' said Ruth, imitating her Jewish mother. 'It's no wonder you're passing out all over the place. All I've seen you eat in two days is a bowl of soup and a bread roll.'

Helen stared at her feet, trying to stave off a cold wave of faintness. 'It seemed so – it still seems so – plausible. Why shouldn't I have killed him? He deserved it.'

'Why indeed? But you didn't kill him. Someone else did and then left him for you to find. That wasn't very nice of them.'

Helen stared. 'Not very nice?' she echoed. 'You don't object to Edward's murder, but you think it was *impolite* to leave his body for me to find?'

Ruth stared back. She didn't need to tell Helen what a shit her husband had been. It wasn't necessary to enumerate his many and varied faults; Helen knew he was a bully, a serial adulterer and a vicious, social-climbing snob whose ambition far outweighed his talent. Helen didn't need anyone to tell her that most of his acquaintance hated, feared and despised Edward.

They were startled by the telephone ringing. Ruth went to answer it, returning a few moments later, subdued.

'Who was it?'

'One of the tabloids, wanting a comment.'

'How did they get this number?'

'Being ex-directory is scant protection against those jackals.' Ruth sighed. 'You'd best stay at my place for a few days.' She stood, picking up the newspaper which Helen had discarded on the kitchen table and jamming it back into her pocket. 'Come on, I'll take you there now.'

Helen shook her head. 'I'm staying here,' she said firmly. 'I'm not going to let them drive me from my home.'

Ruth's cool blue eyes searched her friend's face. A trace of amusement flickered at the corners of her mouth. 'Attagirl,' she murmured.

Chapter Nine

The front door slammed and the baby jerked awake, instantly screaming. Clara Ainsley groaned. Her eyes were red-rimmed from lack of sleep and from crying, her hair, normally so sleek and well-groomed, was caught carelessly in a scrunchy and pulled back into a ponytail. It had not been washed in two days and she couldn't bear it on her face. She carried the baby through to the narrow hallway; he was overheated and cranky – he smelt of curdled milk and warm talcum powder. He had thrown up on the clean babygro she'd put on him not half an hour earlier and she was damned if she would change him again. He had kept up an incessant keening for the day and a half that David had been missing; that constant, penetrating baby cry that will not be ignored, as though he knew there was something wrong. It had set her teeth on edge until she had fled to the upper rooms of the house, but his howls had spiralled up the stairwell, and even when she played a CD blaring rock music she imagined she could hear him. She had stood at the head of his cot, screaming back at him but that only made him worse, so finally she had gone out of the house – left him – because she feared that if she went to him she would hurl him from the nursery window to the concrete path below. She even imagined it – the flight, the sudden, soft thud, the silence. The blessed, longed-for silence.

She had walked to the river and for a while watched the ducks bobbing frantically on the wind-whipped water. It was bitterly cold and she had left the house without an overcoat, but she could not go back, could not trust herself near him yet. On the flimsy footbridge over the river she saw a young couple kiss, as she and Edward had kissed so often, but never so publicly. Once, they had found a quiet spot in the park on the other side of the bridge half afraid and half excited by the thrill of indiscretion, the risk of discovery. They had talked, whispered, shared their food and drink, sipping from the same glass, feeding each other morsels, laughing, touching, kissing like teenaged lovers. He had slept, briefly, stretched out on the tartan rug that her mother had given her as a wedding present, and she had teased him, kissing him awake. He had feigned sleep until she had been ready to lose patience and then he had grabbed her and tumbled her to the rug and returned her kiss with all the passion that once David had felt for her. She and Edward had shared something special, precious, to be cherished, and he had wasted it. Whenever she began to regret her actions on that awful day, she only had to think of what he had thrown away . . . She could not have allowed him to treat her as he had treated the others.

She had returned an hour later, calmer, able to pick up the still screaming baby, able to resist the compulsion to shake him. She shushed him, holding him in the crook of her arm as, one-handed, she mixed him another bottle of milk. He refused it of course, forcing the teat out of his mouth with his tongue in ill-tempered spite and arching his hot little body until her arm ached. She walked. Miles and miles of carpet-wearing, back-breaking walking, trying him with the bottle until finally, exhausted, he began to suck and within minutes had fallen asleep. And then the front door had slammed.

David Ainsley looked both haggard and sullen. He was unshaven and his suit and overcoat were badly rumpled. Clara and David eyed each other, the baby carriage forming a barrier between them. It was an old-fashioned Silver Cross pram in the grand style, too big for the house; soon it would be too small for the baby, but Clara had wanted it and as usual he had given way to her.

'Satisfied?' she asked.

'Far from it.'

'Where've you been?'

'What the hell do you care?'

'I was worried.' The baby had screamed without taking breath since the front door had slammed and she patted his back, thinking, If he doesn't stop soon, he'll choke – then, with a rush of venom – *I hope he bloody does, then David will see what I've been through these last two days*.

'Thought you'd lost both your men, did you?' David asked.

'For God's sake, David!'

'Sorry – I'm not being terribly *adult* about this, am I?'

Clara thought of Edward, so unlike David, both in appearance and in temperament. David's anger – and she supposed he had a right to be angry – seemed like childish petulance. She could not remember, nor even imagine, Edward being anything less than impressive. His anger had been daunting, his criticism crushing, his arguments bruising to the ego. She wondered again why she had ever married David. The notion of love, or even affection seemed outrageous – this sulking, flop-haired child? She made a conscious effort to imagine how Edward would have handled the situation, to frame the words he would have spoken.

'You can't help yourself, can you?'

'Me? I haven't been carrying on a shabby little affair—'

'There wasn't anything shabby about it!' Clara interrupted, flushing, telling herself it was anger rather than shame; but all the same, remembering their meetings at a motel near Heswall – far enough beyond the Cheshire boundary to remove some of the danger, but not too far for her to make the journey by bus, anonymous enough to be safe, hygienic enough to seem wholesome, even guiltless in its laundered sterility.

He was watching her, thinking how ugly anger made her, how little lying became her. 'It was beautiful, then, was it? With him?'

She eyed him coldly. 'Strange you've said nothing until now. You must have known. Even you aren't quite so dense.'

'How *dare* you! Of course I didn't know,' dimly, shamefully aware that he had let the affair go on, suppressing his certain, though largely subconscious knowledge of it.

'Don't play the wronged husband with me, David, I know you better.'

'Are you going to tell me you did it for us, Clara? Tell me you shagged the boss to keep me in a *job*?' His voice rose to a screech and the baby's cries became frightened, a persistent, staccato bleat.

Clara curled her lip in contempt, looking over the baby's shoulder at him, reminding herself to pat rather than hit. 'Don't sully what we had with your sordid interpretation. It wasn't like that,' she said.

'You'd call it something different, would you? What euphemism would you come up with? Love? Please don't ask me to believe you were in *love* with that shit!'

'Edward cared about me!' They competed with the rising volume of the baby's screams.

'Like he cared for all of them – his students who got themselves laid because it would help their grades or because they were flattered by the attention; the junior lecturers and the secretaries and the technicians – the sad succession of women who fell for his good looks and his questionable charm.'

He saw doubt in his wife's face and a spark of triumph made him add: 'All you were there for was to bolster his ego when it felt a little flaccid—' He laughed harshly. 'And for anything else that needed a female hand to firm it up.'

'You disgust me,' she hissed. The baby hiccuped, took another lungful of air and began again.

'Really? Well that makes us even.'

'And what about you, and men like you, hanging on to his coat tails, turning a blind eye to Edward's little transgressions? What does that make you, David?'

'You think he cared for you? He was about to get rid of you.'

'You're talking rubbish. You didn't even know him.'

'Types are easy to read. And Edward Wilkinson was a type. A walking phallus, a supreme ego. He called us all into his office the day he was murdered.' Clara flinched at the word. 'He saved me until last. Told me he didn't think my research into dog whelks was *de rigueur*. "Been done to death," he said. "Molluscs are the province of the great Steve Jones, and he does it *so* much better. Find yourself another niche." He did like his little puns. But then, you'd know that, wouldn't you, darling? He suggested that one of the new city universities might be grateful for someone who would bring a bit of old-style traditional research. "Gives them credibility. A sense of cultural identity." I wish I'd smashed my fist into his self-satisfied, smirking mouth!'

Clara stared at him round-eyed.

'What's the matter, darling? Am I getting through? Are you finally making the connection? If Edward intended getting rid of *me*, that means *you* were on the way out. Don't look so hurt, Clara. After all, mumsy, milky women wafting *Eau de merde*, baby puke and talcum powder weren't exactly *"de rigueur"* with old Ed. He went in for younger, racier models. Who do you think he had spent the afternoon with?'

Clara held the baby too tightly and he squirmed in her arms, fighting for breath. 'How should I know?'

David laughed and she shuddered at the harshness of the sound. 'My God, Clara, was it you? The papers say he was found naked in bed. If it was *you* he was with, then you're what the police call a prime suspect—' He raised his eyebrows, hugely amused by the idea.

Clara stood gaping as he stamped up the stairs to their bedroom, staring at the empty space where he had been and feeling as if her world was disintegrating. Then she followed him, releasing her grip on the baby enough for him to let out a furious bellow. David fetched down a suitcase and a few grey balls of dust from the top of the wardrobe.

'Of course it wasn't me,' she said.

'Not exactly an instantaneous reaction, my love – the denial of an outraged innocent.' He watched her thoughtfully for some moments.

'David, how can you think—'

'That my wife would do such a thing? Well, I have to admit, it took a while for me to accept that you could be unfaithful. Even longer to entertain – entirely the wrong word – the thought that you were shagging that bloody priapus. Now . . .' He paused, gave a small shake of his head. 'Now, I'd believe you capable of just about anything, Clara.'

She watched him for a few moments, too engrossed in her own thoughts to register what he was doing. The baby's crying had abated somewhat and although he whimpered and complained, snuffling unhappily, he seemed calmer. Gradually realization came to her. 'What are you—?'

David threw her a burning, bloodshot look and then continued with his packing.

'You're not going – you can't go!' She grabbed his arm but he shook her off, raising his hand to strike her, then horrified, he lowered his arm.

'You see what you make of me?' he said hoarsely. He was

shaking uncontrollably. 'Well I won't let you do it.' He shut his eyes for a moment and drew a breath, then he continued with his packing.

'You can't! You can't leave me!' she screamed. 'What about the baby! Your son?'

'*My* son?'

'You bastard,' she whispered.

He clicked the clasps of the suitcase closed, fixing her with a shrivelling look. 'Are you talking to me or the child?'

She swung at him with the open palm of her free hand but he caught her wrist and pulled her to him, ignoring the grizzling cries of the baby. 'Read that,' he snarled, fumbling a copy of the *Herald* from his coat pocket. '*Don Juan*, they're calling him – like the pun? Subtle, isn't it? It doesn't actually name you, but there isn't anyone else it could be. How long was it going on for, Clara? A year? More? How many people knew about it? How many lies did you tell me? Did you let him fuck you here? In this house? In our bed? That would really amuse Edward.' He let go of her and ran downstairs with the suitcase. She flew after him, stumbling with her burden, her screams rising above the baby's.

'You bloody spineless shit, David! You weren't so particular when the affair was clean and confidential, secret, behind closed doors. You were more concerned about keeping your second-rate job than holding our marriage together. You're just another of those little men who tried to get what they could from Edward. Leeches. Parasites – petty, small-minded people with no ideas and no talent of their own. And now everyone is going to know it because the Press have got hold of the story and they're going to describe it as it is: Edward took what he wanted and you let him, because you were afraid not to. That's what really makes you angry – facing up to what you really are.'

He flung open the door and barged headlong into Sergeant Hackett. Hackett took a step back, looking past Ainsley to his wife and the screaming child. 'Dr Ainsley,' he said mildly. 'We've been trying to track you down all morning.'

Chapter Ten

It's laughable. The Jehovah's Witnesses say we're different from other animals because we have the power of reason, and a divinity bestowed on us by God. They must never have met story-hungry journalists. I wonder what the collective noun for sharks is — a feeding frenzy? Mindless bunch of pricks! Feed them a line and they swallow the bait, every clichéd word — they'll even fight over it. Give them a good, stiff scandal and they'll print every scurrilous detail: names, dates, hotel rooms, the lot. All I have to do now is wait for the police to pick up on it. They seem to favour the tabloids. Nice to know they keep abreast of current affairs. Well, if it keeps the bastards from focusing on the real target, who cares?

Helen Wilkinson looked up from her work. She resisted the compulsion to go and pull out a chair for Mick Tuttle. He smiled, hovering in the doorway, embarrassed, she knew, by the last conversation they'd had.

'I came to, um—'

'Offer your condolences . . .' Helen hesitated. 'I'm not sure that's entirely appropriate. You know how things were between us.'

Mick dipped his head, neither accepting nor denying the truth of what she said. There was a silence in which he seemed to be considering, then he came into the room, closing the door behind him. He leaned on the door for a few moments, whether for support or to give himself time to gather his thoughts was unclear, then he walked to her desk – a few steps only, but the effort it took him seemed a deliberate letting down of the barriers and in a momentary revelation, Helen realized that this was a physical manifestation of trust. For Mick was hyper-sensitive to the impression his arduous, creaking, leg-swinging movements made on others. He caught the rug with his foot and Helen made an involuntary movement. He smiled, bending to straighten the rucked edge.

'Nice,' he said.

'I brought it in from home,' Helen said, unable to prevent the words from tumbling out of her mouth. 'I couldn't stand the institutional drabness of the place.'

Tuttle nodded. The apricots and blues were, perhaps, a little out of keeping with the mahogany and oak solidity of the building, but this very difference was cheering. He reached the chair by her desk and lowered himself into it.

'I should have come earlier,' he said, 'but—' He seemed at a loss for something to say. He looked out of the window behind her and then nodded at her computer monitor. It was turned at right angles to the room and he could see only one side and a glimmer of bluish light.

'Is that your research proposal?'

'I was given an extension,' Helen explained. 'I thought I'd finished it. But I'd prepared it as a presentation for the seminar. I've had to cut a lot of the good stuff out – the explanatory, the background. I think it weakens the argument.' There was an unreal calm in her discussion of the research proposal, her apparent surprise at being granted an extension even though the reason was the death of her husband.

'Emphasize commercial sponsorship – they'll go for it,' Tuttle said, to fill what was becoming a difficult silence. 'If you want me to look at it—' He stopped, thinking that she might mistrust the offer.

'I'll do a print–out now.' Helen turned away, focusing on the screen. She clicked on the print icon and then, conscious of his close attention to her profile as she worked, she turned back, catching him staring. He looked away and she pretended not to have noticed. 'It was just as well you didn't come earlier,' she said. 'Ruth's expression is that I've been "out of my skull".'

'Understandable.' His eyes dark, almost black, searched hers. There were depths of meaning in that look Helen was not yet ready to fathom. 'I also came to apologize. What I said, that day – it must have sounded like whining self-pity.'

Helen's mind switched to their previous encounter. Monday morning. The day Edward had died. It was something over which she had no control, this instant replay: virtual reality. She watched it as a bystander as it played in her mind.

'I've just had my interview.'

Helen takes a breath. She can imagine how Edward had treated him. 'I'm sorry.' The words are a reflex, a reaction to his evident distress, and they so inadequately convey her feelings that she blushes.

He runs his fingers through his hair and Helen notices with too-rapt attention how thick and dark it is. Mick is deep-chested, handsome, in some ways like Edward, but there is a sensitivity, a compassion in Mick Tuttle that Edward lacks entirely.

'He told me that reclamation of colliery spoil was old hat. Definitely out, he said. As if conservation is some kind of trend to go in or out of fashion. He asked me if I'd heard that just about all of the deep pit mines in Britain had been closed.'

Helen draws up a chair and sits opposite Mick. 'What about open-cast mining?' she asks.

'That's what I said. He laughed. Suggested I look for a more promising area of reclamation.'

'Mick, I don't know what to say.'

'Talk to him,' Mick urges. 'He'll listen to you.'

Helen looks, startled by the frankness of the request, into those dark eyes. His face, which is normally so controlled, as if denying the effort each step costs him, is flushed with agitation.

'I really don't—'

'It's not like I'm asking you to fiddle the departmental budget,' he says, with a harshness that makes her sit up, increasing the distance between them. 'I'm sorry, Helen. I know it's not your fault but – you know what he said to me? "You wear those callipers like a badge of distinction, Dr Tuttle. But in my book there are only two criteria for selection: academic excellence and commercial viability." '

Helen feels a wave of hatred for her husband. She hears Edward's voice as clearly as if he had been in the room, calling Mick by the name he uses only in the privacy of their home: 'The Cripple.' A simultaneous image floods her visual cortex – a knife slicing neatly through the intercostal muscles, meeting the smooth, slippery resistance of heart muscle, puncturing it with a faint pop.

'I do everything I can to make people look at me instead of at these!' Mick slaps his knees and Helen hears the metal joints of his callipers rattle. 'So I'm asking you to try and convince him.'

'I'm not sure I can convince him on my own behalf, Mick. What makes you think I can argue your case for you?'

'I acted like a brat, storming out like that.'

'Edward had that effect on people,' Helen said, shaking herself out of the daydream, the action replay. 'He made them act out of character, one way or another.'

Mick stood, and Helen wondered if she had offended him again. Then he picked up the freshly printed text of her proposal and said, 'I'll phone you when I've had a read through.' He made his way to the door and stood looking at her for a few moments. 'If you need me—' he began.

'I know where you are.'

He stared thoughtfully at her as though he doubted she would ask for help. 'Or I could pop by, see how you are.'

Helen felt a small contraction of her heart. Mick Tuttle

didn't just 'pop by' anywhere. In the first five weeks of the academic year he set up in the lecture hall before most of his students had stumbled to the refectory for breakfast. He volunteered for the early lectures so that he could be there before they started drifting in, he remained seated throughout and waited until they had all left before packing up to leave. He once told her that his first tutorials were make or break for most of his tutees: either they had already accepted him as a person and it was no big deal, or they were offended that they had been tricked all this time by a *cripple*.

Helen blinked, realizing that she had let another silence develop, that he must have seen her drift off like some sad psychotic. 'Yeah,' she said, rallying. 'Fine. I'll make us some coffee.' She tried to adopt the same careless tone Mick Tuttle had adopted. And failed, as he had failed.

'I've just been talking to your boss.'

Hackett slowed his pace, half turned, waited for Ruth Marks to catch him up. He had chance to appraise her in the fifteen metres or so between them. Rangy, lean, fit. A woman who chose clothes for comfort and warmth rather than fashion; today she was wearing faded jeans with ankle length, low-heeled boots. The blue check of her brushed cotton shirt was mismatched by the brown wool of her sweater.

'You know,' she said as she drew level, 'if I had an Alsatian with eyes that shade of madness, I'd have it put down.'

Hackett bit the side of his cheek. 'I take it you didn't get on too well,' he said, electing understatement as a defence.

'He's mad as a rabid hound and twice as dangerous. Are you on your way to hassle some other poor bastard or do you have a moment?'

Hackett was not in the mood for idle chat. He had just finished interviewing David Ainsley, who had confirmed that his wife and Professor Wilkinson had been having an affair. He claimed to have known nothing about it until the news article, and said he wouldn't have the first idea how to break into a colleague's computer, but then he would say that, wouldn't he? Nelson had counselled diplomacy in the matter of the Apocalypse file. Listen carefully, and wait for someone to slip up. Meanwhile, they would ask the computer services department to locate whose PC had been used to modify the file.

Hackett was weary; his home was not the normal haven of quiet and comfort because of his mother's frequent calls, and the new argumentativeness in Lisa. He was worried about Daniel as well; he had become secretive, evasive, refusing to tell them where he had been the previous night – 'Just out.' The fact that this case was keeping him away from home was not easing the situation.

'You've given your statement to DI Nelson, Dr Marks,' he said. 'I'm sure that will do.'

'Please yourself.'

Something in her manner made him ask, 'You *have* made your statement?'

'I made *a* statement.' She gave him a level stare. 'I *told* him bugger all.'

Hackett found her constant amusement obnoxious. He took a breath, ready to say what he thought of her light-hearted dismissal of their murder investigation but she spoke again before he had a chance to begin:

'I don't like him, Sergeant. He has crazy amber eyes and a nasty mind.' She paused, as if regretting the passion with which she had spoken. He thought he discerned a slight shrug, then she resumed in a more bantering tone, '*Your* eyes, on the other hand, are a very nice shade of green. Cats' eyes. Sexy, if you want to know.'

'So my wife tells me.'

Ruth Marks laughed. She edged closer and whispered, 'It's all right, Sergeant. I'm not going to ravish you – you're not my type.'

Hackett huffed a little laugh. 'Despite my sexy green eyes?'

He conducted the interview in the college refectory, partly because it was lunch time and partly because it was the place Nelson was least likely to turn up.

'So,' Hackett said, trying not to show surprise at the four doughnuts Ruth Marks had picked up from the buffet. 'What can you tell me?'

'What do you want to know?' she asked, biting into a doughnut and unselfconsciously licking the sugar from her lips as he watched.

Apparently she wasn't going to make it easy for him. 'Tell me about Prof Wilkinson,' he said.

'An unmitigated, selfish egocentric shit.'

'The newspapers are carrying a story about an affair—'

'Privatization has gone too far if you're relying on the tabloids to direct your inquiries,' Ruth said, sinking her teeth into the jam centre of the doughnut and groaning with pleasure.

Hackett smiled obligingly and began on his sandwich to give himself time to think and Ruth Marks an opportunity to say more. She chewed thoughtfully and then nodded, pouching the mouthful of doughnut into her cheek and mumbling 'Clara Ainsley'. Noting his surprise with a degree of self-satisfaction she added, 'Clara and Ed had been at it for a year or more,' through a doughy mouthful.

'And his wife didn't suspect?'

'Suspicion of adultery is one thing, proving it is another. And Ed was so convincing he sometimes fooled even himself.'

'You knew him well?'

'Too well.' She took a swig of black coffee and swallowed.

Hackett had to look away; there was an indecency in the way she abandoned herself to the enjoyment of her food, cramming the sweet, vanilla-scented cakes into her mouth.

'Is that why you're leaving?' Hackett asked.

For a moment Ruth seemed confused, as if working through the idea in her mind. She picked up the third doughnut and licked it, as a child might lick an ice cream. 'Why I'm leaving . . .' she repeated, then bit thoughtfully into the doughnut, taking time to suck the jam from between her fingers. 'Oh, you mean . . .' She wiped her face and hands with a paper napkin, laughing into it. 'My reasons for leaving are purely academic. I'm afraid *Ed* wasn't my type either.'

'And what were *his* eyes like?' Hackett asked, surprised and amused to find himself flirting with this wide-mouthed, blunt-talking, messy eater.

'Brown, like velvet. But if you caught him when he wasn't ready – when he hadn't time to strike a pose – when he was being himself—' She shrugged. 'They were flat, dead, the inward-looking eyes of a narcissistic and arrogant man.'

'And Helen Wilkinson? Do you like her?'

'I adore Helen.' It was a simple statement of fact. 'Everyone does who knows her well. Ask her students.' She went on eating unaware of the effect it had had on Sergeant Hackett.

'You didn't think that you should tell Dr Wilkinson of her husband's infidelity?'

Ruth laughed, blowing sugar crystals from the doughnut. 'As a *friend*, you mean?' She chewed, swallowed hard. 'Helen didn't need telling any more than David needed telling about Clara. Helen knew. I saw them once, Edward and Clara, by the river. They were having a picnic. He was pretending to be asleep. Just lay there, looking pretty, driving her wild making out he couldn't feel her kisses, her caresses, her plaintive, humiliating pawing of that splendid body of his.' She caught the sergeant's startled look and added. 'What I'm trying to tell you is the man was a sadist. A subtle one, perhaps, but no less damaging for that. If I sound bitter it's because I've seen what Edward could do to people.'

'Why didn't she confront him?'

'Helen? She did, more than once. Which is more than most women would have the courage to do, given Ed's temper.'

'He was violent?'

'Physically, no. But I've seen him lacerate a few tough hides with that tongue of his. Edward Wilkinson made it his business to find a person's weak spot and he would attack it without compunction.' Hackett listened to this, thinking how Wilkinson's cutting remarks must have filleted the delicate tissue of this strangely insecure community.

'You didn't like him?'

Ruth laughed. 'You have a genius for understatement, Sergeant. The question is, did anyone? Except Clara, that is. He was despicable.' She sucked her thumb thoughtfully for a moment. 'Perhaps not even Clara.'

Hackett waited. Ruth smiled at him over the rim of her coffee cup.

'Not even Clara,' he repeated, returning the smile.

Ruth ran her tongue between her gums and her upper lip. 'Valerie Roberts worked as Edward's secretary for ten years, putting up with his sarcasm and his unreasonable demands on her time, smoothing ruffled feathers for him, getting him to where he needed to be – lectures, meetings, or mistresses' beds – on time, properly prepared.' She waited for the distasteful reality of her meaning to hit home, then went on: 'And he was planning to get rid of her and install that silly, vain little bitch, Clara, in her place.'

Hackett felt a tingle run from the back of his neck down both arms. How the hell did she know all this? What was *her* relationship with Professor Wilkinson?

'Ed felt safe discussing sensitive issues with me,' she explained, as though sensing his suspicion. 'Before long I'll be doing glamorous research on state-of-the-art technology in that *most* glamorous of locations, the USA. Ed was a sucker for glamour.' She smirked. 'He told me things he probably never even told Helen.'

'You realize you've removed Clara Ainsley's motive for killing Edward?'

'The fact that he told David he was not to have his contract renewed? God forbid that I should put that round-heeled bitch in the clear.'

So she knew about Ainsley's dismissal, too. He wondered if Ruth Marks had access to the professor's password, and did she feel sorry enough for Valerie Roberts to change the Apocalypse file entries?

Ruth was playing with a little mound of sugar on her plate, all that remained of the doughnuts. 'Try this,' she said, drawing the crystals together into a small, slightly pink-tinged peak. 'Clara thought he was going to dump her.'

'Why would she think that if he's just offered her a job working closely with him?'

She tilted her head on one side, working on the sugar mound. 'Ed played the game by his own rules. He might not have told her – keeping it as a surprise. David gets home from his interview with God on Monday, tells her he's out of a job, she assumes that goes for her, too.'

Hackett watched, fascinated and repulsed, as she took a pinch of the sugar mound and trickled the sticky crystals on to the tip of her tongue.

'Ed would have told her the good news eventually, but it was his way to make them sweat a little, make them prepared to *give* more – so Clara would be more grateful when he did offer her the job, and his total devotion. But what if he didn't

Chapter Eleven

Isaac Smolder wrote in his diary: 'I saw Helen standing in the quad this morning. She was talking to that policeman. She nodded her head, smiling in that sad, sweet way. I don't think she was listening to him, not really. She hadn't put on an overcoat and was shivering. Her breath condensed around her face as she talked, turning back, caressing her skin. I felt a stupefying surge of emotion. I wanted to go to her, to put my arms around her. To make her warm. Foolish, really: one shouldn't go against one's nature, it only brings trouble, complications.'

Although he was close by, she hadn't seen him. He had found this difficult: the need to make contact was becoming stronger, more urgent. He thought that she might understand, but human emotion being something of a mystery to him, he was unwilling to make this bold step, for fear of spoiling what was, for the time being, a delightful indulgence.

He knew that his preoccupation with Helen was becoming an obsession, but he could not help himself. He wondered what it would be like to experience her senses, emotions, urges. He had a dizzying notion that he would like to be inside her head, to feel the shock of synaptic electricity. Would it be different, seeing the world as Helen saw it? Watching her, unobserved, from his vantage point above the quad, her delicate gestures, her aching vulnerability, he thought that for Helen the world must seem a terrifying place.

The door to Helen Wilkinson's office opened and Inspector Nelson slowed his pace a little. He made a mental note – the guy with the callipers. Tuttle closed the door behind him then turned away from Nelson and started his slow journey down the corridor.

Dr Wilkinson's office was opposite the staircase and Nelson glanced at the fire doors as he drew level with them, a survival instinct he'd retained from earlier and more dangerous days when he had spent time in drugs-ravaged housing estates. He saw a flicker of movement, a face pulled back from the wired glass of the door. Nelson shoved the door hard, grunting with satisfaction at the indignant cry of pain.

'You bloody idiot! Who do you think you are?'

'I think I'm Detective Inspector Nelson, Cheshire CID. Who do you think you are?' Nelson turned a nasty smile on the scrawny-looking youth, his eyes flashing an amber warning.

'Oh, I – I'm sorry. I didn't . . .' Then, realizing he hadn't identified himself, the youth said, 'Ellis. John Ellis. I'm just a Ph.D. student. I really don't know – that is I *didn't* know Prof Wilkinson very well.'

Nelson raised his eyebrows, amused. Ellis, he thought. Referred to the Senate House Overview Panel. And who'd asked him for his life story, any road? 'You know his wife better do you?'

'Sorry?'

'Or is she your supervisor – isn't that what you call it?'

Ellis's laughter sounded brittle in the shrill acoustics of the stairwell. For a fleeting moment, Nelson saw someone else, and flinched at the recognition. 'No, nothing like that.' Ellis's

Adam's apple bobbed. 'I – Dr Mallory is my supervisor. I . . . er . . . I was just passing and—'

'Dr Mallory? But his office is in the other building, across the quad. Surely you can't have been just passing.' Nelson's eyes glowed. He could sense terror in the boy – and so far, he'd been quite polite. Ellis blinked. 'Why were you about to visit Dr Wilkinson?' Nelson asked softly.

Ellis opened his mouth to speak, but another voice carried, echoing up the stairwell: 'He came to pay his respects.' Nelson knew the voice – even on such short acquaintance, Dr Marks was not an easy woman to forget.

'Seems to be a lot of it about,' Nelson observed, thinking of the labouring figure of the crippled bloke retreating down the corridor a few minutes earlier.

'What?' said Ruth. 'Respect?' She appeared on the second landing, her shoes making short gasping sounds on the stone tiles of the steps. 'Nice to hear a copper say that. You're not one of the hang 'em and flog 'em brigade then, Inspector?' She was smiling.

Nelson wondered if she used this strategy as a regular thing, wrong-footing the opposition – diversionary tactics. Well, he wasn't about to enter into a philosophical discussion with Ruth Marks. He turned to Ellis who stood sweating, trapped between the handrail and the door. He looked guilty as sin, but then people did when they were questioned by the police; nothing so suggestive in that.

'You were about to tell me why you were here.'

'It's like Dr Marks said. I'm here to—'

'Pay your respects' – Nelson's gaze flicked from the woman to the youth – 'like Dr Marks said.' He stared the boy down, which was not difficult, but Ruth Marks looked back at him amused, interested. Nelson pulled the door open. 'Don't let me keep you, Mr Ellis.'

Ellis blanched, glanced down the stairwell.

'I was about to visit Dr Wilkinson myself, but I'll wait till you've *paid your respects*.' He saw the whites of Ellis's eyes as he looked to Ruth Marks for help, but this time, inexplicably, she held back, apparently content to watch the play unfold.

'I don't think I'll bother—'

'No,' said Nelson. 'I insist. We can't have you making such a long journey for nothing now, can we?'

Ellis wiped his upper lip. Nelson could see he was seriously considering making a break for it, but abruptly he subsided, meekly edging past Nelson, through the fire door which the inspector considerately held open for him, and knocked at Helen Wilkinson's office door; a fumbled, multiple rap because his hand was shaking too badly to control it. Nelson listened to Ellis's mumbled message whilst staring at Dr Marks. Ruth stared back, a look of open curiosity on her face. Ellis shuffled out of the room a few moments later, blushing to the roots of his hair.

Nelson could only imagine Dr Wilkinson's bewilderment at the visit. He stood square in front of the fire doors so that Ellis had to edge around him.

'I'm afraid you'll have to come back later if you're after paying your respects to Dr Wilkinson,' Nelson told Ruth. 'I've got a few questions I'd like to ask her in private.'

Ruth stared past him at the nameplate on the office door. White etched on black. 'No problem,' she said, the corners of her mouth curving up into a smile. 'I've just remembered something I need to do.'

She caught up with Ellis in the courtyard. He was almost in tears. 'Bastard!' he hissed.

'Take it easy,' Ruth said, putting a hand on his arm.

He jerked away. 'Bloody bastard!' he repeated, but he slowed up a little. 'She looked at me like I was mad.'

Ruth laughed explosively, throwing her head back and catching, from the corner of one eye, a blue patch of sky in the jumble of grey and white cloud over the quad.

Ellis stopped, jammed his hands into his trouser pockets and stood hunched over her like an overgrown schoolboy. 'What's so bloody funny?'

'I was just thinking,' Ruth said through her laughter, 'it'd be a nice change for Helen, looking at someone like *they're* mad instead of vice versa.'

Ellis walked on, muttering.

'OK.' She shrugged. 'So you don't think it's funny.'

They crossed the courtyard, avoiding the rainwater puddled on the Yorkshire stone flags, hunching their shoulders against a fresh spattering of sleety rain. The foyer of the zoology building smelled of wet umbrellas and formaldehyde and years of dissections. The fish lingered for the greatest time: skate and mackerel, occasionally squid, always slightly off because the students' inexperience led to dissections taking days instead of hours. Some were returned to the freezer and after several sessions had dissolved into a sodden mush.

Ruth breathed deeply and then asked, 'So why *were* you visiting Helen?'

In the gloom of the poorly lit foyer she thought she saw Ellis twitch. 'Nothing. No reason. I just – I wanted to ask her about my research proposal.'

Ruth moved in closer, trying to read his expression. The foyer was walled in on either side by thick sandstone. Before and behind were heavy oak doors, and the only light was from two dim lamps set high in the ceiling.

'Look, I know I told you Mallory wouldn't be any use to you, but what makes you think Helen'd be any better?'

Ellis looked over her shoulder, his feet moved restlessly and his lower body pointed at an angle away from her. 'I suppose I thought Dr Wilkinson might – might know something.'

'About what?' Was he blushing? His body language suggested extreme unease, but the inadequate lighting protected him from close scrutiny. Ruth quelled an urge to drag him and hold him under the lights. Ellis stirred himself under the intensity of her stare.

'My research grant finishes in the summer. I was hoping to ask her about the availability of posts here. Interview tips, that sort of thing.'

'From Helen?' She shrugged. 'All right, why were you lurking at the top of the stairs? Why didn't you just go into her office and speak to her?'

He fiddled with his tie, then brought his hand down, trying to control the nervous restlessness of his movements. 'Dr Tuttle was in there. I didn't like to interrupt. Anyway, he makes me uncomfortable. I never know what to say to him.' He glanced at his watch. 'Look – I have to go. Thanks for – you know. With that bastard Nelson.' He hurried off through the heavy doors and ran up the central staircase to avoid being called back. Ruth watched him go and mused that the acronym SHOP might have another, quite different meaning.

Ellis ran on, past the postgraduate research laboratory, on down the corridor, sweating. Tuttle had been with her. Mick Tuttle had been waiting in Mrs Roberts's office when he had left after his interview with Professor Wilkinson. He must have heard the row. Did he know? What had he told her? What had the prof told her? 'Christ, what am I going to *do*?' he whispered.

He ran up another flight of stairs, out of breath, close to tears, trying to recall exactly what had been said. Not enough, perhaps, on its own to implicate him, but if Tuttle had seen him in the labs when he should not have been there, he might make connections.

When the doorbell rang, Helen was standing at the bedroom door. She thought she had heard something. A noise.

Something. The police had taken away the bloodstained bed-clothes and duvet. Ruth had done her best to remove the stain from the mattress, had washed and turned it, had put fresh sheets and blankets on the bed, but Helen could see through the layers to the darkening rusty patch. X-ray vision. The stain would remain forever. On the mattress. In this room. On her conscience.

She shuddered as the bell rang again, more furiously. Half a dozen reporters had been waiting for her at the college gates. The security staff had kept them out, but they could not protect her beyond the walls of the college and the reporters had followed her home, continuing their constant barrage of questions as she walked to her front door. Questions about Edward. Their relationship. Had she known about his affairs? About Clara? Could she account for the knife that was missing from the kitchen?

Helen covered her ears against the insistent ringing of the doorbell. She screamed: 'Leave me alone!'

Abruptly, the bell fell silent. A voice, thin, frightened called up to her. 'Helen? Come to the door, love.'

Her heart began pounding. She turned, ran down the stairs, fumbled the chain from the door and flung it wide open. Molyneux got a good picture before the hacks surged forward. Helen blinked in the light of the flash, a vague look of irritation on her face. She turned to the woman on the doorstep.

'You shouldn't have come,' she said. Then: 'You'd better come in.'

She took the overnight case without comment and set it down at the foot of the stairs. 'You'll be wanting a cup of tea,' she said, falling unthinkingly into the old patterns of speech. 'You must be perished.'

'Your dad sends his love—'

'What were you thinking of, coming on your own?' Helen burst out.

'I got the train straight through – and a taxi from the station. I'm not incapable, Helen. I can fend for myself. *He'd* have come but—'

Helen did not want to think about why her father didn't feel able to make the short train ride from Manchester to Chester: 'I think Ruth got some food in,' she muttered, turning to the refrigerator.

'Helen – love.' Her mother waited while Helen continued, frowning, sorting the cheese from the cooked meats, extracting the salad from the bottom compartment.

'Ready-washed – just open and serve.' She read the instructions on the pack aloud as if they could ward off her mother's questions.

'We were worried – your dad and me, when you didn't phone back. We tried to get through—'

Helen started guiltily. 'I unplugged the phone. The reporters. Crank calls . . . I meant to call again – to let you know I was OK.' She shrugged helplessly. Her mother smiled at her over the jumble of packages on the kitchen table, her concern, as always, an accusation.

'Are you?' she asked. 'OK, I mean.' This, said too brusquely, encouraging a simple affirmative in answer, as though any admission of illness or unhappiness – even in bereavement – would be judged an imposition, a play for attention.

'Hmm.' Helen shied way from her mother's caress, saw the hurt in her eyes and regretted it but, powerless to recall the action, instead fussed over the preparation of food. 'I can do you an omelette – or would you prefer a sandwich?'

'Omelette'll be fine. What do the police say?'

'They don't *say* anything. They just keep asking me questions I can't answer.'

'So they don't have any idea who—'

Helen faltered, feeling a cold wave of dread. She wanted to say, *Not unless you count me*, but that would be too cruel, so she said simply, 'No. They don't seem to.' She could not keep the tiredness, the exasperation from her voice and her mother, thinking she was the cause, withdrew. It was a small change, a tightening of the lips, hands crossed protectively across her abdomen, that too-familiar look of disapproval. So, Helen thought miserably, I've been cruel after all.

She reached for the short-bladed knife she preferred for slicing vegetables and recoiled when she saw the empty space in the knife block, where the boning knife should be. The police had returned the others, but they had not found the missing knife.

'Why don't you make us a brew?' Helen asked more kindly, 'While I sort this.'

She chopped the vegetables while her mother performed her tea-making ritual. As she waited for the kettle to boil she filled the teapot and two mugs with hot water from the tap. By the time Helen was ready to whisk the eggs her mother was standing at the sink poised, ready to tip the hot water out of the pot and add the tea bags at the exact moment the kettle clicked off. Of course, she preferred proper tea, loose leaf, like they all used to have, but she could make do when necessary. Helen watched her mother, to distract herself from thinking about the glutinous mix of yolk and mucilaginous albumen in the bowl, to take her mind from the smells of hot butter and fried onions and tomatoes in the pan. She would not allow herself to check for tell-tale flecks of red on the yolks, but added ground pepper and salt, a dash of Worcester sauce and a spurt of cold water, and began to beat the eggs.

The thick, liquid sound, a comforting rhythm in childhood, now made her stomach lurch and roll with every flick of the wrist. She tried not to think of the slimy liquid falling from the fork in ropy strands, but focused on her mother, adding the water to the tea bags, stirring the pot, placing the lid on it, looking around for a cosy and finding none, making do with a tea towel.

She's grey, Helen thought. Quite grey. And she looks exhausted. Only a couple of years earlier she had been dark, as dark as Helen; people had mistaken them for sisters. Now Helen could see in her mother the grey ghost of her future self.

'Can't the police do anything about those vultures outside?'

Helen was nibbling at a cheese sandwich while her mother worked through the omelette. 'I don't know that they want to.'

Her mother's anxious look of enquiry forced an answer. 'A knife is missing from the block.'

Her mother's head began to turn, then snapped back to look at Helen. 'They can't think that you—'

'Why not? I had motive enough. I even wanted to.' This was dangerous territory, this honesty. Who was she spiting, her mother, or herself? She felt herself hurtling towards an admission she did not want to make.

'Helen! You mustn't talk like that.'

'Why mustn't I, Mother? It's the truth. And it was just as I'd visualized it.' *Except for the blood!* She closed her eyes, but the image of Edward dead, white sheets and dark blood, was too strong and she gasped, standing, picking up the plates, throwing her half eaten sandwich into the bin and taking the plates to the sink.

'What do you mean, how you'd visualized it? How could you think such wicked thoughts?'

Wicked thoughts! Didn't her mother know how she had fought over the years to repress the fury inside her — the wickedness — the natural unthinking urge to lash out?

'Mum, you must have seen the papers—'

'Lies. They make up stories to get people to buy. Surely they must be lies, Helen?'

Helen sighed. 'I wish they were; then at least I could get angry instead of feeling this burning humiliation. It's true, Mum. All of it.' She wanted to say more, to explain, but her mother had been charmed by Edward, his middle-class manners and Oxford education, his easy, confident way of making small talk, appearing interested when he wasn't listening to a word. Edward had made sure that they saw her family infrequently and fleetingly, so the illusion had remained intact.

'Helen, we thought – your dad and me – we thought you and Edward were happy. Edward was such a nice man, so clever—'

Helen smiled. Tears pricked at the back of her eyes and nose. 'Handsome is as handsome does, eh, Mum? Anyway, what could you have done? I'm all grown up now.'

'I know love, but you're all we've got—' She faltered, stopped, biting off her words.

Helen plunged her hands into the scalding dishwater to stop herself finishing the sentence in her head: *You're all we've got since* . . . The unspoken implication: *And you're a poor substitute*, the question unasked a million times, but always there, as a reproach: *Why him and not you?*

'I'm sorry love,' her mother said, breaking the silence. 'I never meant—'

'I know.' The silence descended again and Helen's mother picked up a tea towel, ready to help, anxious to make amends. 'Let them drain,' Helen said. 'Why don't you go and lie down? The spare room's made up.' She had made it up for Ruth, whom she was expecting later, but Ruth would understand.

Her mother folded the tea towel with elaborate care, giving herself time to say something, but, unable to find the words. She hung it up on the rail next to the cooker and left the room. Helen could feel the distance between them, the silence, tug at her. She wanted to go to her mother, to comfort her. But how can the guilty bring comfort? What could she say that would change anything? So she waited until her mother was too far away to hear and then she whispered softly, 'I'm sorry, Mum. I'm so very, very sorry.'

A sharp rap at the kitchen window made Helen start violently. She closed her eyes and concentrated on her breathing. A second rap, something metal, perhaps a coin, then David Ainsley's voice, muffled and tearful.

'Oh, God.' Helen leaned against the sink for a moment, still trying to regain her equilibrium.

'Helen, *please*! Let me in.' Not muffled – slurred: he was drunk.

She opened the scullery door, shielding herself behind it, in case of photographers. He stumbled in and she slammed the door.

David stood, swaying slightly, blinking in the light. 'It's quite all right,' he said, enunciating carefully. 'They didn't see me. I waited until they weren't watching. Came down the side passage, the gate was unlocked.'

Helen looked at him, unshaven, his suit badly rumpled, the collar and cuffs of his shirt grubby, and wondered where he had been sleeping. 'You must be bloody mad, coming here.'

He grinned foolishly. 'Create a splendid photo opportunity, wouldn't it?'

She led him through to the kitchen and cupped both hands around the teapot. It was cold. Crystal-gazing, she thought, fortune-telling. And what does the future hold for me? She frowned at the incongruousness of the idea. 'I'll make you some coffee, then you can go home.'

His eyes filled with tears. 'Can't go home.' He sounded like a pettish child. 'You knew, didn't you?' His voice high-pitched, accusing. 'It's in the papers – have you seen? You knew and you said nothing.'

'Are you saying you didn't know?' Helen spooned coffee into two mugs, her eyes fixed on Ainsley. He looked away, muttering something incoherent.

'Sit down, David,' she said.

He dragged a chair out and collapsed into it heavily. 'Bloody bitch!'

Helen set down a mug in front of him and sat opposite. He was, she decided, referring to Clara.

'Clara was another conquest for Edward,' she said. 'He notched them up and then moved on to the next challenge. She'll realize that soon enough, if she hasn't already.'

'Oh, she has,' he said viciously. 'I made sure of that.' This, muttered into his coffee mug as he lifted it to his lips, moving it too fast, miscalculating the distance so that the porcelain clicked against his teeth and a little coffee slopped out, scalding his chin. He wiped it away with the back of his hand, swearing. Then, in a deliberate motion, he placed his hand on hers. Helen jerked away. He looked, startled, into her face, ready to weep. His eyes were bloodshot and sore from drink and crying and sleeplessness. He let his head fall forward, his hair flopping in front of his right eye. 'I thought you'd understand,' he said.

'I think I probably do.'

'The police think *I* did it.'

'Did what?'

'Killed him. Stuck the knife in the bastard bloody homewrecker.'

Edward smiling up from his bed, warm with the afterglow of sex. A kiss, a quick, firm push, and the knife went home. His gasp of surprise and pain . . . His hands grasping the sheets, spoiling their pristine smoothness.

Ainsley flicked his hair from his forehead. 'Some of his files were altered—'

'I know,' Helen said quietly.

'He was going to get rid of me. Us. You'd've had him to yourself.'

'I was past wanting him, either shared or all to myself,' she said. 'I wanted him out of my life.'

'What are you saying?' He tried unsuccessfully to bring the blurred outline of her face into focus.

Helen paused, wondering how much she wanted to tell him, then decided he had a right to know. 'You're wrong about Edward planning to get rid of both of you. He was going to offer Clara Valerie Roberts's job.'

Ainsley's eyes widened. His brain, steeped in alcohol, could not take this in. Then he saw Clara's face as he had told her that Wilkinson was going to have his contract terminated. 'No.' He shook his head slowly, feeling the liquid swirl in the vestibular apparatus of his brain, seeing the room rotate alarmingly even with this slight movement, 'No. She would have said—' She had been shocked, angry, when he had told her Edward had been planning to sack him. Was there also regret? If she had known Edward's plans she would have said anything to hurt.

'She didn't know,' Helen went on. 'But he did plan to retire Valerie early, and he had recommended Clara as replacement.'

'Bloody, sodding bitch!' Wasn't he allowed even the satisfaction that Edward would have abandoned her? 'It's his, isn't it? Why else would he want to look after her? Shag 'em and leave 'em's his motto.'

'I know she's hurt you, David, but you have to look to the future. What about Henry?'

David snorted into his coffee mug, took another slurp. 'Let her take care of the little bastard. Better if he'd never been born.'

Something changed in the room. The cold tap dripped steadily into the sink, as it did before, the pale lemon walls reflected the blue-white glow of the fluorescent lighting but momentarily the darkness seemed to close in and the air grew hot despite the bitter easterly wind which rattled the window sashes. David frowned, feeling the change, chanced a look at Helen. Her face had grown solemn and still.

'I think you should leave now,' she said, quietly.

'I didn't mean—' He reached out to touch her.

'Leave me alone. I can't help you.' She stood and moved to the side of the table. He lunged forward, made to grasp her hands, missed, his hands fumbling at her waist. 'Helen—' She pushed with both palms, flat on his chest but, although he swayed, he did not yield and Helen felt a clammy apprehension. He bent forward, his fingers straying lower now, gripping the tops of her thighs, cupping her buttocks. His face near hers, stale, smelling of cheap wine and vomit. She began to fight, knowing this to be the wrong thing to do, but the smell, the confining proximity of him was too much for her. She shoved hard and he staggered back, catching the base of his spine against the kitchen table.

'Fuck,' he muttered, releasing one hand from her buttock, flailing, knocking a chair over. Helen began to fall, but he caught her by the waist again and she swept her arm in a wide semi-circle, connecting with a crack to the side of his face.

David responded slowly, looking first at her, shocked by the strength of the slap, then raising his hand to his face. 'Bitch,' he said, softly, astonished, as though realizing the truth of it for the first time. '*Fucking* bitch!'

'Go back to your wife, David.' Helen's voice was harsh, her breathing ragged. 'Go back to your son.'

He laughed, belching a sour cloud of alcohol and vomit on his breath then he turned quickly, almost losing co-ordination, but steadying himself against the door frame before he drew himself up in an effort to regain some dignity and stepped carefully into the scullery. He paused at the back door. Helen stared at him. His face was contorted with hatred. 'You didn't realize how much you had in common with Clara, did you? She thinks you despise her for not having a job – relying on my income. And there *he* was, banging away at the both of you. It didn't seem to matter to him. Like a dog, he followed any bitch on heat.'

'*David!*'

'It's a pity you didn't carry full term,' he said, enjoying her outrage, the pain he was causing her. 'Clara's little bastard would've had a half-brother to play with.'

Chapter Twelve

Helen leaned against the back door, trying to think past the trembling that shook her body, above the pain in her ribcage, beyond the screaming in her head, to a small, white patch of nothing, where there was no pain, no guilt, no tomorrow. Edward had told Clara about their baby, had even told her it was – would have been – a boy. And Clara had told David. She felt a surge of fury at Edward's continuing malign influence. When she thought her legs would support her she took a step into the kitchen. She gasped as though struck.

'Mum—'

Her mother looked at her, her head slightly lowered, angry, unapologetic, unembarrassed for the first time since she had arrived. 'What were you waiting for, Helen? For us to read about that in the papers as well? Couldn't you have told us – me?'

'How could I have told you? I've hurt you enough. I couldn't—'

'You mean you wouldn't. I'll get my things,' she said. 'I'll not trouble you any longer.'

Her mother's cold look of dislike was too much for Helen and she burst out, 'Mum!' her voice rising in panic. She took a step, tripped over the fallen chair, and her legs buckled, she felt herself falling, spinning and she snatched at the table top, missed, heard the sound of her fingernails scratch the wood.

Her mother was bent over her, crying. Helen saw a tear fall and felt an urge to catch it, but her limbs wouldn't work. Then she felt a sharp stab of pain in her cheek and everything returned to reality. Helen blinked, thinking, Real? Yes, I think this is real. But the impression lingered for a while longer that if she had caught that teardrop she might have made everything right between them.

'Get Dr Patterson.' Her mother had not spoken. Ruth had arrived at last.

'Help me up,' Helen said. 'Then call Sanjay.'

Ruth gave her a long, speculative look. 'I didn't know you were on first name terms.'

Patterson had wanted her admitted to hospital for observation but Helen had refused and he had compromised with her mother and Ruth taking turns to watch her throughout the night.

'It's a nasty bruise,' he said. 'She's lucky she didn't catch herself half an inch higher or she might have lost an eye.'

Helen lay on the sofa of her den and let the discussion go on around her while she determined what she could say to her mother, how much she dared tell her.

'I'd like to speak to Mum, please,' she said quietly. Ruth and Dr Patterson stopped talking to look at her. They exchanged a glance; the agreement was unspoken and they left in silence. For several minutes the only sound in the room was the impatient spattering of wind-driven rain on the windows.

'I'm sorry, Mum,' Helen said at last. 'I was trying to protect you both.'

'What from, Helen?'

Helen closed her eyes. From more pain, she thought. From

letting you down again. Another loss, with me at the centre. What she said was: 'I was only four months on.'

Before answering, her mother took her hand. 'Only four months.' It was said as a judgement. Only Helen's lapsed Catholicism would allow her to say such a thing. Her mother had read the statement as a dismissal of the worth of the child Helen had been carrying.

Helen tried again:

'He was perfect, your grandson . . .' She couldn't go on.

'Grandson.' Her mother tried out the word. She sighed.

'I know all about foetal development,' Helen went on. 'I knew what to expect. But I was totally unprepared for how perfect he was, how complete. They let me hold him—'

'What did you expect? How did he die?'

'He didn't die. Not in the real sense. Because he'd never really lived.' For a moment they were both thinking of someone else. 'And that's the tragedy of miscarriage.' Helen searched her mother's face. It was closed. Her mother had decided: Helen's failure of faith; her immoral views on abortion; her inadequacy as a wife – the sins of her past had returned to punish her. Just before she looked away, Helen thought she saw an exultant glint in her mother's eye.

'It can't be helped.' This was said firmly and Helen wondered if her mother wasn't referring to that other time, that other tragedy.

Helen closed her eyes, fetched a sigh that became a sob and turned her face away. 'I didn't want him. Not at first. I was furious with Edward.' She knew it would do no good, but Helen needed at least to try and make her mother understand, to see just once, the pain she felt. 'I think he wanted me pregnant so that I was out of the way.'

'The affair?'

Helen nodded. 'And I'd just won backing for my project from one of the pharmaceutical companies. I think he was jealous.' She risked a glance at her mother. Although she looked puzzled, lost almost, the dislike was gone and this gave Helen the courage to continue. 'I did it.' Her voice was no more than a whisper, but her mother's head jerked up as though she had screamed. 'It was my fault. We argued about Clara. I took a swing at him. I wanted to *kill* him!' She paused for a moment, breathing heavily. 'He dodged and I fell. I began haemorrhaging.'

'You didn't mean it to happen.' It was meant as reassurance, a comfort, but the inflexion was wrong. It came out as a question, despite her. Helen felt it as a physical blow.

'Old excuse. Wears a bit thin, doesn't it?' She could not keep the bitterness out of her voice any longer.

Her mother looked away.

'No. I didn't mean it to happen,' Helen went on. 'By then I wanted him. My baby. My son.' Her voice trailed off and the room was filled with the throbbing grief of loss. The two women looked at each other, each aware for the first time the depth of the other's pain and regret, but aware that the years of estrangement had rendered them powerless to breach the gap.

Chapter Thirteen

Nelson seemed preoccupied, even shaken. Hackett tried to engage his attention and, failing, shrugged and drew up a chair for Dr Wilkinson. He leaned back against Mallory's desk, his legs stretched out in front of him, fingers curled around its edge. It had been cleared of its ornaments – living and dead. The tarantula would inhabit some other office until Mallory's temporary exile was over, and the skull, cigarette still drooping insouciantly from between its upper and lower mandibles, now squinted down at them from the shelf opposite.

Nelson had requested an interview with Helen Wilkinson. It was in all the papers; the Don Juan story had taken a new turn: the tragic loss of his wronged wife. They had somehow got hold of information that Helen Wilkinson had miscarried a child in January, and it seemed that her behaviour since had been strange, to put it mildly. The mood of the reports had changed: they were becoming more sympathetic to Helen, and Hackett wondered if she was capable of feeding them the story herself, or had the person who gave it to them a purely mercenary motive?

Hackett looked at Nelson. He was standing at the window, feet slightly apart, hands in his pockets, staring out at the rain.

'Sir,' Hackett said. There was no response. Hackett shrugged and turned to Helen.

'Are you all right?' He gestured to the swelling and discolouration on her cheek.

'I fainted. Fell against a table. I'm fine.' She tilted her head forward, so that her hair hid the bruising under her left eye. The worst of the swelling had been kept down by the ice packs her mother and Ruth insisted that she use, but a purple wedge of colour, and a darker than usual shadow under her left eye showed through the make-up she had carefully applied that morning. Her mother had driven her almost to distraction with her warnings and suggestions that they ask Dr Patterson's advice before Helen should venture outside the house. She didn't want fuss or sympathy. It was understanding she needed, not pity. Helen saw that her mother, conscious that they could never have the easy, trusting relationship that would heal and help them both, had compromised with an overbearing solicitousness, a fuss which creates noise and the appearance of concern through the agency of bustle and agitation, the illusion of communication in meaningless words.

'Why did you want to speak to me?' she asked.

Hackett watched her for some time, before asking, 'You've seen the papers?'

'Yes.'

'You didn't tell us that you'd had a miscarriage . . .' Hackett began gently.

'Why the hell should I?'

'Well . . . because it could be relevant – if you were depressed for example.'

'Of course I was *depressed*. I'd recently lost a baby and my husband was having an affair with the wife of a colleague! Wouldn't you be depressed?'

Hackett looked into her pretty, elfin face. This was something new, this fieriness, this sparky aggression. Ruth Marks

116

had told him that the fey, dreamy, damaged quality that he had seen up to this point was not the true Helen Wilkinson. Is this, he wondered, closer to her real self?

'If it was me,' he said, continuing in a warm, gentle tone, 'I'd want to get back at him.'

Helen tilted her head on one side, seriously considering the notion. 'You don't seem the type for revenge,' she said.

Hackett looked over at Nelson, but he had moved to the door and was standing with his head bowed, apparently deep in thought. Hackett turned back to Helen, irritated that Nelson, who had insisted on the interview, had apparently lost all interest in it. He nodded, even forced a smile. 'You're probably right,' he said. 'But I might be tempted to do something just to make the awfulness stop.'

Helen frowned, remembering the row that had resulted in her miscarriage.

'It must have felt like there was no end to it,' Hackett went on, his voice quiet, its tone mesmeric. 'The loss of the baby. The taunts.'

Helen looked into Hackett's broad, friendly features. Should she tell him how much she longed for one kind word from Edward? One act of gentleness – one word of regret? Could she make him grasp the simple truth that she would have been grateful even to have been left alone to grieve?

'Shall I tell you what Edward said to me after I lost my baby?' She didn't wait for a reply but went on, 'He said that a female's worth is measured by her fecundity and her child-rearing skills. Apparently I failed on both counts.'

'How did you react?'

Helen blinked, startled, as if she hadn't realized she had spoken aloud, then she looked away. 'We argued,' she said. 'Again.'

'Did you ever fight? Physically, I mean.'

'Edward was far too subtle for that. He didn't need to resort to anything so crude as physical violence.'

'But surely, when you lost the baby—'

Helen swallowed. 'That was the only time. And it was me, not him. I threw a punch. Missed—' She took a breath as though she could not get enough air. 'And killed my baby.'

Hackett moved into the chair opposite Helen's. 'That must have been – difficult for you.'

Helen laughed. A sudden, harsh sound, without humour, like a cry of pain. 'Difficult. Yes.'

Unruffled, Hackett went on: 'It wouldn't be surprising if you'd wanted to hurt him the way he'd hurt you.'

'Edward was fireproof,' she said quietly. 'Nothing could hurt him.'

'Something did,' he said quietly. 'Someone.'

I did, Helen thought. A thousand times after that day. In daydreams. Fantasies so real that she would have to seek Edward out, to convince herself that he really was all right. And sometimes, when she found him in his study, or watching TV, or reading in bed, notes scattered around him, a supercilious look on his face, it wasn't relief that she felt.

Once, she had found a kitchen knife – *the* kitchen knife – in her bedside cabinet and didn't – still couldn't – remember putting it there. So many times she had taken the boning knife from its slot in the block and sharpened it, taking comfort from the song of metal against metal, and lulled by the rhythm, she would go through every step, from start to finish, carrying out her intention in her mind and soul and heart because she hated him with an intensity that could not be described in words. Only in action.

'I um . . .'

'Yes?'

There was a pause and then Helen said, 'I don't know who killed Edward. But I'm not sorry he's dead.'

'Sir?'

Nelson twitched at the sound of his name, then shook himself. 'Oh,' he said, looking around the room. 'You've let her go.'

'Are you OK?'

Nelson's eyes were watery, their colour less intense than usual. 'That bloke, Ellis,' he said. 'He was hanging around again. When we brought her in. What is it between them? Are they having an affair an' all?' He tried to make a joke of it, but he was haunted by the first impression: Ellis, shadowy in the recess of a door further down the passageway. Something about the eyes, visible, shining even in the dim light of the doorway. Something . . . something about the hunch of the shoulders, the constant edgy activity of his hands that made Nelson think of his son. He had stopped, transfixed, had almost called out to him and then Ellis had moved into the light and darted away from him and the illusion had fragmented.

'What did you get out of the mistress?' Nelson asked, rousing himself and walking to the window. Helen Wilkinson was crossing the quad, followed by the tall figure of Ruth Marks.

'*Clara's* more carved up about Wilkinson's death than *her*,' Hackett replied, meaning Helen.

Hackett had interviewed Clara Ainsley earlier, at head-quarters; it seemed kinder than bringing her into the university where speculation and gossip had already reached fever pitch. A neighbour had agreed to look after the baby for a couple of hours. She looked a hundred years old. Hackett was reminded of the winter when Lisa got one damn cold after another and would cry all night and most of the day. Even when she was quiet, they would need go to her and check that she hadn't suffocated on the terrible congestion in her lungs and nose. Sheila, haggard, wild, frenzied, had been driven to the point of screaming in the end, and he had felt the urge more than once himself, despite the fact that, for ten or twelve hours of the day he would be away from the noise and the upset.

'Guilt, or grief?' Nelson asked.

'She claims she saw him at the university, after he'd completed the staff interviews. Told him they were finished. She thought he was messing about with someone else.'

'I wasn't about to let him treat me like the others,' she had said. 'Like some tart he'd picked up on a street corner.'

Nelson grunted. 'You have to admire his energy, don't you? A pity, though, dumping him like that, when he was planning to set her up in her own little office, right within pawing range.'

'I got the impression she felt the same way.'

Nelson sniffed, turned, and found himself staring into the empty eye sockets of the skull. 'Spilt milk,' he said. 'On the other hand, we only have her word for it that she dumped him. What if it was the other way round?'

'He was setting up the secretarial job for her, why would he get shot of her?'

Nelson nodded, irritated that he'd missed the obvious. 'OK, what if she *thought* he was going to dump her? One of his little games, like Marks said.'

'Then she's just about untethered enough at the moment to've taken a knife to him.'

The rain and sleet had abated for the time being and although small, sodden melts of snow clustered around the bases of the daffodils, the sky was a flawless cobalt blue and the sun sparkled on the raindrops that trembled on the buds of the birch trees.

'Hey, slow down!' Ruth put a hand on Helen's arm and Helen paused.

'Forty-five degrees,' she said.

'What?'

'The flower buds of the daffodils – they're angled at forty-five degrees to the stems. There must be a reason, don't you think?'

Ruth glanced around and then edged Helen towards the doorway of the environmental biology building. 'Helen, don't do this. Don't start flaking out on me again.'

Helen frowned. Still considering the puzzle of the daffodils, she made to go through the door, but Ruth stopped her. 'It's all a smokescreen. Avoiding unpleasant truths by going off on a tangent like that.'

Helen's office was housed in the comparative modernity of the Edwardian building, the patterned tiling of its floor had long-since worn thin and many of the tiles were cracked, but it held a certain charm; its square, unfussy design was well suited to the department's needs: a combination of office accommodation and laboratories – indeed, it was one of the few purpose-built departments in the university. Helen entered and walked past the stairway leading to her office, towards the staff common room.

'Where are you going?' Ruth demanded, standing in front of Helen and placing both hands on her shoulders.

'I have to get my coat. Who would tell the Press all those things, Ruth? About the baby. Who would know?' She stared into Ruth's face as though she would find the answer to her question in the fine lines around her friend's mouth, or in the blue-grey of her eyes.

'Ed didn't exactly keep it a secret,' Ruth said.

'But the details – in the papers—'

Ruth shrugged. 'Clara? David? Who knows? Helen, it doesn't matter.'

'It does matter.' Helen shook herself free. '*It matters.*'

'All right. I'm sorry. It matters. Now will you tell me where you're going?'

Helen's eyes roved around the main entrance. It was empty except for a porter and two postgraduate students who were checking the wooden racks of pigeon-holes for mail. She moved toward the common room again with Ruth following, and Isaac Smolder eased back into the shadows, unseen, listening.

'Will you just *tell* me?' Ruth demanded.

'I don't confide in many people, Ruth. There aren't so very many people I feel I can trust. I confided in you.'

'Yeah, so?' The two women stared at each other for a full half minute, then Ruth, suddenly assimilating the implications of what Helen had said, burst out: 'Is this an accusation? You think I'd spread those sordid stories about your husband's grubby little affairs? Jesus, Helen! Who helped you sort yourself out when you lost the baby? Who suggested the switch to tissue culture when you couldn't bear the sight and smell of blood any longer? Who smoothed your worried brow and took your calls at two in the morning and convinced you otherwise when you found the knife in your bedroom cabinet – a couple of weeks after you lost the baby – and you thought you'd done the bastard in and hidden it there, remember?'

'Don't let her speak to you like that,' Smolder breathed.

Helen turned her wedding ring round and round on her finger.

'Who looked after you? Told you what was real and what was in your head?' More than once, Ruth had tracked Edward down – in a meeting, or a seminar – and insisted that he talk to Helen, because she had convinced herself that this time, she really had done it, that he was dead. 'It was me, Helen, all those times. Your old faithful friend. Always there, like a big St Bernard, lolloping after you – whistle and I come running. I don't drop hairs on the carpet and I don't cock my leg on the furniture – the perfect family pet.'

'Don't patronize me, Ruth.' The words spat out, angry.

'Then stop talking like a bloody lunatic!' Ruth said with sudden ferocity. She closed her eyes for a moment. 'I'm sorry. I really am. But you are making me *crazy*. What are you trying to do? Drive away the only friend you have in this temple of misogyny? Is that what you want?'

'You don't have to put up with it – don't have to stand for that sort of treatment any more.'

Helen felt the need of her mother; she knew it was childish and pathetic, knew how unsatisfactory the encounter would be, but she wanted comfort, uncompromising love, even though she knew her mother was incapable of giving it. Anyway, she had returned to Bolton on the 9.30 train; Ruth had dropped her at the station after Helen had persuaded her to go home with the promise that she would visit at the weekend.

'I just want to know what happened,' Helen said, her voice calm.

Ruth grabbed her roughly. 'I'll tell you what happened. Someone did you a fucking great favour. Edward is dead and you're free to do whatever the hell you like. Get used to it and stop whinging.'

Smolder almost broke cover. Almost shouted to Ruth Marks to take her mauling hands off Helen. But he knew that now would be the wrong time. Once, animal activists had got into his laboratory. Security had discovered the break-in and called the police before they'd had chance to do much damage. All of the cages had been unlocked and the doors were wide open. He had arrived two hours later and from a total of over a hundred experimental animals, only a couple of rats had escaped; the rest, habituated to captivity, had remained pass-ively in their cages, doing no more than sniffing anxiously at the open space where the door should have been. All he had to do was secure the latches. Helen would not go far. He could wait.

Helen stared at Ruth, shocked by her outburst. The two students had turned to look at them and the porter took a tentative step towards them. He cleared his throat. 'All right, ladies?' he asked.

Ruth let go of Helen. 'Fine,' she said. 'Everything's under control – isn't it, Helen?'

Helen shrugged and smiled, embarrassed. They were arguing, why was that? As Ruth said, it was crazy. 'That bloke Nelson has a funny effect on me,' she said, then turning back toward the entrance, she added, 'I think I'll take a walk.'

Ruth hesitated, then followed, a few steps behind, uncertain of her welcome, but Helen dawdled, despite the cold of the day and she was soon walking beside her friend, wondering how someone as strong as Helen could allow herself to be so manipulated and misused.

'I've been thinking,' Helen said. 'About the people on the list.'

'The Apocalypse file?'

'Could they have done it, Ruth? Would anyone kill, just to keep their job?'

'It isn't just a job to some of these people. It's home, career, status – and Ed would most likely have worked on their inflated egos – he really had a way of flaying the flesh from the bone, and Marks's Paradox states that *in*flated egos are easily *de*flated – the rate of deflation being directly pro-portional to the original distension.'

Helen laughed, and Ruth drew her arm through her own. Her hand was frozen and Ruth turned into a more sheltered area with paved paths and raised flower beds, riotous with pansies and polyanthus. 'Look at Mallory,' she went on. 'He must've seen it coming, but he was devastated when Ed told him his contract wouldn't be renewed.'

'How do you know?'

Ruth grinned. 'Valerie hates gossip, but she's soft-hearted. Take a sympathetic line and she'll tell you anything you want to know. "Poor Dr Mallory, after all those years of devoted service . . ." You get the idea. And talking of Valerie, she had a motive of her own.'

'Ruth! You can't be serious! Valerie Roberts—'

'Never underestimate the fury of quiet women, especially quiet, middle-aged women. They feel the slings and arrows, the contumely of the young and arrogant far more acutely than the rest of us. And they don't suffer them lightly.'

Helen looked into her friend's face and Ruth stared back for a few moments, then they both burst out laughing. 'All right,' Ruth agreed. 'It's a ridiculous notion, but reasons for murder often are ridiculous, or at least they seem so to the outsider, the objective, rational observer, because they haven't had to put up with the years building up to the event. Ten years, in Valerie's case.'

'Even so,' Helen said. 'Valerie . . . What about Clara, or David? If Edward didn't tell her his plans, she might have lost her temper.' She shrugged. 'And David has not been exactly rational since the news broke.' Her hand went involuntarily to the bruise under her eye.

'Bloody madman.' A sudden cloud darkened the little garden where they had been pacing for the last few minutes and they heard the first hailstones fall like broken rosary beads on to the stone flags. 'Shit,' Ruth said eloquently, and they ran for cover.

They found themselves inside the Horace Shelby library, shaking melting ice from their hair and continuing their speculation. 'Either of them could've done it,' Ruth said, her voice echoing in the high, empty space of the foyer. 'And what about Mick Tuttle?'

'*Mick?*' Helen blinked.

'It's no secret he hated Edward. He's strong enough. If he surprised Ed in bed—'

'Come off it, Ruth. He may be strong, but he could hardly be described as fast. And how the hell would he surprise Edward in bed wearing those callipers?'

Ruth pondered. 'If it was nearer Christmas Ed might've thought it was the ghost of Christmas future coming to haunt him – but you're probably right, Mick isn't a strong candidate. It'd help if we knew who'd altered the files. Who had access to Ed's password?'

Helen flushed slightly. 'Valerie, Me, Clara? Anyone with a bit of know-how can get access to a password, Ruth. And to make it really easy, Ed used to keep it on a slip of paper in his wallet – I've found it lying around on his desk a few times. He never agreed with the computer services' policy of expiring passwords periodically – said he'd only got used to one when they forced him to change it.'

'Ellis is a keen computer user, isn't he?' Ruth said, in answer.

'So what?'

'So he might know how to hack into Ed's files – to alter them.'

'But *why?*'

'I'm working on that. We know he had a blazing, ding-dong, toe-to-toe, eyeball-to-eyeball confrontation with Ed the morning of the murder. If we knew why, then perhaps the rest would all come clear.'

Chapter Fourteen

The entire plan was perfectly executed. The practice run through had been just like the real thing, except that his eyes wouldn't stay closed. I couldn't bear him staring up at me from under those unevenly closed lids, like a tipsy judge, so I held them down with two fifty pence pieces until they stuck. I can hear those two coins jingling in my pocket as I walk, I took them with me, a memento, and a private joke. What are they? No more than loose change. But what have they done? Where have they been? Next time I speak to the police, maybe I'll buy us a cup of coffee with these fifty pences. 'Sugar, Inspector? No, I can't imagine why anyone would want to kill poor Edward. Please – let me get these . . .' Or maybe I'll keep them as makeweights, ringing out like leper bells: Unclean! Unclean!

'I'd like to question her with her GP present,' Hackett said.

'Who?'

The discussion of strategies had been going on in this distracted fashion for a full fifteen minutes, with Hackett making suggestions and Nelson either missing the point or deliberately obstructing him, and Hackett was beginning to weary of it.

'I'm talking about Dr Wilkinson.'

An innocuous statement in itself, but there was a suggestion of impatience, a whisper of insubordination. Nelson flashed a warning, his eyes kindling to gold for a brief moment, but quickly fading to dun-brown. 'I'd like a chat with Ellis – a real chat, I mean. Formally.' There was no emphasis on the 'I', no indication that he had heard Hackett's suggestion at all.

'Why?' Hackett asked.

'*Why?*' The heat of Nelson's glare was searing, but still he could not force an apologetic 'sir' from Hackett, so Nelson went on: 'He's shifty, hiding something.'

'So is half the academic staff of the college, from what I can make out.'

'Got guilt written all over him.' Nelson had meant to say 'all over his face' but it wasn't just his face. Ellis reeked of guilt. It oozed from his pores like sweat from a sick man. It was in the nervy, twitchy movements of his hands, in the constant tightening of his jaw muscles, it showed in his bitten fingernails, and in the dark circles under his eyes. 'He can't even look me in the eye when I speak to him,' Nelson said, unable to articulate all those other things, which he intuited rather than addressed as conscious thoughts.

Hackett glanced up, startled. Since when did Nelson require eye contact? He generally took sustained eye contact as a challenge to his authority.

'He lies,' Nelson went on. 'Obvious lies. He can't even be bothered to lie convincingly. Said he was looking for Mallory when I caught him hanging around her office yesterday, but Mallory says he's been trying to catch up with the lying toe-rag for a couple of days. And he was here, loitering outside, just before Wilkinson's interview.' He saw Hackett's questioning look, but Nelson was not a man who liked to be questioned, and he certainly wasn't the sort of officer who invited opinion from his inferiors.

Hackett took a breath. 'We've got Helen Wilkinson practically begging us to let her confess.' Apparently he had decided to tell Nelson what was bothering him, with or without his blessing. 'Ainsley's so beside himself with rage at his wife's infidelity he can't bring himself to set foot inside his own house. What makes you think Ellis—?'

'Don't use that tone with me,' Nelson snarled. 'Your inquiries into those two haven't exactly come up with a shitload of confessions. Helen Wilkinson is falling over herself to confess, and all you've got is "I'm not sorry he's dead." '

Hackett was mildly surprised: Nelson must have been listening, at least to that part of the interview.

The two men fell silent, Nelson trying to gauge his opponent, but unable to see past the impenetrable stare that reminded him so much of that damned stray cat his wife had brought in that it made his right foot itch for contact. Nobody seemed to know much about Hackett. He was respected, had a reputation for fairness, but he was a family man and not much of a drinker, which meant he socialized only as much as was necessary to avoid causing offence. So, he remained something of a mystery.

'You spoke to Wilkinson's secretary,' Nelson said, deciding that trying to read those unflinching green eyes wasn't really worth the effort.

'Twice,' Hackett replied. 'Once about the staff interviews and once about the professor's files being messed about. He certainly didn't mince his words on their relative performances in the Research Assessment Exercise – and of course the merging of faculties means some departments simply won't be viable.'

'Let's get her in again, see what she knows about our Mr Ellis.'

'What about Dr Wilkinson?'

'What about her?' There was no mistaking the look: Nelson was not about to tolerate any further discussion in the matter. Hackett, however, was not a man to give up without a fight.

'I just think you should consider—'

He got no further. Nelson was on his feet and shouting and Hackett, permitting himself a heavy sigh, decided he had better do as he was told.

Mrs Roberts had been brought in for further questioning after Ruth Marks's revelation that she was earmarked for early retirement. She was, after all, the person most likely to have access to Prof Wilkinson's password, and hence the Apocalypse file. At first, she had denied any knowledge that Edward was planning to pension her off, but she was a woman not used to deception, and the dishonesty had proved hard for her to sustain, especially when they had discovered that she had made discreet enquiries to the heads of several departments about the availability of secretarial posts. She confessed, then, but although she had admitted to lying about the security of her job with the professor, she had been unrepentant. It was not, she had told them, because of any inadequacy of hers that Professor Wilkinson had planned to get rid of her, thus implying that the inadequacy was all his. She vehemently denied having tampered with the Apocalypse file and although they had been certain that she was hiding something, they could get no further.

Mrs Roberts was discretion itself. Hackett had unwittingly prepared her for the ordeal, by manifesting in the short walk from her office to Mallory's a terseness, ill-temper and rudeness that was untypical of him, but which approximated, if rather pallidly, to Nelson's own style of interrogation.

Yes, she told them, a number of academics had exchanged heated words with the professor. No, she did not know the details of their disagreements. 'I think,' she said, settling back in her chair in a physical intimation that she would sit here all day if need be, but she would not betray a single secret to the inspector, 'you really ought to be addressing these questions to the staff concerned, and not to me.' Nelson let her go after half an hour, disgusted.

Ruth Marks was more forthcoming, although not particularly helpful, as it turned out. She stood at the threshold of Mallory's office, her arms quite relaxed at her sides. 'Well,' she said. 'Isn't this a transformation! Incredible, isn't it, what a flick with a duster and a new perspective can do to enhance a place?'

Hackett covered a smile, but Nelson was not in the mood for levity. 'Dr Marks—' he began, but Ruth swept past him and began a deeper assessment of the alterations they had made to the office.

'The tarantula, for instance. Now I knew that wouldn't appeal to you, Inspector Nelson. All those beady eyes on you.' She gave a sensuous little shudder. 'And the skull. To be frank, if it were my office, I'd rather have it sitting on the desk scowling out at my visitors than on the shelf glaring at me.' She tilted her head. 'But you know best.' She perched on the edge of Mallory's desk, staring thoughtfully up into the empty eye sockets of the skull. 'Most people assume it's an attempt by the old curmudgeon at humour, but in fact it's a reminder of *what could happen*. The cigarette? It's the last one from the very last pack of Capstan Extra Strength Mallory ever smoked. There's even a family resemblance, don't you think?'

Nelson, who was not incapable of patience when the occasion demanded it, had listened to all of this, intrigued that the doctor seemed to know so much of the personal histories of her colleagues.

'Perhaps you can be as informative on the subject of John Ellis,' he said, thinking aloud.

She laughed, shaking her head. 'In the departmental hierarchy, Ellis, as a doctoral student, ranks just above an amoeba. Amassing a body of knowledge about a staff takes time and energy.' Her eyes twinkled and Hackett again sensed that edge of sexual mischievousness he found both stimulating and disturbing. 'I don't like to waste my energy,' she added.

'Nevertheless, you did lie for him.'

She raised her pale eyebrows and placed one long-fingered hand across her chest in a dramatic gesture.

'Yesterday. He wasn't there to pay his respects.'

'Oh,' she said, pretending wide-eyed innocence. 'You mean his little visit to Helen. Wasn't he? Are you sure, Inspector?'

Nelson stared at her, feeling a creeping heat spill from his neck on to his face. What was it about the damned woman that constantly put him off balance?

'I can't say I know why he wanted to see Helen. He didn't confide in me,' Ruth said soberly.

'What do you know about him?'

Ruth turned down the corners of her mouth, thoughtful now. The flippancy, the sly humour vanished, if only momentarily. 'He's a postgraduate student, doing doctoral research in behavioural ecology. Animal physiology. Invertebrates. Mallory's his supervisor – he'd be able to tell you more.' She gave a short laugh. 'On the other hand . . .'

'He's worried about this research project or thesis, or whatever you call it?'

'He's built a certain notoriety for himself on the basis of a bit of dodgy maths. If he can't back it up with actual data, he's going to upset a lot of people who have personal investments in his theory.'

'Investments – you mean cash?'

'Not up front, but he's working on the trendy – and possibly lucrative – idea that population dynamics is linked to a self-regulating mechanism within the biosphere. Mother earth protecting us from ourselves – a comforting notion, and quite popular in these post-Darwinian, post-atheistic, quasi-religious times.'

'What, you mean Gaia, that sort of thing?'

Ruth's eyebrows shot up. 'You astound me, Sergeant!'

'My son's into all that New Age stuff. Can't get him to church on Sundays, but he believes in Gaia, all right.'

'I shouldn't worry too much, Sergeant. For Gaia, read God. *Homo sapiens* is neurotic by default – ever since we became sentient we've been trying to make sense of why we're here. It – sorry, *she* – Gaia – is simply a more trendy variant on the theme of deity. God with science PR – Saatchi and Saatchi style.'

'I'm sure this is fascinating,' Nelson said, 'but can we get back to Ellis?'

Ruth narrowed her eyes at the inspector, and for a moment, Hackett thought she might clam up, but after a pause which made her point eloquently, she went on: 'John has upset the vast majority of behavioural ecologists, physiologists, zoologists, environmentalists – in fact just about every species and subspecies of biologist except the crackpots who would like Gaia to be true. He has quite a following on the Internet – you should see the e-mail he gets – and if he's right, which any real scientist must seriously doubt, he could revolutionize our view of population dynamics.'

'And if he doesn't find the proof for his theory, all these people will be disappointed?'

'Crushed. Humiliated. Mortified. Devastated. And you know who they'll blame.'

'What would happen to him?'

'He'd be finished before he really got started.'

'So,' said Nelson, 'he's a worried man.'

'They all are, about one thing or another. The Senate are talking in terms of 30 per cent wastage – redundancies – in a university, I ask you!'

'*You* don't seem particularly worried, Dr Marks.'

'Me?' she slid a sideways glance at Hackett. 'Didn't your sergeant tell you?'

Hackett shifted his weight from one foot to the other, but he continued staring ahead as though preoccupied with other thoughts.

'I'm off to the United States as of August. I've been invited on to an interdisciplinary team working with neural nets – specifically the development of a part biological and part silicon-based brain. I'm going to be helping to develop the wetware – that's the biological side.' She laughed. 'Don't look so horrified, Inspector. It won't be a human brain, although they do use human brain cells – from donated cadavers. The brains are packaged and shipped to the research facility before the neurones start to degenerate. You can keep clusters of cells alive for a very long time, given the right tissue fluids and stimulation.'

Hackett had never seen her so animated, so enthused about anything. He had thought her incapable of rising above her cynicism, but this was something she believed in. Nelson, however, had heard enough. The whole concept of digging out people's brains and then sticking them in jars and giving them electric shocks was sickening. He returned to his original theme: 'So you didn't fall out with Professor Wilkinson on the day he died?'

'One of the few who can say that, hand on heart, and mean it,' she replied, solemnly miming the action.

'Would Ellis have cause to argue with the professor?'

Ruth considered. 'Edward loved to pick fights with people, just to show how completely he could win.'

Nelson sensed that she might be willing to say more, given the right encouragement. 'You 'em – couldn't speculate as to why Ellis might argue with the professor?'

'I could, but would it be ethical?'

'We really would appreciate some help here, if you think you can give it, Dr Marks,' Hackett intervened, seeing that Nelson had almost exhausted his meagre reserves of patience, and sensing that the doctor may have something worth hearing.

'I'm afraid I haven't got a confession to the murders for you, Sergeant.'

'But—' Hackett prompted, thinking that her sharp perception really must rankle, if she's as unguarded in what she says to her colleagues.

She smiled. 'But I will tell you this: John Ellis is a troubled soul.' She had their undivided attention. 'He has bad dreams.' Nelson invited her to be seated and he took up position in Mallory's chair behind the desk, leaving Hackett leaning against the cabinet of beetles. 'At first they were simply rehashed versions of his argument with Edward, but apparently he's started having a recurring dream. Now I know it's only a matter of days since Edward was murdered—'

Hackett thought, How easily she says that word. Most people couldn't bring themselves to use it at all, and those that did would hesitate, or look away, a reflection of their embarrassment or disbelief, but Ruth Marks used the word unflinchingly. For her, it was just a word, the most suitable one for the situation.

'But poor John has been sleeping badly and whenever he falls asleep, he has this dream. He describes it as a "terrible dream". He finds it deeply troubling. He can have it four or five times a night, and he wakes from it in terror. It's disturbed his sleep patterns so much he's taken to catnapping during the day – and the instant he falls asleep he starts to dream.'

'A nightmare,' Nelson murmured, and Hackett and Ruth both glanced over at him, but he seemed engrossed in some abstract thought. 'The content of this recurring dream?' he asked.

Ruth remembered Ellis's lightly covered terror as he told her:

I'm sitting on jagged rocks, at my feet is a net full of oysters. I'm opening the oysters with a knife and scooping out the pearls. Helen Wilkinson is watching me and I suddenly realize that I'm using the knife that killed Prof Wilkinson to prise open the oysters. I can't stop, because I don't want to draw attention to the fact and I don't want to upset Helen, so I carry on, opening the shells and casting the pearls into the sea, which is lapping at my feet. I've counted one hundred and twenty-five so far.

Then Helen is gone and Edward is standing over me. He says 'How many?' and I answer, 'One hundred and forty-seven.' He dips his hand into the water and scoops out a pearl, then he drops it into a beaker of water. But it isn't water, because it fizzes and Edward says, 'Drink it down. It'll set you right.'

I want to run. I know, you see, that the drink must be acid to make the pearl dissolve, but I can't move. I take it and he makes me drink. It tastes bitter. Then I wake up.

There was a silence of three or four seconds and then Nelson demanded, 'Well?'

Ruth raised her eyebrows. 'Well what?'

'What the hell is it supposed to mean? What am I supposed to make of it? Does it mean anything?' Nelson demanded. 'You must have some idea!'

Ruth shrugged. 'You're the detective. You work it out.'

Chapter Fifteen

If Ruth had listened, if Sanjay Patterson had let her speak, Helen might not have told Mick Tuttle. But fear had made Sanjay timid. 'I'm not your priest,' he had said, regretting it even as he spoke. 'Whatever you tell me cannot be held an inviolable secret.' He had almost followed her into the hallway of the old house which served as both surgery and home to the practice partners, but Sanjay had fought hard for what he had achieved and he was not about to risk losing it over a scandal. He was ashamed to think this way, but he couldn't change the fact that he didn't want to hear what Helen Wilkinson had to say. It was, he knew, by an uneasy intuition, dangerous in a way that Inspector Nelson, for all his ill-suppressed violence could never be: what she wanted to tell him was the stuff of ruined reputations – perhaps not his, although such secrets, once out, had a way of tainting all they touched, even incidentally. He did not want that risk; the burden of sharing her secrets would, he was convinced, prove too hazardous.

This refusal to share her secrets, even as an observer, had come as a shock to him. Until the moment that she had begun to take him into her confidence he had convinced himself that he would do anything to help. He had seen Helen through the first few months of pregnancy; the morning sickness, her doubts about having the baby, and her eventual acceptance of it. Her husband's affairs had been common knowledge throughout the university. He had admired Helen's courage and dignity and sympathized with the hurt her husband caused her. He had attended her when she had been discharged from hospital after the miscarriage and had been deeply affected by her quiet strength despite an intense and poignant sense of loss. But friendship could be taken only so far, and only so much could be expected of him professionally, he reasoned. Nevertheless, he could not disguise the fact that he had failed her.

Helen had returned to her office just after four without any specific task in mind, but unable to face fighting through the disorderly ranks of reporters outside the college gates in order to go home. They would, she knew, be there no matter how long she put off leaving but she needed time to recover from Sanjay's rebuff. She didn't blame him; within the confines of the university, an Asian doctor was viewed in the same light as a woman academic: exotic, an amusing diversion from the norm, but to be treated with caution and regarded with suspicion, since either or both could bring the deadly spores of liberalism and change. So, although Sanjay had a good Celtic surname, inherited from his Scottish father, he was not, in the eyes of the college establishment, entirely to be trusted.

A phone call from Edward's father had demonstrated unequivocally how entirely she was alone. She was crying when Mick came into the room; weeping silently, tears of loss and confusion and self-doubt and exhaustion. The cynic in her asked what precisely she had lost and Edward's image was supplanted by a fleeting vision of her baby, small enough to fit into the palm of her hand, so terribly, immutably still.

After a brief confusion over the bruise on her face, Mick

accepted her explanation and made coffee in silence, giving her time to recover. She mumbled a 'thank you', accepting the mug, and he lowered himself into the chair opposite her, waiting for her to begin.

'I'm sorry,' she said. 'I thought I was finally getting myself together. I've just had a call from Edward's father. He and his wife are staying at the Chester Grosvenor.' She looked wildly about the room. 'Oh, Mick – what can I tell them?'

He didn't reply at first, but regarded her thoughtfully, his dark eyes brimming with sympathy. 'You don't have to tell them anything. They just want to be near their son, and now you're the closest they can get.'

Helen shook her head. Tears glistened on her lashes. 'They want answers – they've read the papers, heard the speculation. The knife missing from the kitchen, the infidelity, the miscarriage – oh God!' She covered her face with one hand. Mick gently prised the coffee mug from her grasp and set it on the desk, then he knelt beside her, ignoring the pain in his knees and the chafing of the leg brace against his calf muscles.

He put both arms around her and held her to him, drinking in the scent of her hair, feeling the heat of her tears soaking through his shirt, torn between her need for comfort and his own for contact with her.

After a time, she subsided. The coffee was cold and he made some fresh, wincing as he got slowly to his feet, testing the strength of his joints before putting his weight on them. Helen washed her face at the little vanity basin and he passed her a towel from the hook next to it – not standard issue, something soft and fluffy she had brought in from home, another small indication of her subtle non-conformity. They returned to their seats and at first she avoided his eye, but after a few minutes she looked up tentatively, nursing the coffee mug between her hands.

He looked back, his calm eyes unflinching, unjudging.

Sunlight came and went in breathless bursts, barging out in brilliant ebullience and then disappearing, swallowed up by clouds which threw occasional drops of rain on to the windows. In these brief rushes of dazzling light, his eyes danced with colour, tawny flecks and hints of hazel and chestnut sparked from the dark, almost black depths of his irises, colours of warmth and compassion. Helen swallowed, took a breath and began. 'Edward's parents worshipped him. He's an only son. I mean, he was. They have a daughter, but—' She shrugged. 'It seems archaic – implausible – doesn't it, that boys should still be valued above girls?'

'It's sad, and it's wrong, but implausible? No.'

'Edward always had whatever he wanted, so he never learned that there are some things you can't – shouldn't – have. He assumed that what he wanted was his by right, and his looks and his public school charm ensured he always got it.'

Edward was young when they had first met, and she still in her teens, a student, insecure. Edward had made something of a pet of her, liked to coax a smile from her. Not such an easy task in those days. She had felt singled out, blessed; his attention was a mark of distinction, it gave her confidence and eroded her self-hate. So when he had pretended not to know her on her arrival at St Werburgh's, she had been hurt – stricken even. Of course, it had been a pretence, she realized that when the excitement of his subsequent gallantry and courtship of her had begun to fade; after the gloss of marriage had accumulated a few months' dust. Then she began to see Edward for what he was, and she despised the trick as infantile, cruel, a measure of his superficiality. Perhaps not all at once, but in small, shocking revelations, she saw his vanity and his monstrous narcissism.

When she first knew him, as a student and acolyte, he had an angelic look in repose, which she had mistaken for innocence. She couldn't have known then that the statuesque composition of his features had been carefully rehearsed in a mirror. With age, he had managed with this conscious control of his facial muscles to maintain a smooth, almost flawless complexion, but the few lines and wrinkles he had been unable to avoid betrayed his inner self, emphasizing the meaner aspects of his nature. The deep grooves at the corner of his left eye gave him an effortless expression of superciliousness, and a line, fine and indistinct as yet, from his right nostril to the corner of his mouth would, had he lived, have become a more or less permanent sneer.

'His parents couldn't see the flaws in his character, the casual cruelty, the way he used and manipulated people,' Helen went on. 'For them Edward was – always will be – perfect.'

'And you can't make all the things he did and said unhappen. You can't tell them all those things in the Press are lies, is that it?'

Helen sighed and nodded, relieved not to have to explain this, at least. She took a swallow of coffee to slake the terrible dryness in her throat. 'After the – after I lost the baby,' she frowned, fighting for control – 'I couldn't think straight. Sometimes I couldn't remember what I'd done or said. There were blanks. Blackouts. Some days, I couldn't find the energy to get out of bed. And all the while he was carrying on his affair with David Ainsley's wife' – she couldn't bring herself to say the name – 'and tormenting me with my failure, as he saw it.'

Mick gave a low, choked exclamation.

'There was only one thing I wanted at that time.' Helen was completely calm as she reached this part of her story. 'What I wanted was to see Edward dead. I wanted to kill him myself. I even planned how I would do it.' She brought her gaze level with Mick's. 'A knife between the ribs.'

Mick's expression was serious, attentive, but it held no hint of repugnance and this gave Helen the courage to continue. 'It was a fantasy, Mick, no more. Then one day I found the knife – the one that's disappeared from the block – the one the police are looking for. I'd put it in my little cabinet by our bed. Except I couldn't – still can't – remember putting it there.'

Her look of pain and confusion made Mick reach out and take her hand. 'What did you do with it?' he asked.

'I returned it to the block. But, Mick, it's gone again and the police think—'

'And *you*, Helen. What do you think?'

She passed one hand wearily over her eyes. 'I wish I knew, Mick. I wanted to, I passionately wanted him dead – for the death of my child. I wanted to kill him.' She looked at Mick. A life for a life. It wouldn't be the first time she had felt that way. On that other occasion she had failed, but only just. And this had been better planned, carefully rehearsed. 'I'm so confused. I can't separate the fantasy from—' She frowned; she had been about to say, 'from what really happened', but she didn't know what had really happened, she didn't even know if she had been there. The frown deepened. 'I keep thinking, every time I open a cupboard or a drawer, that I'll find the knife hidden—' She stopped. The whole thing seemed too wild, too crazy.

He considered, then nodded to himself, accepting her reasoning. 'How about checking over the house together?'

Helen looked up, startled. His hand, warm against hers, strong, increased its pressure slightly. She smiled, thanking him silently. 'I suppose if we searched together . . .'

Isaac Smolder watched from his office window. Mick had returned to his office to collect some work, and Helen waited for him in the quad, alone for several minutes.

Those eyes! She glanced up at the hundreds of glinting panes, reflecting fleeting cold light, and seemed almost to look through and beyond Smolder. Yet he was certain she could feel his presence.

He felt once more that compulsion to know her thoughts, to see inside her mind. What would she do without Edward? He was foul, destructive, and yet Smolder suspected that she felt the need for the dubious security of his tyrannical control. He nodded to himself. He thought he was beginning to understand Helen: her confusion, her timidity and abhorrence of change had led her to accept less than she deserved.

Her hair fell forward curtaining her face. It gleamed with a warmth that seemed almost to challenge the feeble sunlight. He willed her to see him. To acknowledge his presence. She stood with her head tilted on one side, as if listening; an unconscious pose, but beautiful, like a carefully composed photograph, and he had a sudden, wild urge to capture that unstudied, natural moment.

He caught a movement in the doorway from the main building and glanced down, simultaneously pulling a little away from the window, out of sight. Someone had joined her. From his vantage point above the quad he had seen a number of comings and goings: Helen and Ruth; Helen and Ellis; Ruth and Ellis; Helen and Sergeant Hackett, but none was stranger, none more devastating than this. Helen with Mick Tuttle. Smolder felt a pain radiate like a starburst in his chest. He wanted to tear at it with his fingers, to excise it, but instead he turned back to his room and as he began writing his journal entry, the suffering in his face seemed no more than a dyspeptic spasm.

Ruth Marks tore another cob of bread from her roll and smothered it with margarine. She opened the tiny jam pot, still holding the knife and watched the drama unfold. Ellis had flounced in moments before. His eyes were raw-looking and the dark circles beneath them attested to his lack of sleep.

He threw an acid-damaged and dirty lab coat on to a table nearby, shaking with rage. Teacups were overturned and two of the technicians at the table jumped up, knocking over their chairs and protesting loudly.

'Who took it?' Ellis was red in the face, barely in control.

A voice somewhere behind him grumbled, 'It's bloody disgusting, bringing that filthy rag in here.'

Ellis wheeled on the man, a fellow graduate student whom Ellis did not like. 'Mind your own bloody business.' Breathless with fury, he turned back to the table. 'Who took my money?'

A post-doctoral student, dark-haired, lightly tanned from a brief trip to his parents' time-share in Spain, relaxed, sure of his welcome, strolled over, carrying a tray. 'What's up?' he asked, casually pushing the lab coat to one side and sliding the tray on to the table.

'Ellis is bitching again.'

The graduate student had spoken up a second time, deliberately baiting Ellis. He was bigger, a rugby player, also fitter than Ellis, and he had put up with about as much griping and foot-stamping as he was prepared to from the smaller man.

'I just want to know who stole my money!' Ellis shouted, addressing those seated at the table, as an appeal to their decency and a means of deflecting the anger of the rugby player.

'No one stole it.' The woman who had spoken, a small, mousy-haired Masters student, riffled through the pockets of the filthy lab coat and finally fished out a one pound coin. 'We swapped it for a couple of 50p's.'

'You took my money. My personal property.' This was an old grouse: in the research lab, a good deal of 'swapping' went on, but most people, both students and staff, were philosophical; the odd filched biro or stick of chewing gum had to be balanced against a pleasant working relationship with the rest of the crew. Ellis could not, had never, accepted this approach to life. What was his was private; no one had the right to touch his property, borrow his lab coat, rummage through his pockets, or swap one coin for another – it was intrusive at best and criminal at worst.

One of the technicians spoke up, smiling foolishly, 'I needed 50p for the coffee machine. You know it won't take one pound coins—'

'You bloody bastard!'

The post-doctoral student seemed unruffled by Ellis's exhibition. 'Listen, man,' he said, smiling the crooked smile that the girls found so irresistible. 'You've got to get used to give an' take in a research lab. Graham didn't mean anything by it. Chill out, will you?'

Ellis's eyes bulged. Ruth could see a blood vessel standing out on his temple.

'He'll burst something,' Ruth muttered, scooping more jam on to the last little ball of bread without taking her eyes from the scene.

'You give it back. I need those 50p's. You had no right! They're my personal property!' He was screaming now.

Graham, the technician who had taken the coins rolled his eyes. 'Oh for fuck's sake, John, get a *life*.'

Helen telephoned Ruth from home, some hours later. Mick had helped her search every inch of the house – supervised her might be a more accurate description – since she had insisted on Mick checking with her every cupboard and drawer, every bookshelf and box file, no longer trusting the evidence of her own eyes.

'Do you want me to come over?' Ruth asked.

'No . . . I think I'll make an early start in the morning, see Edward's parents and then go and visit mine – try and shake off the tabloid hacks for the weekend and get my research submission completed. Thanks for your comments, by the way. I'll incorporate them into the discussion.' She blushed, hearing her words as Ruth would hear them: forced, stilted.

'About to schkip town, huh, schweetheart?'

Helen smiled. She could imagine Ruth drawing her lips back from her teeth to get the Bogart lisp just right. 'I've told Sergeant Hackett where he can reach me. He suggested leaving a few lights on and slipping out the back way.'

'*Nice* man! You know, if he wasn't already spoken for, I'd set my cap at him myself.'

'I've told him you have a key, in case of emergencies – I hope you don't mind.'

'To my place, or yours? Hey! And what about Mick Tuttle?'

Helen was stunned for a moment. She *had* given Mick a key to the back gate so that he could let himself in and out without being noticed by the reporters camped outside. 'Mick?' she faltered.

'Well, did he pop in for coffee as he'd threatened?'

'Oh!' Helen laughed, realizing her mistake. 'Yes. He was very sweet.'

Ruth made balking sounds at the other end of the line. '*Sweet!* Helen, really. Why don't you call him *nice* and be done with it?'

'What do you mean?'

'Sweet, nice, bland, nondescript, boring, tedious, vapid—'

'Yes—' Helen interrupted. 'All right. I get the general idea.'

'Well – talk about damning with faint praise.'

Ruth had been impatient that Helen persisted in her self-doubt, or rather in the possibility that she might really have killed Edward, and Helen now discovered a lingering and, she knew, unwarranted resentment against her for refusing to go through the house, 'checking for non-existent evidence' as Ruth termed it. Helen's annoyance was tempered by embarrassment, tinged with relief that she and Mick hadn't found anything, as, paradoxically, she had known they would find nothing. Mick had left exhausted and she suspected in pain, but he had taken her seriously, had understood the need to convince herself once and for all, that the knife – the murder weapon – was not hidden somewhere in the house.

'If you *do* find the knife, I'll fall on it myself as an act of penitence for not having believed you,' Ruth said.

'I wish you wouldn't make jokes like that,' Helen said, wincing.

'Who's joking? Look at it this way,' Ruth replied. 'They say some women fantasize about rape – not my scene, I have to admit – I see myself more as a dominatrix, but that's not my point. Just because they fantasize about it, does it mean they actually *want* to be raped? No. Because in their fantasy, they're in control. They know exactly who the guy is – they fancy him more than likely. They determine the moves, the duration, what he does or does not do, because the fantasy is theirs. The *real* thing is someone else's fantasy, and it's brutal and ugly. Like murder.'

'I need some sleep, Ruth,' Helen said, to avoid getting into an argument. She knew she would feel different about Ruth after a good night's sleep, but for now, she could not face her.

'So,' Ruth said. 'You don't want your old buddy, your mucker, your pal—'

'Look,' Helen replied, interrupting what she feared would become another of Ruth's thesaurus mode monologues. 'If you'd really like to—' She regretted the words even as they tumbled out of her mouth. She really did need sleep, she had not been lying about that, but before she could sleep she needed to think about Mick and her unexpected reaction to his presence in the house. His proximity as they searched through the seemingly endless boxes and bookcases had acted as a balm. A male presence that did not threaten or challenge, but which soothed and reassured, it was all the more shocking when they had touched as he climbed the ladder behind her to check the top shelf of the bookcase in her study and the contact had felt like an electric charge.

There was a brief silence, then Ruth said, 'I don't know about you, but I'm bushed. I've been holding John Ellis's hand for the last few hours.'

'John? Is he all right?' Helen wondered if Ruth had been trying to find out more about the row he'd had with Edward on the day he died.

'Don't ask. Suffice it to say that counselling neurotics takes its toll, you know?'

Helen felt the muscles at the back of her neck tighten. 'Yes, I suppose it does,' she said.

A pause, then 'Oh, Jeez, Helen, I'm sorry. I didn't mean—'

Helen relaxed. 'It's all right, Ruth,' she interrupted. 'We're both tired.' It was a typical Ruth comment, unintentionally hurtful, retracted in an instant and probably worried over for hours afterwards. 'Forget it.'

'No,' Ruth insisted. 'I've put my size sevens right in it again, haven't I?'

Helen laughed. 'Who's being neurotic now?'

'Last offer. Do you want me to come over and keep you company?'

'Ruth, I'm fine. I've got a bit of sorting to do, then I'm going to bed.'

'Before you do, check out the fridge. You'll find something mouth-watering.'

'Ruth!'

'So, tell me you've eaten.'

Helen laughed. 'I promise I'll check out the fridge before I go to bed, Mama. But I can cope for one night on my own.'

There was a hesitation before Ruth said, 'To tell you the God's honest truth I was hoping you'd say that. What I lust after most just now – picture this, if you will – is to curl up with a large gin and tonic (heavy on the gin) and tipple myself into oblivion.'

Chapter Sixteen

Nelson's close scrutiny seemed to burn his skin. He could feel it in tiny splashes, not enough to leave a mark, but sufficient to make his arms and upper body jerk in a hundred minor spasms. Like hot fat, it seemed to continue burning, layer on layer, until he could feel it freckling the pale flesh of his face, marking it. His cheek muscles twitched with each explosion of heat; he would be scarred by the encounter.

He covered his own eyes to protect them from the light coruscating from Nelson's in short, searing radioactive bursts. He knew there were gamma rays emanating in deadly particle-waves, penetrating the dermis, mutating irretrievably the Malpighian layer, burrowing deeper into his body, poisoning his liver and destroying it. He knew with a feverish helplessness that toxins were building up to dangerous levels.

Orange light pierced his fingers, he could see the glow even though his eyes were shut tight. He breathed hard, sobbing with each breath, and Nelson kept up his incantation of muttered words, arcane magic.

He fled to the window and stared out through the mesh, willing Nelson away. The entire room was now bathed in the unnatural sodium glare, it intensified and pulsated, gaining power from his neural circuits, piercing the protective carapace of his skull, probing the delicate pathways of thought, shorting the synaptic connections, destroying millions of cells in the ferocity of its heat.

A sudden scream roused Nelson and he became aware that he must have been staring at the boy. The stand-off had resulted again in a wordless battle of wills, the unspoken hostility that had characterized their every meeting. He moved quickly across the room, anxious to stave off another outburst, soothing, calming, softly calling the boy's name.

'You're killing me!' the boy screamed. 'You're burning through my *brain!*' He turned to the metal grill on the window and plucked at it despairingly.

Did she mean to hurt him, Smolder wondered. Could she really be so taken with that phoney, that invalid, that cripple? She always was easily moved to pity. Stray dogs, mangy cats, ragged people, the flotsam and jetsam of life. And now this – it's too obvious, too hackneyed, this elevated compassion, and for him!

He was consumed with disgust. She used her vulnerability like a pheromone. What is it? Some kind of exhibitionism? Wasn't she satisfied that she was free? What was she trying to do – drive him crazy? Smiling at that policeman – after all, he's oh so polite. And now that damned mutant, Tuttle! Letting him talk to her. Listening to him, taking his advice, throwing her door open to strangers. She'd be giving the Press an exclusive before long. He flung down his pen, unable to concentrate. He knew what was right for her, why couldn't she see that?

Helen lay awake for a long time, listening to the muffled sighs and occasional creaks of the old house. She tested her feelings as one might test a bruise – gently, approaching the tender area obliquely. She had felt safe tonight with Mick, protected in a way that she had longed for, but never felt with Edward. Protected physically, yes, but there was something further; approaching trust, another aspect, a warmth, an emotional security, an effect that Mick had summoned like a charm by his unquestioning, unjudging presence. With Mick, there was no need to keep up the defences she had built high to keep Edward at bay.

Soon, she would tell him the rest: about Robbie, but also about the night she had gone out, looking for the man she held responsible for his death, and finding him, had—

The moon flashed suddenly from behind a cloud, and she saw again the sharp glint of light on metal, the slow, arrogant walk, the easy smile, and she experienced the same searing rage that had made her want to kill.

Helen groaned and turned over. Pale, cold moonlight shimmered dimly through the curtains, casting shadows from the pear tree on to the window. She had arranged to meet Edward's parents the next morning and she had no words of comfort for them, no tears, no regret to share with them, no sense of loss. And now she was being drawn to the one man in the college whom Edward had despised more than any other! For hours she watched the pear tree's shadow see-sawing in the wind.

The exchange was quick, money for a twist of something wrapped in silver foil. 'Bold as you like,' the locals said, but this was not bold, it was discreet, a business transaction. No one wanted to get caught and, the trade completed, he left. Daniel Hackett couldn't see the harm in that. He wasn't shooting up in anyone's doorway. He didn't rob grannies on their way home from collecting their pension, and he resented being made to feel like a criminal just for the sake of the occasional tab of E, and maybe enough weed to roll a couple of spliffs.

Nevertheless, he walked quickly away from the housing estate. He'd been relieved of his purchases more than once, on the dusty route back to the outside world, and if there was nowhere to run, it was best to give in with good grace – less chance of getting hurt.

The wind whipped up bits of grit, and he turned his face away to protect his eyes. In the darkness, chip papers and polystyrene boxes lifted and skittered along the road towards him, sinking as the wind dropped, as if in exhaustion, only to rise and dance a few fluttering yards more with the next gust. He tasted grit in his mouth and thought, this is excitement. This is real life; the comfortable, lazy existence his parents called living was like a long sleep, a living death.

A noise to his left made him whirl round, but it was only a tin can, skittering along in the wind, bouncing hollowly from gutter to roadway and back, overtaking him in its bustling urgency to be elsewhere. It was darker than the streets of home: lads with air rifles put out the street lamps, sometimes for sport, and sometimes for money, or a little twist of paradise – the pushers didn't like to be too closely observed. Daniel laughed suddenly and started to run, chasing the tin can in the wind.

Nelson drove around the city aimlessly, first heading for home, but the thought of the empty house was unbearable, and he turned the car towards the city centre and the County Headquarters. The sight of the shabby, glass-fronted building depressed him further and he drove past, unable to stop the automatic glance upwards, the check on which offices were lit.

He flicked on the radio, punching the off button immediately to silence the nasal whine of a jilted cowboy. Finally, unable to stand his own indecision, he pulled over and jumped out of the car in a fury, and landed a satisfying kick to its offside front wheel, screaming 'Fuck!' a few times for good measure.

A car full of youths cruised by, windows open, stereo thumping an insistent, meaningless beat: noise to attract notice. They hung out of the windows, laughing, asking if he had a flat tyre. 'Use the spare!' one wag yelled. 'The one keeping your trousers up!'

Their laughter, the noise, the erratic swerving of the car was enough. Instantly, Nelson was back in control, he didn't need to remind himself that he was a professional, these boys had brought him seamlessly back to himself. He watched their car edge past at a strolling pace and memorized the registration number, even smiling a little as he put the call through to Traffic to have them pulled over and checked for drugs and booze.

Feeling much better, he drove on a little further, then swung off the road by Grosvenor Park and eased the car into the kerb in front of St John's Church.

The night was cold and the wind blew in petulant bursts, subsiding from time to time, before whipping up again to bring in a few spots of icy rain. Between the clouds, the Plough was just discernible, shimmering in the orange-tinged sky. He locked the car and walked down the narrow path between the ruins of the old collegiate church and the park. Its closely mown lawns were damp and sparkled in the ghostly light of a low energy street lamp.

Nights like this, he used to ache to be home. But that was when Beth was still alive. He always called her if he was going to be late and the miracle of it was that she never seemed to mind. She had made an adventure of those nights, listening to the radio while she ironed or sewed. Sometimes she would bake bread.

He still couldn't walk past a bakery without having to suppress a bubble of emotion, remembering the warmth of the house as he opened the front door, the air fragrant with yeast and malt and the faintly beery promise of the loaves proving by the hearth. And Beth, waiting for him, so cross with herself if she'd dozed off that he'd quickly learned to slam the door as he came in, so as not to disappoint her.

She was truly lovely, his Beth, with her thick brown hair and her creamy skin. Full-lipped and generous-spirited. She had seemed to glow with an inner happiness during the pregnancy. Her skin was furzed with the faintest hint of down, an ethereal phenomenon, which he could feel with his fingertips and his lips, but which suggested itself to the eyes only as a reflection of light from her face, like a golden aura.

And with the baby, she had died.

Not immediately, it wasn't a sudden demise: she wasted away, body and soul. Soul first, before the rest, in stages, one merging with the other until he couldn't be sure exactly when she reached the point from which she could not be recalled. It was as if the child had drained all the life out of her. She ignored it and of course it had keened like a lost kitten, endlessly, hopelessly. Even when he had succeeded in coaxing her into holding it, she had only looked at it with a kind of dull disgust.

Nelson thrust his hands deep into the pockets of his raincoat and trotted down the steps, slowing at the bottom to negotiate the stone sets that glistened, treacherously wet in the lamplight.

Baby Blues, the doctors had called it. In those days they had simply waited until the woman snapped out of it, hormone imbalances and biochemically induced depression as yet unheard of. So it went on for two years and eventually their

GP had prescribed antidepressants, and the boy learned in infancy, to mistrust when he should have known only certainty; even the provision of comfort and food, which he should have been able to take for granted, were provided sporadically, unreliably, for in Nelson's absence, when he went to work, or to buy groceries, there was no one to remind Beth, and Beth needed reminders. More importantly, the boy learned that he had no right to love. He was neither loved for himself, nor for what he did. His mother was unpredictable, except in her coldness towards him, and so he learned also to fear. He could not know that as he looked up with those huge fearful eyes, his fear and unhappiness was both an accusation and a reproach, but Beth felt it, and finally she could take it no more.

Nelson turned instead of crossing the footbridge and followed the path beside the river. At this late hour the riverside was deserted. His footsteps echoed in the quiet moments when the wind was still. He continued, deep in thought, only dimly aware of the sound of his footsteps ringing out on the flags and the biting cold nipping at his ears and his fingers.

He had found her, lying on the sofa, a bottle of whisky empty on the floor beside her – his whisky – a bottle of paracetamol beside it. Ever practical, she had placed a bowl beside her on the floor, but she hadn't the strength to lift her head, so she had lain in vomit half the night. The boy had been playing quietly on the floor beside his dead mother, and Nelson's overriding urge had been to yell at him: *Why didn't you stop her?*

They had pumped the child's stomach in case he had swallowed any of the pills and Nelson had felt a perverse, shameful, sadistic satisfaction in the boy's pathetic cries as he balked on the tube.

She had left a note: *'I thought it would be so perfect—'* The sentence was unfinished, the note unsigned.

Nelson paused at the bandstand to catch his breath, and looked down at the black water. He hadn't allowed himself to think of this since the day it happened, since Beth's suicide. He had blanked out the details of that night, but it was there, always, like a haunting, if not the images of Beth, grey, repugnant in death, as she had never been in life, then the feelings he couldn't suppress: pulsating, fearful waves of emotion. He thought of all the times he had sat, staring at the boy in silence, hating him for taking Beth from him. The boy had curled up, shielding his eyes, hiding from him, from the hatred that must have flowed from him in tidal surges. Nelson uttered a cry of anguish and jerked away from the rail, walking quickly in the direction of the weir, wanting its roar to silence these newly awakened thoughts.

'He's burning into my brain!' the boy had babbled. 'His eyes. The fire. Make him stop! I can't think. *Help me!*' The screams had pursued Nelson into the corridor, down the stair-case, out into the car park of the hospital. They echoed now in his head. He felt they would follow him – accusing him, cursing him for ever.

Helen surfaced briefly from a light sleep of confusing dreams, sighed and sank again. Moonlight and shadows played over her face, the dark jagged lines of the twiggy branches, and the pale blue reflections from raindrops on the window, drip-ping like melting wax down her cheeks, distorting her features.

Her eyes opened and she was instantly awake, totally con-scious. The hairs on the back of her neck stood up. A faint noise, no more than a creak and a dull thump, had roused her. She held her breath, waiting, listening, and imagined the intruder on the other side of the door, also listening, tense. The phone was in the hall, and that would be cut off by the intruder, but perhaps she could get out of the house by the patio doors. She eased herself into a sitting position and then stood. A floorboard creaked under her foot and she drew in a breath, her heart pounding. The presence grew stronger, an almost palpable menace filled the room. Helen saw the door handle begin to turn. She hadn't locked the door! She looked over her shoulder at the patio doors. If she got out she would be trapped in the back garden – the key to the side gate was in a drawer in the kitchen – would anyone hear her if she screamed for help? But if she surprised the intruder . . .

She went to the side table by the front window and picked up a statuette in bronze, a slender woman in diaphanous, clinging silk, but surprisingly, comfortingly, heavy. Helen moved to the door and raised the figure. As the door opened she prepared to strike, then gasped in dismay and relief as the tall, muffled stranger yelped:

'What the f—?'

Ruth.

'I might've brained you!'

Ruth took the bronze statue from Helen's trembling hand and placed it on one of the bookshelves.

'I should bloody well brain *you*,' she growled. 'So much for alcoholic oblivion. Know where I've been?'

Helen stared at her friend. 'Ruth, what the hell are you doing here? Why didn't you call first – or at least ring the bloody doorbell?'

'You sound pissed off, Helen.'

'I am! You scared the shit out of me.'

'Good,' said Ruth. 'Why didn't you say something, Helen? Warn me?'

'Warn you about what? For God's sake, Ruth, I thought you were—'

'What? The murderer? Or the dear departed Edward?' Ruth laughed, and Helen shuddered at the harshness of the sound.

'He wasn't particularly dear to you, though, was he, Helen, though his departure was dearly, devoutly hoped for.'

'Ruth, what *is* it?' Helen had never seen Ruth so angry.

'I've spent a couple of hours in the company of the lovely Sergeant Hackett, accounting for the fact that my computer was used to alter the Apocalypse file.'

'Oh.'

'Oh. Is that it? I lie through my teeth to protect you and all you can say is "Oh".'

Helen went straight to the phone in the hall. There was no point in apologizing to Ruth in her present frame of mind. Neither Inspector Nelson, nor Sergeant Hackett were available – hardly surprising since it was the middle of the night, but the officer she spoke to suggested Helen come in and make a statement at a more acceptable hour. Helen hung up and turned to face Ruth.

She was still angry, but some of the heat had gone out of her and she was left with an overwhelming sense of disappointment. 'Don't you trust me, Helen? After all we've been through together?'

'Ruth,' Helen reached out to touch her friend's arm, but Ruth flinched from her.

'You let me speculate about the people on the list – Valerie Roberts, Ellis, Mallory. Did you think it was some kind of game? Were you laughing at me, trying to make a fool of me?'

'Ruth, no!' Helen knew that Ruth's flippant humour and twisted irony were defensive measures, an armour against the snipes of colleagues who regarded women scientists as little more than window dressing, light, mindless froth, and yet, with typical inconsistency, condemned her research as unfeminine, immoral, projecting from it a terrifying future of cyborgs and cybernetic control. 'I just didn't want to involve you. I thought I could help a few people by altering Edward's records.'

'David as well – such Christian goodwill, Helen.'

'He has a child to support. And there's nothing wrong with his work. Edward simply wanted him out of the way—'

'Whose child?'

Helen was stung, but hadn't she thought the same herself? That Henry was Edward's son?

Ruth glared back, furious with her, ashamed of her own outburst, at a loss for words, wanting to make things right between them, but wanting also to make Helen see how much she had wounded her.

Helen sighed. 'Come on,' she said. 'We'll try for oblivion together.'

Ruth hesitated, then, shrugging, followed Helen through to her study. Helen poured two large measures of whisky and handed Ruth one glass. She took it begrudgingly.

'You're thinking what right have I got to judge other people's work. Who am I to say David should stay on and Mallory go, right?'

Ruth flopped into a chair and scowled at Helen. 'It might've crossed my mind.'

'The Senate were going to get rid of Mallory with or without Edward's say-so. He wanted to break the news himself, that's all, wanted Mallory to think it was all down to him.'

Ruth recalled Mallory's undignified exit from Ed Wilkinson's office on Monday, shouting, red-faced with rage, and thought, not for the first time, that few would mourn the professor's passing.

'If I'd changed Mallory's entry,' Helen went on, 'the Senate would've been on to it immediately. While I was waiting for you in your office, Valerie Roberts came in. She was looking for you. Poor Ruth, folk are always seeking you out to unburden themselves. She told me she'd lied to the police about Edward wanting to keep her on. She was afraid they'd find the file and suspect her – well, I know it's ridiculous, but

I wasn't thinking straight. I was trying to put things right, Ruth. Trying to redress the balance a little. I thought maybe if the selection committee accessed the file they might be influenced – respect for Edward's last wishes, that sort of crud.'

A glimmer of amusement lit Ruth's features and Helen lifted her shoulders and gave a rueful smile. 'Pretty naive, huh?'

Ruth's faint spark of humour became a grin and they laughed. Ruth took a swig of whisky and washed it around her mouth before swallowing with a slight wince. 'Thing is, Helen, they're likely to suspect *you*, now. After all, you get a promotion out of it.'

Helen almost choked on her whisky. 'I didn't change *my* entry, for God's sake!'

'*The thing is*,' Ruth repeated, 'will the police *know* that?'

Helen chuckled. 'For someone who's at the cutting edge of intelligent computer systems you know very little about the basics of the software.'

'I'm strictly wetware, the *bio* of bionics. And anyway, neural nets aren't programmed in the same way as your standard UNIX system.'

Helen bowed her head, conceding the point. 'They can tell which entries have been edited and which haven't.'

'Well,' said Ruth. 'That's all right, then. So long as you're in the clear.'

Helen's smile faded. She wished she were in the clear, and that it was all as simple as checking databases – if her own memory were only as accessible! What was it in her that so mistrusted people that she wouldn't even tell Ruth that she had altered the files? Was it because she feared that the hidden part of herself might become visible to Ruth, and that, through Ruth she would be forced to see the awful reality of what she was, and of what she had done?

Chapter Seventeen

Nelson seemed subdued, perhaps even reflective. The brooding anger was there still, unmistakably, seething beneath the skin but it had an altered complexion. He looked ill, and when Hackett had commented, had said he'd spent most of the night thinking. Hackett believed this, although he would have given Nelson's ponderings another name: the inspector's present fixation on Ellis as a suspect was becoming an obsession and Hackett believed it was more than tenuously linked with his superior's visit to the hospital the previous evening. The inspector had shaved, but badly, and his skin, always uneven in texture and suffused with an angry glow, was nicked in several places and had a shiny, scalded appearance. His breath smelled of peppermints, but there were undertones of heavy alcoholic consumption and his movements were a little too controlled, a little too precise.

Hackett understood Nelson's frustration. It wasn't as if they didn't have anything to go on – there were, perhaps, too many people who would have liked to see Professor Wilkinson dead. And it wasn't as if the exhaustive list of suspects had watertight alibis – Helen Wilkinson had given conflicting stories as to where she had been at the time of the murder; first she had said that she had been with Ruth Marks all afternoon, then she had remembered that she had left work a little early and stopped briefly at the supermarket before walking home. David Ainsley and his wife were, separately, neither wishing to corroborate the other's story, at liberty and unobserved at the approximate time of death, he working in his study at home and she walking the baby in (as it turned out) a fruitless effort to lull the child to sleep. Ellis, whose behaviour was growing increasingly bizarre, had been working in the computer suite at the Horace Shelby library, again unobserved. Hackett wondered at the insular and rather lonely life these academics seemed to lead, that they could spend hours of each day sequestered in some silent spot and no single soul to know or care where they were or what they were doing. Perhaps it was a symptom of the escalating paranoia surrounding the reorganization of the departments, together with the consequent 'staff wastage'.

Whatever the cause of the overwhelming atmosphere of secrecy and suspicion at St Werburgh's, it didn't help their investigation, when all they had were a few fingerprints, too smudged to be of use. The murder weapon was still missing and the high hedge at the front of the Wilkinsons' house and an even higher brick wall which enclosed the back had prevented even the most assiduous neighbourhood watchers from observing the murderer entering or leaving the premises.

'So, Nelson said, breaking the silence at last. 'Is she covering for Ruth Marks?'

'Ruth has the least to hide. She's leaving for a much better paid and resourced job in the States in a few months. She wasn't even listed on the Apocalypse file. What motive would she have?' They were seated at opposite sides of the desk in Nelson's cramped office. Helen had just left the headquarters after being interviewed. It was still early; Nelson had called Hackett in as soon as he'd got the message she had left during the night. 'What motive?' Nelson repeated to himself but he couldn't even begin to think it through, the way he felt. 'What about one of the others?' He smoothed a hand over his face. Both felt hot, febrile, and his hand trembled slightly. He felt terrible.

'Like who, for instance?' Hackett asked, distracted momentarily by the tremor.

'Clara Ainsley, for instance,' Nelson said with choleric impatience. He was grateful, however, when Hackett began thinking aloud: he believed he might be sick if he were forced to say any more.

'Helen's unlikely to cover for her, of course,' Hackett said. 'She wasn't on the files, either, but Helen could be telling the truth when she says she was trying to help out the professor's secretary and do a few people a good turn in the process. Which means the alteration of the Apocalypse file might have nothing at all to do with the murder. Now if Clara thought Edward was going to get rid of her, what would she do? She said in her interview that she saw Wilkinson at the university, but Mrs Roberts says she wasn't listed in the appointments diary – and her story checks out. Of course, we know Mrs Roberts has no great affection for Clara, and that she has lied to us before. Neighbours saw no one enter or leave that afternoon. But the prof didn't commit suicide, did he? So someone must've been there, and it's entirely feasible that Clara saw him at home, and not at the university.'

'In which case she's got some explaining to do.'

Nelson screwed up his eyes, the light was hurting his head, and his guts were in turmoil. He knew his hangover could only get worse, and if he had to suffer, he wasn't going to do it alone. 'Fetch her in and talk to her again,' he said. 'Give us a call when you're done. I'm going home for an hour or two.'

Hackett was glad of that, Nelson would not be much good in an interview the state he was in, and with any luck he'd think to shower and change before he came back. He wondered whether his boss had a single moment of contentment or peace, and thought that his own situation, despite its complications, must seem idyllic to a lost soul like Jack Nelson.

Hackett called in DC Tact to assist in the interview. Clara responded to the young constable's vagueness, mistaking it for vulnerability. She combed her hair and insisted on getting changed before going with them. A university friend agreed to look after the baby until she returned and as she slammed the front door shut, Hackett noticed that she had dabbed on a little make-up, but it couldn't entirely cover the dark shadows under her eyes and the grey tone of her skin. She declined her right to a solicitor, and the interview began at 9 a.m.

'You say you saw Prof Wilkinson at his office on Monday,' Hackett said. His hand rested on a red leatherette-bound book.

Clara looked from Hackett to Tact. The constable was looking at something a fraction to her left with such intent curiosity that Clara had to resist an urge to turn and follow his line of vision.

'I've already been through all of this,' she answered.

'You told him you were finishing the affair,' Tact added. 'Is that right?'

Clara lifted one shoulder. 'It's already on record.'

'In his office?' Tact had grey, unblinking eyes that seemed to penetrate whatever he looked at.

Clara blushed.

'You told him you were finishing your affair, in his office,' Hackett repeated, approving of the line Tact had taken. 'Within earshot of the professor's secretary.'

Clara looked down at the table top. 'That's right.' She sat up very straight and folded her hands demurely in her lap. 'I thought—' She stopped, seemed to consider the line she was about to take unwise.

'What did you think, Clara?' Hackett asked, leaning forward.

'I wasn't about to let him treat me that way—'

'Treat you what way?' said Tact.

Two bright spots of colour grew and deepened on Clara's finely chiselled cheekbones. 'I thought he – I'm sure he was seeing someone else. I didn't want him to take me for granted. I couldn't bear to have people feel sorry for me as they did Helen.'

'I don't think there was any danger of that, do you?' Hackett said, slouching back in his chair, pausing so that the insult had more impact. 'Helen was his wife, she had a right to pity when her husband was unfaithful.'

Tact drew down the corners of his mouth. 'Mistresses don't have the same rights to sympathy,' he added, shaking his head regretfully.

Clara's eyes darted about the room, avoiding the two police officers. Her eyebrows were drawn together in a worried frown, and there was something in the set of her mouth that suggested tears were imminent.

'Prof Wilkinson's secretary has no record of you going to see him on Monday,' Hackett said, opening the red book and identifying it for the tape as Professor Wilkinson's appointments diary.

'I didn't need an appointment to see Edward.'

Hackett saw her swallow deeply and remembered from somewhere, the telly, or a course in interviewing techniques, that this was a sure sign that the interviewee was lying. Not that he needed to deploy such clever and close observation skills, since he had questioned Valerie Roberts on this matter by telephone that very morning.

'Mrs Roberts says *everyone* needed an appointment to see the prof that morning – even his wife.'

'She would say that, wouldn't she?'

'She did say you visited the prof that morning, or at least that you were on your way to see him. But someone was already with him, and you left.' Tact was staring in that focused, yet unfocused way over her left shoulder again.

'I er . . .'

'Come on, Clara,' Hackett said, gently. 'We're just trying to get at the truth here. You were fond of the professor, weren't you? You must want us to find out who killed him.'

Clara mumbled something, and Hackett asked her to repeat it for the tape. 'I said, I wasn't just fond of him, I loved Edward.'

'Well then,' said Hackett.

She looked into the sergeant's broad, friendly face. She was in no doubt that what he wanted most was a conviction. Wasn't that what all policemen wanted – an early arrest and conviction? And wasn't she the easiest target? He didn't care about Edward, or her, or Helen. Results were all he cared about.

'I had intended seeing Ed, but when I arrived he was having a terrible row with John Ellis.' She paused. 'No, that's not quite accurate. Edward's voice was only raised sufficiently to make himself heard over that lunatic's ranting. Ellis stormed out, screaming at Ed, threatening him, calling him names. "I won't let you do this to me. I'll sort you—" Surely that fat cow Roberts told you? I didn't want her listening in on what I wanted to say to him. It was private.'

'So you decided to see him later at home.'

Clara stared at Tact and he stared back. How could she ever have thought that he might be an ally? 'No, of course not. I was too busy with the baby.' But she had delayed too long, and the hesitation was tantamount to an admission.

'When did you see him, Clara? What time?' Hackett asked. 'He went home after lunch. Some time between 1 and 2.30.'

She bowed her head.

Hackett leaned forward. 'Someone murdered Edward Wilkinson, Clara. Was it you?'

'No! Look I don't expect you to sympathize, but I've been bereaved, too—'

'I know this is difficult for you, Clara,' Hackett said. Then left a silence that lengthened, almost half a minute. They all felt the pressure of it; half a minute is a long time for silence between strangers. Clara felt it most.

'I – I'm not sure of the time,' she said, her voice almost inaudible at first. 'Half one, two, perhaps. But I left Ed safe and well.'

She looked up at Hackett and her lashes were wet. 'I said some terrible things to him. I confronted him, said I knew he was being unfaithful to me. How could he *do* that to me?' Hackett searched her face, but the irony of what she had said seemed beyond her understanding.

'Now I don't know – maybe I was wrong. I don't understand why he didn't just tell me he was going to look after me – why he let me think those awful things about him.'

'More games?' Hackett asked.

'Maybe he *was* seeing someone else and wanted you as well,' Tact suggested.

She looked at him sharply, but he had that bland, vague look on his face. She shrugged. 'He didn't deny it. But then Edward never denied anything. "Never apologize, never explain." ' She fell silent. He had been calm, that afternoon, sardonic. It didn't seem to matter to him that she was leaving him. She was screaming, hysterical, but he smiled and smiled and—

'Did you have intercourse with Prof Wilkinson that afternoon?'

'Of course not!' Clara gaped at Hackett, shocked. 'What do you take me for?' The heightened colour drained from her face suddenly and she gasped. 'Oh, my God. David said he'd been found in bed. You mean—?'

'Do you know who he was . . . seeing – apart from yourself, that is?'

She shook her head.

'What time did you leave?'

'I don't know.' Clara's hand went to her hair and she tugged at a strand, worrying and twisting it. 'I was only there about a quarter of an hour. I couldn't speak to him when he was like that.'

'Like what?' Tact asked.

She turned from Hackett to the young DC. 'Cold, distant, cruel.'

'He was found naked in bed,' Hackett said. 'Semen on the sheets. Clean sheets, fresh on that morning. He wasn't alone, either – Forensic have got two types of pubic hair, and some fair or mousy hairs on the pillows, along with a few from his head. And from what Dr Wilkinson says, since her miscarriage there'd been no sexual contact between her and her husband.'

'D'you believe her?' Tact asked.

'No reason not to. She hated his guts.'

Clara had been taken down to the cells after a tearful phone call to her babysitter. She would not hear of social services being called in and had agreed to keep the baby until Clara was released. Hackett and Tact had retired to the canteen to take a late, but well-earned breakfast.

Tact shrugged.

'Come on, Jem, let's have it.'

Tact carefully assembled a piece of fried egg, a sliver of bacon and a square of fried bread on to his fork, then dipped the lot in the yolk before sliding it into his mouth. 'I don't know what women see in that type.'

'Takes all sorts,' Hackett replied. 'Wilkinson was a clever – some say a brilliant man – women find that attractive.'

'No, I can understand that. But all the rest. The cheating, the lies, the power play.' He shook his head. 'Maybe that's where I'm going wrong.'

'Love life not on the up and up, Jem?'

Tact narrowed his eyes, but chose not to grace the comment with a reply. 'Clara has no alibi, and plenty of motive,' he said. 'Aren't you eating those mushrooms?' Hackett was already regretting the fried breakfast he'd just eaten. He shoved his plate over and Tact scooped the mushrooms on to his own plate and continued. 'She now admits she saw Ed at home on the afternoon of his death and argued with him.'

'Closest we've had to an admission since the investigation began,' Hackett said. 'But Ellis *did* threaten the prof, so maybe we should have him in again.' Nelson would be well pleased. It was time to call him anyway.

Hackett accompanied Nelson to the university-approved accommodation at eleven o'clock on Saturday morning. It was a rambling Edwardian building, divided into flats and bedsits. The owners had made an effort to keep the paintwork in reasonable condition, but the occupants had put their own distinctive mark on the windows: coloured glass ornaments, stickers exhorting passers-by to legalize cannabis, to ban hare coursing, or organophosphates, or the second runway – this last was faded, the Sellotape yellowed and peeling from the window pane. Hackett reminded himself that this concern for the environment, mingled with rebellion against the constraints of conformity, were a natural progression, a modern equivalent to the rites of passage. It was just that Daniel, as the son of a policeman, had more to kick against than most teenage boys. He felt briefly consoled.

The front door was open. The two policemen wove past a motorbike and a rusting VW Beetle parked on the concreted front garden, and went in. For the moment, all was quiet. Several bikes leaned against a large grey cupboard in the hall, in varying states of disrepair. The house smelled of lubricating oil, accumulated dirt and fried food. They climbed the stairs and knocked at number seven and were admitted by a dishevelled and disorientated Ellis.

A quick glance around the grimy surfaces of the room confirmed Hackett's suspicions: that Ellis was undisciplined, disorganized, clever perhaps, but without the indispensable dedication and single-mindedness required to bring his projects to a satisfactory conclusion. The room, in short, was a mess. Several days' dishes lay encrusted in the sink, several weeks' washing unsorted, smelling rankly at the foot of the unmade bed. Books and papers were strewn without apparent organization around the spindly kitchen table that served as a desk. A few old-fashioned third-of-a-pint bottles lay on their sides around the room, the blue, slightly crusted contents which had been set at an angle in each had shrunk from the sides, desiccated, as were the remains of the tiny insects which had fed off it. A few of them were tangled in the cotton wool bungs and several more clung to the filter paper which must have served some purpose to the once-thriving colonies.

Nelson, Hackett knew, had made the same observations and come to the same conclusions he had. The inspector had stared for some moments at the logo on Ellis's T-shirt, proclaiming *E-quality for all!*, waiting until Ellis was visibly squirming before asking with guileless charm, 'Something to do with *women's lib*, sir?'

They had taken Ellis to headquarters for questioning. Nelson had, with uncharacteristic candour, briefed Hackett regarding the shift to the station: its twin aims were to silence Mallory's bleating about needing access to his office, and to encourage Ellis to be more forthcoming, a possibility Nelson felt was more likely in the unsettling atmosphere of an official interview room.

Ellis sat, startled by the glare of Nelson's eyes. He even seemed to crouch, neck forward, head down like a rabbit on a roadway. He tried to listen to what the inspector was saying, but the clamour of buzzing and sing-song twittering in his head were distracting. The words formed like bubbles on Nelson's lips, they floated upwards, like lysosomes: tiny organelles filled with self-destruct enzymes, poisonous packets of annihilation.

'Something's been bothering me,' Nelson confided. Ellis turned his head, listening to the whispering somewhere to his left, trying to make sense of it. 'You keep turning up all over the place.'

Doesn't he know the word 'ubiquitous'? Ellis thought dreamily. His hands brushed at some invisible speck of dust or fleck of ash on the worn surface of the interview room table. He giggled.

Nelson squinted at him, and Ellis saw that he was fighting a hangover the size of Cheshire. The signs were all there, pallor, a faint sheen of perspiration on the forehead, photophobia. The inspector's hands were folded in front of him on the desk, so he couldn't make out the incipient signs of DTs. And Nelson had sneered at his E-quality T-shirt – bloody hypocrite! Nelson massaged the stabbing pain in his right temple and went on with the little speech he had planned. 'You argued with Prof Wilkinson the morning of the murder – well, that' s not unusual. Most folk, from what I gather, had a fair old ding-dong with the prof that day.' He shook his head sadly, carefully. 'That's one of the things that's making our job so bloody difficult.'

Ellis nodded, sympathizing with Nelson's predicament; he knew their task had been hampered by the complexity of the situation, by Professor Wilkinson's despicable treatment of so many people. He had it in his power to help the police, but he did not like the way Nelson looked at him.

'Of course, the professor wasn't what you'd call a popular character – and that's another problem. But not yours, eh?'

Ellis blinked, unsure. Didn't they know that part yet? He relaxed a little. Perhaps he was safe after all.

'I mean, your funding is guaranteed to the end of your doctoral research. When is that? End of summer?' At Ellis's confirmative nod, Nelson went on: 'So by October you should have your thesis all boxed, locked and loaded.' He saw the hesitation before the nod. 'It is going to schedule, is it, John?'

Ellis swallowed, unable to speak.

'It is going to plan?'

Whose plan? Ellis thought. He hissed a 'yes', and Nelson went on: 'Still, it'd be nice to have something set up for the autumn, eh? Is that why you wanted to speak to Dr Wilkinson? To ask her to put in a good word?' Surprised by Ellis's continued silence, he felt the need to clarify. 'Twice, when I've been to interview Dr Wilkinson, you've been lurking about.' He flashed Ellis a shark-like grin. 'You see the kind of conclusions a man like me might feel compelled to—'

He stopped, shaken by that awful similarity he had noticed before, the likeness between Ellis and his son. Ellis was tall and thin, as was his son, but there the physical similarity ended. Nelson's son had his mother's thick, brown hair, but Ellis was mousy and his hair curled in frizzy tufts. Ellis's skin was slightly pock-marked and uneven, whereas the boy's, despite his pallor, retained the creamy smoothness that reminded Nelson so painfully of Beth. A moment later, with a shock of realization, he had it. The similarity was in the intensity of expression, the tilt of the head, as when his son was listening to his voices. It was in the fear – apprehension might be a better word – the terrible—

'Sir?' Hackett stepped forward from his position by the doorway and placed a hand on Nelson's shoulder.

Nelson shook him off, impatient with himself for this

weakness, this unpleasant reminder of his own fallibility, and angry at the sergeant's presumption. 'You must see how it could look, John?' he finished belatedly.

'How it could look,' Ellis echoed, tilting his head, listening more intently. If they didn't know, he might be in the clear. But ideas had been coming to him recently. Dangerous ideas, and they made him afraid. He hadn't felt this way since his A levels, since that other, terrible time . . .

'You've been . . . edgy – let's call it that – since we arrived. It does make me wonder – bound to.'

Ellis sighed, but made no reply.

Nelson changed tack. 'There was a disagreement, a fracas – call it what you like – yesterday in the um, refectory.' It embarrassed Nelson to use such words, words like *refectory*.

Ellis sat completely still. The whisperers, by some miracle, were beginning to be comprehensible to him.

'Over money, was it, sir?'

'Who told you?'

'There were lots of witnesses.'

Ellis nodded. *'Technicians!'* He felt a little glow of pleasure at the disdain in his voice, and found that he could now hold Nelson's gaze.

Then Nelson produced two fifty pence coins from his pocket. There had been ten such coins in the machine when it was opened. Unexceptional, ordinary fifty pence coins. Nelson, used to working on his instincts, had taken two at random and bagged them. Ellis could see them clearly through the plastic, but couldn't read the label. He leaned forward, reaching for them, stopping himself in time. 'An *evidence* bag?'

Nelson scrutinized the bag, resting his elbow on the table top, and speculating as if to himself. 'Prof Wilkinson's eyes were closed.'

Ellis stared, dry-mouthed at the inspector. What was he saying? What did he know?

'There's some people can't even keep their eyes closed when they're asleep, let alone...' He focused on Ellis, staring intently. 'Did you know that, John? The eyes tend to flit open – or at least half open. Now like I say, Prof Wilkinson's eyes were closed. Looked asleep almost, but for the blood.' Nelson tilted the bag and the coins jingled softly, sliding together into one corner of the bag. 'In the old days they used to keep 'em closed with pennies – the big old ones, not the piddly post-decimalization lightweight toytown tiddlers. The big, solid old-fashioned type – you probably wouldn't remember – with Britannia ruling the waves on the one side and often as not King George on the other. About the size of 50p's they were, only round of course.'

Ellis looked into those dangerous eyes and knew it was hopeless trying to explain. His life was falling apart; his research was treated as a departmental joke by everyone except his supervisor – and that was only because he was so out of touch he couldn't see that it was a heap of shit. Everyone was waiting for him to fail: he had been so close to scientific eminence – and now nobody respected him, even the technicians tormented him. Suddenly he could stand it no more. He leapt to his feet, knocking his chair over. It shot back, bouncing off the far wall. He flung himself towards the door and Nelson, sluggish with lack of sleep and his steadily worsening hangover, was too slow to prevent him. Hackett grabbed the boy as he scrabbled at the door handle, and swung him round by the collar and the hem of his jacket. Nelson set the chair right and Hackett lowered Ellis into it. He was crying, muttering about *needing* the coins, that they didn't have the *right*, on and on. Nelson let him, waiting for the waves of nausea and the pounding in his head, brought on by the surge of adrenaline, to subside.

When, at last, Ellis was quiet, he said, 'Now then, Mr Ellis, perhaps you'd like to tell me exactly why these two coins were so important to you.'

Helen sat at the kitchen table of her parents' home, trying to make sense of the dream that had woken her from her afternoon snooze. Her father had taken his tea and his copy of the *Manchester Evening News* through to the sitting room as she came into the kitchen, muttering something about catching up on the final scores on the telly. Helen tried not to feel the painful thud of rejection, but her face betrayed her and her mother said, 'Now don't look like that, Helen. Your dad's had a hard week, that's all.'

Helen nodded, a hard week had been the standard excuse for years for her father's avoidance of her on her weekend visits. When she had been able to persuade Edward to come with her he had made more of an effort to be sociable, to hide his feelings for her. She realized that her parents had seen Edward as a substitute, and now she had taken even that away from them. Her mother set about making tea and Helen, calmed and reassured by the familiarity, the predictability of the ritual, prepared herself to answer her mother's questions. She would not tell her about Mick, not yet – there was nothing to tell. Despite which, Helen found herself thinking of him constantly.

'You've had time to do some thinking, then,' her mother began.

'I suppose.'

'So what have you decided?' The question was posed over the shoulder, face-to-face questions being difficult for Helen's mother, as if she thought them impertinent, and eye contact rude.

'I haven't decided anything, Mum. I still don't know . . .'

'You're still not sleeping. Not eating?' Since she could not show Helen the affection that she really needed, her mother had fallen into the habit of nagging her about her health: at least it gave the appearance of concern.

'A little, of both. Oh, Mum, I am trying, really, but—'

There was a silent build-up of tension and Helen was a pocket of heightened energy. The air seemed almost to crackle with it, as before an electrical discharge, then:

'When your brother died—'

Helen gasped. Her mother had broken an unspoken rule which, until now, had been inviolate. 'Mum, please.' Her voice was barely audible. She felt a prickling in her scalp, a tingling sensation ran from her chest to her fingertips. She tried to get up, but her legs would not support her.

'What happened to him was a tragedy.'

Helen was finding it hard to breathe.

'We've tried, Helen, but we can't put it behind us, not entirely.'

Helen shook her head, to dislodge the image of her brother screaming in pain and clutching his head.

'We can't blame you.' As if blame, the apportioning of responsibility, would make it better, easier to bear. Even in this, there was bitterness, and she felt that she had somehow failed them.

'If we'd stayed and to hell with what his friends might think, maybe we'd've been able to stop him – or do something to help.' This was a well-worn track spiralling inwards to a claustrophobic centre. They blamed themselves for Robbie's death. They might have stopped him taking the pill that killed him, where Helen had failed. They couldn't blame Helen, and yet they did blame her, needing someone to share the burden, despite all their rationalization, and this increased their guilt.

'It's such a bloody *waste*!' Helen burst out, suddenly angry. A waste and a shame, and what happened after was a shame and a waste of two years of her young life. It had happened, and life would never be the same, but they still had to live it. Helen looked into her mother's face and saw the sadness of the years etched deep, and the unrelenting anger that she, their daughter, whom they had trusted with their most precious gift, had proved unfit, had taken from them their only son. For them, moving on, making a new life would be a betrayal.

Helen had suffered two years of black despair following his death. Although her actions had taken her from her family, denied her the opportunity to talk about what she had done, for even though she tried, she had been unable to explain to her mother that she would rather have died than let Robbie go through that terrifying pain, she did not regret what she had done after his funeral.

It was unplanned. She had wanted to see him, to understand how he operated, and she had driven her car from the quiet suburban street where they lived to the terraced houses of the estates on the rough side of town. She sat in her car, watching him in the dark winter night, and he had turned and smiled at her. That smile! His casual arrogance that made her want to kill, because he was alive, vibrant, and Robbie was dead. She had buried her kid brother the day before, and this thug was able to walk the streets, selling his poison, turning a profit.

Accelerating through the rain, the drops of water seemed to elongate as they streaked past her window – warp speed – but not fast enough.

Her mother broke the contact, disconcerted. She avoided Helen's eye, as one avoids the eye of someone disliked, and Helen disentangled herself carefully, feeling a solid pain in her chest, as real as the fading bruise on her face.

She returned home late on Sunday night, and to keep her mind from the thought that this would be the final separation from her parents, she mulled over the dream she had had the previous day.

In her dream, Helen saw herself wearing a coarsely woven dress, sitting at a table while other women took food from her plate, each making the ritualized statement, 'At prisoner's request.' On waking, she had thought immediately of Margaret Atwood's book, *The Handmaid's Tale.*

Am I blaming myself for his infidelities? she wondered. Then she remembered that Edward's mother had said something about her 'allowing' Edward to have affairs. Perhaps that had been the trigger.

They had looked older, both of them. They had dressed carefully, as they always did, and were as well groomed, but the sleekness was marred; they were irretrievably diminished by the loss of their son.

'Edward wasn't a child,' Helen had told them. 'He didn't ask for permission.'

In the dream, the women asked her how she felt. She had replied 'Hard. Full.', and they had given her sideways looks, as if they knew she was pregnant.

Helen had been told in the dream that once a month the members of the community were allowed to vent their true feelings on an effigy of the 'lord' who ruled them. The lord was Edward. He rode on a white horse up and down the pavilion. The women charged on foot at a straw-stuffed doll which was dressed like Edward. They stabbed it again and again and Edward smiled down on them, unharmed, shielded in some magic way. Then the weapon was placed in Helen's hands and the pavilion fell silent. She looked at the long, thin steel pin, at its globular head, she knew she had the power to destroy him.

She had walked slowly, quietly through the hushed crowd while the lord on his horse had looked on in amusement. She went to the straw effigy and stabbed it again and again, the long shaft of the pin piercing through the breast and stopping only at the post to which the doll had been tied.

From each tiny puncture hole, a bead of bright red blood appeared.

Helen shuddered, and roused herself from her morbid thoughts, but the dream would not be shaken; she found herself returning to it again and again, wondering if she could have killed Edward during one of her blackouts – she had them even now. From time to time it happened that she would become aware of her surroundings, *coming to*, it seemed, and the discovery would be unexpected. She could not remember having gone into a particular room or, more disturbingly, having travelled from home to work. At these times she always had a dizzying sense of danger, and the danger was within herself.

Chapter Eighteen

Jeff Townley had been looking forward to taking a short walk to the smoking room, but he now pushed the cigarettes to one side. In the last week Dermot Molyneux had come up with some first-rate pictures of Helen Wilkinson. Aside from the haunting *House of Death* picture, he had managed somehow to catch Ainsley, the cuckolded husband, and his wife, Clara. Touching one, that: her carrying the baby, looking startled and vulnerable. The Wilkinson picture and the last one of Clara Ainsley had been syndicated to most of the tabloids, one of the quality papers and the BBC. Dermot had earned more than enough in one week to pay for a new computer with hi-tech imaging software, a bed scanner, a modem to connect him to the office, a zoom lens and a lightweight camera holdall. As Dermot enthused about his latest piece of information, Jeff thought about the offer Ralph Milton had made to work with the photographer on a *Herald* exclusive. Dermot had refused – this time – but Jeff had serious doubts that he would be able to entice him to stay past the end of his one-year contract.

He eyed the packet of cigarettes longingly. Gone were the days when he could light up without fear of provoking a storm of protest. Smoking was now strictly limited to the smoking room, but what the hell good was that when he needed a fag to help him think here, now, in his office, talking to a photographer who was probably about to waste company time and money, but whom Jeff couldn't afford to upset?

'Wait a minute, hold on! Go back a few paces.' He had lost concentration for a second. 'You reckon this "contact" of yours says an arrest is imminent? Is that what he actually said, *imminent?*'

'She,' Molyneux corrected, his vanity unable to resist setting the facts straight. 'And she said she thinks they'll charge him.'

'She,' Townley repeated.

'Well . . .'

'Molyneux,' Townley said. 'Dermot. Don't, please, don't try to work that one on me.'

Molyneux raised his eyebrows. He knew what his boss meant: the coy smile; the roguish grin; the look from under his impossibly unruly hair. That was something for the *gairuls* as his father called them. 'Sorry, boss,' he said. 'Look, I know the story's straight. They took this guy Ellis in and questioned him. They've tied some new evidence to him, so my contact says. No—' He held up both hands to placate Townley. 'I know what you're thinking, and I can tell you she's sure.'

'Not just trying to impress the *man?*' Townley asked, extending the vowel to a Belfast drawl – the closest he could approximate to Molyneux's soft Dublin burr.

'Sure, she was trying to impress me,' Dermot said quietly, 'but don't you think I'd check me sources?'

Townley was affected by the pained restraint in Molyneux's voice. He buckled under the strain and reached for the packet of cigarettes, opened it and slipped one from the pack. Only two left. He rolled the pristine cylinder between his index finger and thumb, resisting – just – the urge to lift the cigarette to his nose and sniff the *Nicotiana tabacum* like a connoisseur sampling the aroma of a good Havana cigar. Molyneux was watching him hungrily, and Jeff surmised it wasn't the cigarette he was interested in.

'What the hell,' he sighed. If he refused, Milton or one of the other nationals would encourage Molyneux to go for the story. 'If you don't turn anything up by tomorrow, the story is dead, is that clear?' Townley pointed with the filter end of the cigarette.

'And, Molyneux,' he called, as the Irishman headed for the door. 'Take a tip. You're far more convincing when you drop the BS.'

Molyneux grinned. 'I couldn't take a tip from you, boss.' He nodded at the cigarette. 'Those things are lethal without them.'

Townley surprised him with a laugh. 'That's just what my wife keeps telling me.'

Helen was interviewed at 2 p.m. on Monday. A pro-vice chancellor, the Dean of Faculty and Alice Chambers were present. They asked their questions kindly and with due deference, and twenty minutes later confirmed that she would be offered a post as senior lecturer in the new School of Life Sciences. She received a call in her office at 3 p.m. It was Ruth.

'You'll be staying, then.'

'Where else would I go?'

'Where indeed? I have to say you don't sound exactly thrilled. It *is* a promotion, Helen.'

'I know. But I don't feel much like celebrating, given the circumstances.'

'Ouch.'

'Sorry.'

'No, I'm sorry. Shall I come round this evening?'

They agreed to meet at 7.30. When, ten minutes later,

Mick Tuttle phoned, Helen felt an unexpected flutter of nervousness. She was smiling to herself as she hung up, but snatched the receiver back at the last moment. The line was dead. What to tell Ruth?

They met in a restaurant in Watergate Row. Helen had walked the mile and a half to the city centre, doubling back on herself a couple of times to be sure she was not followed. She passed the squat, sandstone cathedral building of the university's namesake, St Werburgh, and approached the stone cross at the meeting of the old Roman roads.

She mounted the steps to her right, on to the raised wooden walkway that led to the restaurant. Ahead, a series of archways seemed to overlap, layering the covered path with increasing darkness. She could have continued along the road way and come up the steps at the end of the Row, but she was shivering, despite wearing a thick woollen coat, and the Rows, enclosed on one side by shops and offices and on the other by the black and white wooden railings so characteristic of Chester, are sheltered from the worst of the weather. Helen felt safe, unobserved within the twilight of wooden planking overarched by a low, plastered roof. The black paintwork of the studded timber doors, icing-thick with centuries of repainting, were reassuring in an indefinable way; perhaps giving a sense of perspective, of proportion to her present difficulties.

As she drew near to the restaurant at the end of the Row, she glanced across at the copiously inscribed upper floors of God's Providence House. 'In God is my strength,' she muttered vaguely. Taking a breath, she stepped into the warmth of the bar.

Helen had never seen Mick so relaxed. He was warm, funny, and a remarkably good mimic, a skill he used to good effect in his description of his own interview with the panel.

The restaurant was quiet and the tables well spaced. Its wooden floors, oak panelling and low beamed ceiling sufficiently worn and battered to lend an air of permanence and solidity which added to Helen's feelings of security and safety; perhaps they had a similar effect on Mick.

He paused, studying her for a moment, then said, smiling, 'Go on then, ask.'

Helen blinked. 'Ask what?'

'Whatever it is that's making you look so bewildered.'

'Is that how I look?'

His smile broadened, then he concentrated on his meal for a few moments to allow her time to think. He had chosen a vegetarian meal, deferring to her sensitivity with unshowy consideration, and Helen had been surprised that her appetite had been sustained throughout the first and well into the main course.

'I suppose,' Helen began cautiously, 'I was thinking how different you are outside the university walls.'

'Different?'

She blushed. 'It's hard to explain.'

He gave her a lop-sided grin. 'Just hard to say.'

She raised her eyes to meet his and felt a thrill of something she scarcely recognized. Happiness? She shrugged.

'At St Werburgh's I've always got something to prove,' he explained. 'You know what it's like. In a way we're both regarded as physically handicapped – you because of your sex, me because of my callipers, whereas here' – he glanced around the restaurant – 'nobody would really care if I was held together by elastic bands and lengths of string, so long as I could pay the bill.'

Helen frowned. 'I'm sorry we make you feel that way.'

'*You* don't, but enough do.' He reached across the table and squeezed her hand. 'Don't let it worry you. I can outlast them.

I've got incredible stamina when it comes to that sort of challenge.

'The good thing is, we'll both be working for the newly Recreated School of Life Sciences – or R-SOLS, for short.'

Helen laughed, nearly choking. 'Arseholes?'

'Present company excepted,' he said, deadpan.

Dermot Molyneux moved swiftly and silently, shadowing Ellis as he made his way from his lodgings to the other side of the city. Dermot knew, before they had reached the halfway mark, exactly where they were heading. The evening was cold and blustery and ridges of velvety grey herringbone cloud formations had built up on the underbelly of the storm which was gathering from the east. It was a long walk and he was thankful for the lightweight material and broad shoulder straps of his new camera bag. He always felt a barely reconcilable sense of hilarity and excitement when following a mark: on the one hand it seemed ludicrous, boys playing at spies; on the other, it was risky, and had even, on occasions, proved dangerous.

The house was now bereft of reporters; interest in the story had waned when, after a whole week, the police had made little progress. The last of the nationals had left on Sunday afternoon, disgusted to find that they had wasted the weekend freezing delicate parts of their anatomy waiting for something to happen, when in fact the house was empty. If it hadn't been for two of the more reckless (or more desperate) journalists bunking over the gate at the back of the house and peering in at Helen's study, they might have stayed a little longer and witnessed the arrival of John Ellis. Dermot held back at the corner of the street and got a good shot with his new, lightweight 100–300 zoom, of Ellis in profile as he hesitated, looking both ways before slipping down the side entry leading to the back of the house. He switched lenses as he walked towards the house, working by touch, while keeping a keen eye for Ellis returning.

There was little cover in the street, even though there were plenty of gardens, for in this area of the city, the houses were all occupied, either by the families of the professional classes or they housed the upper range of bed and breakfast accommodation, and as such were reasonably well kept. Dermot reflected that he would be likely to attract unwanted attention creeping through gardens with a camera, and so he strode down the street purposefully. As he drew level with the house, he had to come to a decision: walk on by or go in. There was really no contest: Townley had given him a day to find something worth putting on the front page and the closer he could get to the Wilkinsons' house, the more likely it would be that a good composition would present itself.

The house was semi-detached and each pair in the street was flanked by a side entry. He darted into the passage, glad that he had worn his air trainers, since the high walls on either side echoed and magnified every sound. At the back gate he listened for half a minute before trying the latch – it was locked.

He lifted his bag strap over one shoulder and swivelled until the bulk of the weight rested somewhere between his shoulder blades, then he reached up – not too much of a stretch – to the top of the gate, bracing one foot against the brickwork, a couple of feet up. He swung his right leg over the top of the gate and then eased himself into a sitting position, checking for signs of activity before dropping down quietly into the garden.

It was well kept, unlike the front of the house. Tiny daffodils and pale yellow primroses were massed with stubby-looking purple crocuses which struggled to keep their heads above the mat of grass at the base of the trees. The wooden framed greenhouse stood at the end of the lawn, painted dark green, it was filled with both mature plants in pots of various sizes and seedlings in trays. Beyond the greenhouse, through an archway of climbing roses in delicate new leaf, were carefully laid out oblongs of freshly tilled soil. There was a shed, too, at the far end of the garden, covered in ivy and some variety of climbing rose. The archway would provide good cover, but it was some 25 feet from the house –

Ellis's face appeared at the kitchen window. Dermot ducked behind the bins, hidden behind a screen of close-growing evergreen. He braced himself, sweating, listening for the sound of the back door key turning in the lock. Silence. Ellis had not seen him. He altered the *f*-stop on his camera, and estimated the focus he would need: there wouldn't be time for adjustment. The house and most of the garden were in shadow at this time of evening, which should cut the reflections.

A scurry of footsteps in the passageway almost made his heart stop, then he realized they were going away from the house. 'Stay calm, Dermot,' he told himself. 'Only the neighbour going out the back way.' He counted to three, then rushed at the window and fired off three shots, ducking down below the window frame panting, almost laughing to himself. Three near perfect shots, and of what? Ellis delivering some sort of confectionery for Helen Wilkinson? 'Jesus, Dermot,' he told himself, 'you'll have to do better than that!'

When the key finally *did* turn in the lock, Dermot had plenty of time to hide himself in the little enclosure of evergreens. Ellis let himself out, apparently unaware of the photographer's presence.

Ellis locked the back door, preoccupied with his itinerary for the evening. He had one or two things to organize before he was finished, and he had to remember to drop the keys off at the pre-arranged place – they would be needed later.

David Ainsley had been watching the house for an hour. He had sat, motionless, on the once grand, but now cracked and mossy steps of the empty property, peering through the dense mesh of twiggy fuchsia and leafy hawthorn which had long since overgrown its function as a hedge. The hawthorn, though small and scrubby, was beginning to take on the form and height of a small tree. Still, the shrubs gave cover enough and he could observe, whilst unobserved himself, using the patience and the observation skills he had learned from fifteen years of field and laboratory study, that no lights had been turned on or off, no windows opened, and nobody had entered nor left the house opposite. When he was quite sure it was safe, he stood, giving the blood a moment to circulate through his cramped limbs, then, absently wiping the dust and detritus from the seat of his trousers, he crossed the street and let himself in. Half an hour should do it.

Dermot waited three or four minutes before venturing out. He tried the back door, but Ellis had been sure to secure it. An interior shot of the *House of Death* would be quite a scoop, he decided. It would more than make up for the disappointment of Ellis and the fairy cakes. He scanned the windows of the upper stories. One on the first floor was open a crack, and he decided to see if he could find a step ladder. The shed was locked and there was nothing hidden inside the greenhouse. He was about to abandon his half-hearted attempt at unlawful entry when he heard footsteps approaching the back gate, and for a moment he froze. If he used the pathway to gain his hiding place by the bins, he might be heard. He retreated quickly across the lawn, leaving clear footprints on the wet grass, but perhaps Ellis would not notice. He hid behind the rose arbour just as the gate opened.

Dermot risked one quick shot: the wind was blowing in his

direction and should carry the click and wheeze of the shutter and auto-wind away from the house, but his heart thudded so loudly in his chest that he was seriously worried it would give him away. Not Ellis, but the same three keys on a simple fob with a yellow tab. What was going on? He waited a couple of minutes and was contemplating sneaking up to the house, when a movement at the study window caught his attention and he fired off another shot. The light was going and there was probably too much shadow to make it worthwhile, but he already had one clear picture and he could try and improve the definition in the darkroom, or on the computer.

He waited a further five minutes, wondering whether to leave or to try for another picture. He failed to notice the face at the attic room window which overlooked the garden, didn't see that *he* was being observed.

'David.'

She had lost weight. Lost the sheen of good health and even better grooming which had cost him so much, financially, and later, after she met Edward, everything he had ever wanted in life.

'Five minutes, I'm on my way.'

Clara held the baby to her. He was asleep, exhausted no doubt, as she must be exhausted. She placed the baby carefully, almost fearfully into his cot beside the bed, then turned to look at her husband.

Ainsley eyed her cautiously, wondering how she might react. For a second she seemed ready to fly at him, then she smiled briefly and, sweeping an overlong lock of hair from her forehead with the back of her hand, she said, 'I'll fix you something to eat – you must be starving.'

'No. I won't stay. I needed – some things.'

She laughed, a tentative, nervous sound that ended almost

in a sob. 'Yes, you did rather leave in a hurry.' She half turned. 'Your cheque book's in—'

'I have it now.'

'David, I wouldn't—' He had sounded harsher than he had intended, and she seemed wounded by the implication.

'I know,' he said, relenting. 'I know, Clara.'

'Your things— in boxes. Downstairs. You really don't have to—' A desperate edge was creeping into her voice.

'Yes,' he said, firmly. 'Yes, I do. I have to.'

Her mouth worked and she almost lost control. She looked about her, as if trying to find a distraction from her extreme distress. 'Where've you been staying?'

'Rutherford put me up for a few days, then I found a B&B.'

Rutherford, who so abhorred Ainsley's smugness, was unable to resist his deep unhappiness. His wife had murmured a warning about appearing to take sides, but had agreed that they could not allow David to continue sleeping in his office. He had quickly recovered from the heavy drinking – too ashamed to let Rutherford's children see him stumbling about the house, shambling and tearful – and from there, he had started piecing together a new life, of sorts.

'This is such a big house,' Clara said. 'We needn't be in each other's way.'

It was said timidly, and Ainsley felt a sharp pain below his sternum. He pulled the drawstring on the third bin liner full of his clothing.

Clara laughed shakily. 'Funny,' she said, 'I always thought you didn't care about clothes. And look at all this.'

He half smiled, reaching to lift the first bag. Her hand closed over his, tightened, pulling against him. Their eyes locked, hers pleading, tearful, his grey and clear once more. Beyond tears. She saw that it was hopeless.

'I need you,' she said, looking away, and a tear fell on to the black plastic of the bin bag.

'I know,' Ainsley said quietly. 'But you don't love me. It's not enough, Clara.'

She nodded silently, moving out of his way. 'The police took me in for questioning on Saturday.'

He held his breath, waiting for the confession.

'I was with Edward, at his house, the afternoon he was murdered.'

'You don't have to tell me this—'

'I went there to tell him it was over between us.' She laughed, softly, tentatively, glancing over at the baby's cot to check for signs of restlessness. 'The police think I was the last to see him alive, and you know what that means.'

'Clara—'

'They can't prove anything. They haven't even got enough to charge me. They let me go after eight hours. They searched the house – our house – but of course they found nothing.'

'I don't know why you're telling me this.'

'I had to leave Henry with Cloë Sallis. She wasn't pleased. But the alternative was to bring social services in. She says he slept for six hours. That's more sleep than I've had in the last three days. It was humiliating, David, having to ask for her help, for that reason. She knew, of course. Everyone does.'

'It's not my problem,' he said, avoiding her huge, hungry, tearful eyes.

'No,' she said, with an effort of control. 'It's our problem. We can deal with it.'

'I'll see that you and the boy are provided for—'

'Your *son*!' she screamed with sudden ferocity. 'Henry is your son!'

He looked at her with real pity this time. Then, shaking his head, started to take his belongings down to the hired van below.

Chapter Nineteen

They walked part of the way back along the Roman walls. Helen had been prepared to slow her pace to a shuffle and was surprised that Mick was able to stride along with her; she even had difficulty keeping up at times. The wind by now was fierce. It buffeted them, changing direction with capricious inconstancy, slamming into the walls and creating vortices which snatched the breath from their mouths. They conceded defeat, retreating, laughing, to the relative calm of the street below.

'Maybe we should phone for a taxi,' Helen suggested.

'Are you tired?'

Helen saw the concern in his face and felt a slight shock in the realization that he should think her frail. Did she really look so ill? 'Not unless you are,' she said, somewhat defensively, but was unable to suppress a smile when he laughed. 'Smugness doesn't suit you,' she added.

She was relieved that there were no reporters in evidence outside the house. 'Best thing I ever did, going to my parents for the weekend,' she commented.

'Best thing ever?'

She paused, with her hand on the gate, feeling that the genuine curiosity he had shown in asking the question deserved serious consideration. It seemed that her absence had deterred the reporters, resulting in a huge improvement in her quality of life. Also, a candid exchange between herself and her mother had been long overdue. She knew now that she could never be to her parents what they wanted her to be, simply because she was not Robbie. This had been a painful revelation, but it had also been a kind of deliverance from the years in which she had hated herself and had tortured herself with futile yearnings: if she had supervised him more closely; if she hadn't been so keen to appear the cool older sister; if she had called the ambulance sooner, or her parents . . . And yet there was unfinished business – the waste of two years of her life. It would shock her mother to know that Helen only considered it a waste because she hadn't achieved what she had set out to do. Helen was ashamed of her feelings, but she could not make them go away, and so she had told no one and tried not to think about it. Sometimes it worked, but not always.

Someone had finished the job for her while she was in prison – a drugs-related shooting, the police had called it. Helen had felt thwarted; she had had her chance and blown it. There was something within her that was dangerous, bad.

Still, in all, the letting go of years of self-recrimination had given Helen strength. She had mended no bridges, dressed no wounds, but at least now she was reconciled to the fact that she would have to learn to go on alone, since her parents were stuck in the past, experiencing the same grief, the same pangs of suffering and remorse as they had more than ten years before.

She smiled. 'If not the best, certainly it's the most sensible thing I've done in years.'

Dermot would have given a week's wages for a close-up of the expression on her face as she glanced up at the bedroom window before she opened the gate.

Helen made coffee while Mick fiddled with the radio in an attempt to tune into Jazz FM. Mission accomplished, he sat back and watched Helen through half-closed eyes.

'Unbelievable!'

Mick roused himself from a pleasurable, if imagined, caressing of the curve of Helen's neck. 'What is?'

'Not what, who. Ruth.' Helen straightened up from the fridge. In one hand she held a bottle of milk and in the other a white cardboard box. 'She keeps bringing me little delicacies, trying to "tempt my palate", as she calls it. This looks like the latest. Fancy sharing a pudding with me?'

They had skipped the apple crumble or bannoffee pie on offer at the restaurant and Mick had worked up a renewed appetite fighting against the wind on the walk back to Helen's house. 'Mind you don't drip!' he warned.

Helen set the box down on the scrubbed kitchen table. It seemed one of the cakes had leaked jam, for the base of the box was oozing sticky red juice.

Doughnuts, Helen thought, smiling at her own squeamishness a week before when she had watched Ruth eating one after another in the canteen, licking the jam from between her fingers. Helen cut the string, choosing scissors rather than a knife – carrying a knife still made her scalp crawl – and opened the lid.

'My God.' Mick had spoken. He looked up into Helen's face. It was frozen, ominously still.

Inside the box, on a square of balsa wood was a white laboratory mouse. It was splayed in a way that always made Helen think, with her Catholic upbringing, of crucifixion. Each tiny paw was pinned through its centre and stretched out, to place the body wall under tension and facilitate the dissection.

Helen began to shake so violently that he feared she might convulse. Mick stood and put both arms around her, pulling her away. Once outside the door, Helen came to as if waking from a hypnotic trance. She mumbled something about feeling sick and he let her go, knowing that his slow ascent of the stairs would only impede her.

By the time he reached the bathroom she was already rinsing her mouth out. She had splashed her face with water.

'Helen,' he asked, 'who would do this to you?'

'Did you see?' She ignored his question, focusing on something in the middle distance. Something so real and tangible, that he almost fancied that he could see it too.

He frowned, nodded. Yes, he had seen. So much blood! Whoever had done this, had killed the animal by severing a vein and allowing it to bleed to death slowly. Then it had been expertly dissected. The oesophagus and rectum ligatured with cotton before being cut, then the stomach and small and large intestines had been carefully lifted out of the body cavity, displaced to the left and arranged in a lyre shape to display the mesenteric blood vessels fanning across the transparent connective tissues in a delicate arrangement of red blood vessels and off-white adipose tissue. All this, he had seen, but what she had meant by the question was the last part of the dissection, the part she had been meant to notice: the pouched uterus exposed – showing, beneath the thin, pink muscle of its walls the clear outlines of seven fully formed foetuses.

Sergeant Hackett's eyes roved about the room, searching for something unusual, something that might serve as a clue to who or why. The kitchen was neat and orderly, a prosaic picture of banal domesticity – except for the package at the edge of the table.

'The blinds?' he asked.

'I drew them when I arrived,' Ruth answered. Helen's first instinct, as before, had been to call her friend before she called the police. 'I'm sorry if I've done wrong, sergeant, but the last thing Helen needs right now is her picture in the paper again.'

He nodded, a neutral acknowledgement of the facts, taking in, subliminally, the lack of one knife from the wooden block next to the window, a gap tooth, unsightly, obtrusive in its absence. It had not been found, despite an extensive search of the Wilkinsons' garden and all the gardens adjacent to it – they had even sifted through the mulch in the drains along the street, but the murder weapon had disappeared, dropped in the canal or the Dee, where it would rust quietly until nothing remained but a reddish sludge.

There were no signs of a break-in, and the SOCO had found no fingerprints on the cardboard box.

'Who's got a key to the house – apart from Dr Wilkinson, that is?' Hackett asked.

'Me,' Ruth answered. 'Her mother, I think. That's all.'

Mick Tuttle cleared his throat. 'I have a key to the back gate.'

Ruth stared. 'I had *no* idea!' she exclaimed, and Hackett thought he caught an expression somewhere between amusement and exasperation.

'Helen was concerned about the press interest. The side passage generally wasn't watched too closely.' He shrugged.

'Do you have a key to the house?' Hackett asked.

Mick shook his head.

Ruth opened her mouth to ask a question, then changed her mind, smiling a little to herself.

Hackett asked the question for her. 'When did she give you the key?'

'A couple of days ago.'

Hackett wondered if the professor was not the only Wilkinson who had been having an affair. Mick returned his stare calmly.

'Any ideas about who might've—' Hackett waved in the direction of the white box.

Ruth shrugged. 'Virtually everyone knows about Helen's miscarriage after the newspaper articles, Sergeant.'

'But who would bear a grudge against her?'

Ruth sighed, spreading her hands in a gesture of helplessness. 'Her students like her. She's reasonably well-liked among her peers – bearing in mind that St Werburgh's is a bastion of chauvinistic, misogynistic fundamentalism.'

'Could be someone's jealous that she got a senior lectureship.' Mick had spoken and Ruth fixed her gaze on him. Her eyes ice-blue, now analytical. She seemed to measure him against some paradigm and find him wanting. 'Could be,' she replied, and Hackett tried, unsuccessfully, to discern whether it was mistrust or dislike that filtered through the cool blandness of her expression as she scrutinized her colleague.

A thump overhead broke the silence and with it the wordless exchange between the two academics. Hackett was out into the hall first. Helen was supposed to be resting in her study, downstairs. He mounted the stairs two at a time, not pausing to think of the danger he might be running to.

Helen stood at the door to the bedroom where her husband's body had been found. She was pale to the point of deathliness. On the dimly lit landing her face seemed to glow with pearly light. She smiled tentatively.

'I'm afraid I stumbled,' she said. 'I'm feeling rather weak.'

Ruth pushed past Hackett and helped Helen to the staircase.

'What are you doing up here?' Hackett asked.

'It's her bloody house, Sergeant,' Ruth answered angrily.

Hackett had to concede. It was, as Ruth Marks said, Helen Wilkinson's house, after all, and he supposed this restless prowling was only to be expected given that her property had been invaded in this way. 'Violated' was the word that came to mind. Nevertheless, Hackett walked to the end of the landing to check the two doors which stood slightly ajar. One, a box room: spartan, empty, soulless; Edward Wilkinson had used it as a study, but apparently had preferred mostly to stay in his university office when pressure of work, or Clara demanded. The other door led to the front bedroom. Hackett felt an unaccustomed premonitory dread as he put his hand on the door handle of the bedroom and eased the door open.

The room was empty, undisturbed, except by some turbulent spectre of fear which he felt had emanated from Helen.

When he returned to the kitchen the SOCO was clearing away the last of his gear and Mick Tuttle was pouring black coffee into mugs. He raised the pot and Hackett nodded his thanks. Helen was sitting at the table, staring at the spot where the box had lain; a damp patch remained, cleaned of blood, but darker than the rest of the old pine. A faint smell of bleach hung in the air.

The atmosphere Hackett had sensed in the room upstairs was here, too. Stronger, a solid almost tangible presence. The SOCO glanced uneasily at him as he secured the clasps of his equipment case and Hackett set about trying to find something to say. Then the shrill chirrup of his mobile phone shattered the silence and everyone jerked convulsively before relaxing, grateful for an end to the oppressive stillness.

Hackett spoke briefly, sharply, questioning, and then he was gone, taking the SOCO with him and leaving the three remaining occupants of the room bewildered.

Chapter Twenty

Hackett arrived outside the Victorian frontage as the ambulance was leaving. 'Smoke inhalation,' Nelson said. 'Plus a bloody great skull fracture. He's lucky they got to him in time.' He nodded in the direction of a small knot of firemen, greasy and black-faced, who had just come out of the house and now seemed to be conferring about what action to take next. Two of the men turned and went back into the house, stepping over the fire hose which trailed inside the building.

'Any other casualties?'

Nelson shook his head. The flare of the sodium street lamps and the sharp glitter of blue-red, blue-red in rotating splinters from two police cars and a fire engine cast unflattering shadows on his ravaged face. It was raining heavily now, battering down. The unpredictable gusts of the storm had made the job of fighting the fire more difficult, but it seemed to be contained more or less to one room and the fire service appeared to be bringing it under control. The one window billowed orange-tinged smoke into the night, but there were no flames.

'His darkroom,' Nelson explained, hunching his shoulders against a cold trickle of rain that had found its way down the back of his neck, and thrusting his hands deep into his pockets.

Two hours later they were inside Dermot Molyneux's flat, crunching over debris and tasting the bitter, oily remains of the fire on their tongues. It was not yet light and both men carried powerful torches.

Tim Dignan, sweating, his face smeared in soot, followed them in. 'The fire started in the darkroom,' he said. 'Arson, no question of that. And there's been some damage done before the fire was set. From what we can tell, he came to long enough to get out of the darkroom, but he passed out in here.'

'Where was he found?' Hackett asked.

'Near the phone. But the wire had been cut. The fire built to quite a pitch in the darkroom, but he'd got the door shut and that contained the worst of it – till the window shattered with the heat, but luckily people started to notice by then.'

Nelson was prodding about in the debris. A family grouping – they'd have to be informed. A collection of CDs greasy with smuts. Bands he'd never heard of, but guessed must be Irish from the Gaelic titles.

'Were there people around to notice after midnight on a Monday night?' Hackett asked.

'Studentland this, Terry. They keep late hours.'

Hackett nodded, glancing over at the door to the darkroom, which stood open, its paintwork blistered and blackened in places. Most of the damage in the main living room of the flat was from smoke and water. He didn't envy the poor sods who'd have this lot to clear up.

'Aren't you supposed to get as much of the valuable stuff out before it's wrecked?' Nelson demanded. Equipment, some of it expensive by the look of it, lay broken on the floor.

Dignan took a moment before answering. 'We try to put people before property,' he said, narrowing his eyes slightly, and looking hard into the rheumy eyes of the policeman. 'The photographic equipment was wrecked by whoever started the fire. What did you think? That we came in here wielding fire axes and smashed the place up?'

'Life's bloody work,' Nelson went on defensively. 'Wanton bloody destruction.'

Hackett wondered what had brought on this rare exhibition of empathy in the inspector. 'Surely not wanton, sir – I mean, if it served a purpose?'

Nelson fixed him with a look that would have pinned a lesser man to the wall. Hackett returned a bland, if vaguely expectant stare.

Nelson did not actually concede the contest, but his next words were spoken with an unexpected mildness. 'Perhaps "wanton" wasn't quite the word I was looking for,' he said, returning to a desultory prodding of Dermot's personal effects. 'Can that door be made secure?' He nodded towards the entrance to the flat. The door, though still on its hinges, swung open, while the lock side of the frame lay twisted on the sodden carpet.

'We'll see to it before we leave,' Dignan promised.

Nelson frowned, flashing the beam of his torch to one side of the door. 'Can anything be done about this?' Nelson asked.

Hackett and Dignan exchanged a surprised look.

'Done about it? Salvage, you mean?'

Nelson threw Hackett a withering glance. 'Evidence, I mean.' He directed his torch at the mess that had once been Molyneux's PC. 'Might be worth getting young Tact to have look at it.'

Hackett thought there would be precious little to look at, but he had to agree, it might be worth taking a squint.

It isn't much of a room, John thought. All the same, it had hurt when that crazy policeman had looked around it with that expression of disapproval, of disgust even.

He picked up one of the culture bottles and shook it. The flies lay in clusters on the oatmeal growth medium, stuck fast, not one living specimen remained. He shook his head. It had all made perfect sense. He gathered the other bottles to his chest, sweeping them to him, anxious that this evidence of his failure should not be found, smudging the pristine whiteness of his T-shirt with dust. Never mind, there would be time to change. He was in control now. Back in control.

He threw the bottles into the waste basket and carried it downstairs, jingling as cheerily as a milkman. Nobody saw or heard him – the tenants, most of whom were students, had already gone out for the night, and he had the house to himself.

Gusts of spiteful wind spat large chilly drops of rain. He hurried to the back, where the bins were kept, slipping once or twice on patches of slimy moss on the path up the side of the house. By the time he was indoors again, a heavy shower was drenching the street and rainwater gurgled from a crack in the down-spout next to the front door.

He ran back upstairs, shivering, and slammed the door of his flat behind him. It was cold. It was always cold in this room. He stripped off his T-shirt, now smeared with rust from the bin lid, overlaying the greyish dust from the bottles. He threw the shirt on to the pile of dirty clothing at the foot of his bed, then, seeing the contemptuous expression on Inspector Nelson's face again, he bunched the lot into a ball and stuffed it into the bottom of his wardrobe.

Dispossessed of its clutter, the room looked sparse, grey, ordinary. He had once been proud of his *Drosophila* cultures, and of his skill in handling them – they weren't easy insects, not if you wanted the best from them, but he could etherize, sex, and type fifty in less than five minutes. Where other students routinely lost flies into the lab when they came round unexpectedly, or else they over-anaesthetized them, or they made up their culture medium too wet, so the insects fell prey to fungal infection, or too dry, so they died of starvation, or their eggs, desiccated, failed to hatch, John's *Drosophila* were robust, reliable experimental subjects – even the wild ones he'd brought in from his field studies.

He didn't know why he'd kept them for so long after everything had turned so disastrously against him, and he had allowed his carefully labelled batches to die. He had intended to throw them away, but, somehow he couldn't bear to, and after a while, they had provided a perverse form of comfort to him, like the smell of his own sweat, and the pile of unwashed clothing at the end of his bed.

He turned on the gas fire – no sense in being uncomfortable – and dragged a clean T-shirt over his head. Nearly ready now. He wondered if Helen had returned home, and tried to imagine her reaction. Shock, anger perhaps. He hoped she had understood the message, otherwise it had been nothing more than a petty act of spite.

Helen, alone at last, bolted the doors front and back of the house before returning to the bedroom. Soon first light would glimmer over the rooftops of the houses; already there were a few restless stirrings in the eaves of the front gable, where sparrows were nesting. This was something to be done under cover of darkness.

She overcame her reluctance to cross the threshold, taking a breath before stepping into the room. Her heart thudded painfully in her chest and she turned her head away from the bed, avoiding the image that she would see: Edward, half sitting, chest bare – no, she *would not* think of it.

She crouched beside the little wooden cabinet and braced one hand against the door, taking another breath, holding it, easing the catch with her thumb, opening the door a little at a time, cautiously as though afraid of some terror waiting to escape. A picture of the mouse, splayed, butchered, flashed into her mind and she felt her gorge rise. She pulled the door wide in her distress, dislodging the contents of the cupboard. Magazines, books, an audio cassette fell to the floor. And with them a knife. The blade was dulled, clotted with blood, and the handle smeared with the same rust-coloured stuff, dried and flaking.

Earlier, she had picked it up with her bare hands and thrust it back into the cupboard, now the thought of touching it filled her with dread, a childish horror of the supernatural. How had this happened? They had looked in every room, every possible hiding place, she and Mick together. She stared at the appalling spectre of the knife until she thought if she waited a moment longer she would go mad, then, carefully, she opened the food bag she had brought from the kitchen and tilted the magazine on which the knife had been resting. It slithered into the open mouth of the plastic bag with an unholy sound which drew from her an utterance of disgust and distress. She carried it at arm's length through the house, unable to countenance the thought of having it upstairs with her, close to where she would be sleeping, but equally unable to rid herself of it. What if the police came back, searching bins, digging up the flower beds as they had done before? She would put it somewhere out of the way until she had thought about what to do. Could she trust Mick, tell him? Or Ruth – would she think she had finally lost touch with reality?

She fetched up in the kitchen. The police had already searched here, dusting for fingerprints. Yes, here would be best. She opened the third drawer from the top of the sink unit, the drawer in which she kept oddments, keys, wrapping paper, measuring tape, bits of string. The knife nestled like a dangerous animal on top of a coil of coarse string. Helen wanted to bury it beneath the clutter, but she could not bring

Chapter Twenty-One

Ruth slept badly, dreaming of boxed doughnuts that turned into squirming, screaming mice as she bit into them. So when the doorbell rang, waking her from a new permutation in which Helen was performing an operation on Tuttle's legs without anaesthetic, explaining with cold rationality that all that was required was a little self-control on his part, she tumbled out of bed gratefully.

Nelson and Hackett were taken aback at her wild appearance.

'You,' she grunted, ungraciously, and retreated, scratching her head and yawning. She left the front door open which the two policemen took as an invitation and stepped inside. The hallway was cold, a grey, nondescript replica of rented accommodation in any town and city just about anywhere. The two men exchanged a look and then followed her upstairs.

Her flat was a maelstrom of ideas, themes and colours. Where Ellis's room had been chaotic, an undisciplined mess of unfinished work and insanitary slovenliness, without purpose, Ruth Marks's flat seemed to reflect a mind that held so many enthusiasms that it rebelled against the constraints of order and ordinariness, so that dour prints of Munch's work were displayed on the same wall as a poster of patchwork intensity by Klimt and watercolours of the Cheshire countryside were hung next to Picasso prints. On her crowded bookshelves popular fiction vied with texts on neural networks and the silicon brain. Hackett scanned the mantelpiece; it was cluttered with postcards, curling with age and filmy with dust. He concluded that Ruth Marks was something of a hoarder. Wooden carvings of the three wise monkeys were arranged in a semicircle, in a conspiratorial huddle, partly obscuring a photograph of Helen Wilkinson, bundled up in a dark over-coat, and looking upwards in a dreamy pose. The remains of a Chinese take-away lay discarded on the low table next to the sofa, bringing a faint savoury whiff of stir-fry and the jaded smell of cold bean sprouts. Over all hung the too-familiar sweetish smell of marijuana.

'Dr Marks,' Nelson began.

Ruth had her back to them. She scratched at her side with one hand and waved Nelson down with the other. 'Give me a minute, will you? I've had a bloody awful night.' She stumbled to the far end of the room to a bank of steel shelving, which was covered by blue trellis-work at one end, dividing off the kitchen from the living area.

Nelson was content to give her time while he took in details of her living arrangements. Her PC rested at one end of a folding dining table, in a rather elaborate turret-style bay. Journals and papers lay on the table and were arranged with seeming purpose around the typist's chair by the computer. At the other end of the table was a microscope with a bin-ocular viewer. In a cabinet designed for displaying glassware and ornaments, there were more of the little bottles they had seen in Ellis's flat, but these contained vibrant communities of tiny insects which seemed to stream constantly in solid black rivulets along thin strips of filter paper, from the cobalt blue food matter to the cotton wool plugs. There was room for flight, too, in this microcosm of existence which Nelson found strangely claustrophobic.

Ruth had set a pot of coffee to filter. She stopped suddenly, setting down the mug she held with a clatter, and turned, her eyes wide. 'Helen?'

'She's all right, as far as we know.'

Ruth looked from the inspector to the sergeant, then drew the lapels of her slightly shabby dressing gown together and, tying the cord more tightly, reached for a loaf of bread from a large earthenware pot. She continued her breakfast preparations in a thoughtful mood. Within minutes the flat was filled with the dually tantalizing smells of coffee and toast. Hackett wondered fleetingly if this was an attempt to mask the smell of marijuana, but recalling the doctor's insatiable appetite for carbohydrates, he decided that the food preparations were intended to satisfy another, quite different need.

Ruth carried the meal through to the living area, nodding vaguely in the direction of a large, grubby linen-covered sofa. Nelson took up position at one end, sipping at his coffee and eyeing Ruth with a speculative stare.

Ruth cleared some textbooks from an armchair covered in the same material as the sofa, and dropped them at her feet; apparently she remained immune to Nelson's intimidatory tactics. 'So,' she said, 'if it's not Helen, why are you here? What's happened?'

Their solemn expressions warned her it was grim news, and Hackett was almost relieved she hadn't made some flip remark which Nelson could use to cruel effect later.

'I'd like you to tell us about John Ellis's relationship with Prof Wilkinson,' Nelson said.

'Relationship?' Ruth was ready to laugh but some instinct guided her to caution. She eased herself on to the armchair and rested the mug on the arm. A little coffee had slopped over the edge and she wiped it on the linen before saying, 'Ed's narcissism may have bordered on the psychotic, but he was strictly hetero.'

Hackett saw a muscle twitch in Nelson's jaw at the use of the word 'psychotic', but he remained admirably calm. 'He saw Mr Ellis on the day he died. We know there was an argument. Ellis made threats,' he explained carefully. 'We also know that Mr Ellis's research grant was guaranteed until autumn this year, so the row couldn't have been about funding. But they did have an almighty ding-dong and Ellis left the place screaming abuse at the professor. We'd like to know why.'

'Why don't you ask him yourself?' Ruth's tone was uncharacteristically wary, even apprehensive.

'He's beyond questioning,' Nelson replied.

'Beyond – are you saying—?' Ruth asked sharply.

'John Ellis took an overdose of barbiturates and alcohol yesterday evening,' Hackett explained. He felt Nelson tense beside him. 'He died sometime between 3 and 4 this morning.'

'Poor, stupid bastard,' Ruth murmured.

'We have photographs,' Nelson said.

Ruth sipped her coffee. 'Photographs?' she said.

Nelson took two black and white pictures from his pocket and handed them to Ruth. Ellis entering the Wilkinsons' house. Ellis placing a white cardboard box in the fridge.

Ruth studied them for a long time. 'Compelling,' she said at last.

'So, you see why we would like to know exactly what went on in the meeting between Ellis and Wilkinson on the day of the professor's murder.'

'Oh, I see,' Ruth said, passing the photographs back to Nelson. 'You think John killed Ed in a fit of rage and then did himself in out of remorse, is that it?'

'We're not jumping to any conclusions, Dr Marks.'

'Why not ask Valerie – Ed's secretary—'

'Yes,' Nelson said. 'We know who she is. Prof Wilkinson gave Mrs Roberts strict instructions to work on a recording of a report he wanted typing up, so she was wearing head-phones at the time. She heard voices raised, but not the details.'

Ruth smiled. 'Discreet as ever. Good old Valerie.'

'Dr Marks?' Hackett prompted, when it became apparent she did not intend to say more.

'I don't honestly see what I can tell you, gentlemen.'

'Oh,' said Nelson, softly, 'I think you do.'

Ruth looked uneasily from one to the other.

Nelson's smile was like cheese wire: thin, sharp and poten-tially dangerous. 'We've spoken to Alice Chambers. She says the Dean of Faculty got an anonymous e-mail yesterday.'

'The message?' Ruth asked impatiently.

'Said Ellis had been cooking the results. It suggested a comparison of his lab book with the data he's due to publish in his thesis. Miss Chambers said she had called Ellis to a meeting with the Dean of Faculty and one of the pro-vice chancellors. It was scheduled for ten o'clock this morning. They wanted a satisfactory answer to the allegations made.'

'Which of course the stupid little prick wouldn't be able to give them,' Ruth said bitterly. She shook her head. 'And you think I sent the message, is that it?'

'Anonymous mailings are traceable, given the right expertize and a little co-operation from the electronic mailer,' Hackett said, repeating what Jem Tact had told him just over an hour earlier.

For a moment, Ruth seemed furious, then she sighed. 'Helen's right, I'm not much good with the minutiae of cyber-technology. Academic life isn't nearly so cosseted and woolly as you might think, Inspector. These days it's about fulfilling quotas of one sort or another, a side effect of the Research Assessment Exercise we've just undergone. Staff have to justify their existence by pointing to recent research of national, or preferably international importance, but they also have to find ways of bringing money into the department. Then there's the increased teaching load to cope with. Lecturers don't always have time to do their own research, so they put their doctoral students under incredible pressure to come up with something they wouldn't be ashamed to put their name to. Of course they don't have time to supervise the work properly, so sometimes mistakes are made which aren't noticed, and occasionally – more times than I'd care to think too deeply about – results are fudged.'

'You discovered that John Ellis was "fudging" his results?' Nelson asked.

'The dream put me on to it – counting so many pearls and then giving Ed a different number. Lies, you see. They trip you up, unless you're damn good at it. Ellis was disorganized, a bloody disaster when it came to collecting reliable data. Computers are remarkable machines – give them something reasonable to work with, say a quarter of your results, and they can manufacture a whole new set on a random basis, fill in the blanks. You can even write in a variation about the mean that fits in with the statistical evidence. Saves all the hassle of doing the reps—'

'Reps?' Nelson cut in.

'Replications – repeats of the experiment to check your first set of results wasn't just a fluke. But most fiddlers just leave out the odd result that doesn't quite fit with the trend, or which might make their statistical significance less than impressive. That way their graphs turn out as nice straight lines or curves instead of dog-legs or something resembling a temperature chart. Ellis had dropped a few inconvenient points from his graphs, and to be frank, I don't think he had the skill to do the job properly.'

Nelson stared fixedly at a point somewhere over Ruth's left shoulder, then he nodded to himself. 'Miss Chambers says the panel was a formality. He would have been dismissed from the department immediately.'

'Well,' Ruth said, running her fingers through her hair, 'on this occasion it gives me no gratification to be proved right. None at all.'

'If that's how you feel, why report him?' Nelson demanded.

Ruth was shocked. 'I'm a scientist. I search for truth – I'm sorry if that sounds callow, unworldly, but it's how I feel. What Ellis did discredits the whole scientific community. His research was bullshit, and I have to put up with enough of that from my peers without sanctioning the lies of a second-rate doctoral student. Anyway, if he'd published, the statisticians would've punched a hole the size of Antarctica through his data. And, there were other considerations: the reputation of the university would have suffered; 30 per cent job losses might've become 50 per cent. I didn't want that on my conscience.'

'Very public-spirited of you, Dr Marks,' Nelson said.

Ruth smiled. 'Didn't think altruism was a part of my biological make-up, did you, Inspector? Well, you'd be surprised.'

'You seem to be saying that the argument between Ellis and Prof Wilkinson was about Ellis fiddling his results,' Hackett said. 'And yet there is no record of a complaint against him in Wilkinson's computer files.'

'I thought you'd seen the *shop* entry.'

'Senate House Overview of Progress.'

Ruth stared, her eyebrows raised, astonished that they could have overlooked so obvious a clue. Hackett took a breath, shook his head and exhaled. If it wasn't so bloody tragic, it'd be funny. 'Our original assessment was correct.'

'I'm afraid so,' Ruth said. 'No acronym. Just plain, old-fashioned slang. Edward was going to shop the silly little sod. His mistake was letting Ellis know that.'

Nelson snorted. 'Didn't you say postgraduate students rated somewhere below an amoeba, Dr Marks? Why would Prof Wilkinson be interested in the petty cheating of a student who wasn't even under his supervision?'

'I think what I actually said was that he ranked just *above*, but you're right, most professors would have neither the time, nor the interest in the students under their aegis. Edward, you must remember, liked to control people.' A small puff exploded from her lips. 'People, Events, Policy. Edward's version of a PEP – and he got a good return on his equity. Look how far he'd risen in a relatively short period of time. Edward was also something of a sadist. He was probably just toying with the poor sod, but he didn't bank on Ellis's instability. *The value of investments can go down as well as up.* I can understand why Ellis would want to kill Edward, but I really can't say why he'd kill himself, unless he thought he couldn't live with the shame of fucking up his research so publicly. After all, as far as your murder investigation goes, he was virtually in the clear – it isn't as if you'd made a great deal of progress with the case prior to his suicide, had you?'

A thoughtful silence settled on the three, and Nelson, exchanging a glance with Hackett, rose to leave. He placed his coffee mug on the floor beside the sofa and straightened up. Perhaps it was the harshness of the light, or perhaps it was simply that he hadn't slept for a day and a night. Whatever the reason, Hackett saw Nelson not only as a hard practitioner of the law, not above bullying, cajoling, or deceit to achieve a result, but as a lonely, unhappy and ageing policeman bewildered by the changes imposed on him by the emphasis on work quotas and lack of funding, equal opportunities and political correctness, and to compound the perplexity of his situation, he had no home life, and a son he didn't understand and couldn't love.

'The photographs—'

Hackett turned to her. He got the impression that Dr Marks had blurted this out, that she was, for once, uncertain of her ground, but he had been so absorbed in analysing Nelson that he had missed her facial expression. 'Where on *earth* did you get hold of them?' she finished.

'A journalist from the *Chester Recorder*.'

'Press? I thought those bloody vultures had all flown. Picking over the bones of some other tragedy.'

Nelson flashed her a look of – of what? she asked herself. Aggression – she was used to that from Nelson – but was there also resentment? 'Ellis tried to kill the "vulture" who took these pictures,' he said, shocking her out of her puzzled study.

She stared hard at Nelson. '*Tried* to—'

'Torched his flat.' Nelson's eyes blazed suddenly as if with some reflection of the inferno. 'But we recovered the pictures.'

'How? I mean, if he set fire to the flat—'

'Molyneux had sent the pictures by computer fax. Scanned them into his computer and then zipped them along the information superhighway to the *Recorder*.' Molyneux's boss, Jeff Townley, had brought the photographs personally, as soon as he found them on his return to the office in the morning. 'That's how we found Ellis so soon. If it hadn't been for the photographs, the body might've been undiscovered for days.'

'As I said,' Ruth observed dryly, 'computers are remarkable machines.' She frowned suddenly, chewing at the inside of her cheek. 'The photographer?'

'In a coma,' Hackett answered. 'He may not make it.'

As they left, clumping down the grey stairs unaccompanied, Hackett said, 'I can see why Ellis'd want to kill the prof, and it makes sense he'd have a go at Helen if he thought she'd dropped him in it with the Senate. But I don't understand why he'd bash the photographer over the head and try to destroy the photographs when he intended going home for booze and barbs.' He sensed a watchfulness in Nelson and murmured, 'Sorry, sir.'

'For what?' Nelson turned viciously on him and they stood at the foot of the stairs, locked in another duel of egos.

Hackett shrugged. 'Nowt.'

'It certainly looks like Ellis planned to go home and top himself,' Nelson said, picking up where Hackett had left off. Transgression forgiven, Hackett thought, relieved. 'So why would he give a monkey's backside if he'd been snapped in the act?'

'Doesn't make an awful lot of sense,' Hackett agreed.

They lingered a few moments longer outside Ruth's house in a pool of rare warm sunshine. 'My feeling is, Ellis's trick with the mouse and the attack on Molyneux are unconnected.'

Hackett was less certain. He thought they were connected, though indirectly.

Hackett stopped off at the Countess of Chester Hospital on his way home; he couldn't rest until he had seen the young photographer. He checked his watch as he went in: Nelson would want him back at headquarters by mid-afternoon, but he hoped the house would be empty so that he could shower and get a couple of hours rest. He needed to talk to Sheila about Daniel's continuing rebellion, but he also needed sleep, and right now that would have to take priority.

Molyneux was in the Intensive Care unit. A WPC had been posted outside the glass-fronted ward, with strict instructions to check and verify the identity of anyone entering. She duly scrutinized Hackett's warrant card, but waived the formality of a phone call to headquarters.

'No need, sir. Saw you on telly with DI Nelson.'

Hackett stepped into the antiseptic air of the high-dependency unit. The nursing staff moved about quietly, checking and adjusting the bewildering complexity of digital instruments, occasionally exchanging a word or two with the exhausted, silent figures seated next to most of the beds, afraid to leave, determined that if their mother or husband or child was to die, they would not die alone. There was no rush, no panic, even the lighting was subdued; the atmosphere was one of quiet efficiency. There were five patients in all and Hackett quickly found Molyneux. He had a visitor. Hackett recognized him immediately as Jeff Townley, the editor of the *Chester Recorder*. He had turned up at Molyneux's flat when one of his reporters, sent to cover the story of the fire, telephoned him and told him who the victim was.

Townley looked pale and tired. He had a heavy growth of stubble on his chin, and looked uncomfortable with it. He held a packet of cigarettes in his hand as though he had been distracted in the act of taking one out of the pack. A blood vessel throbbed in his temple and he gave the impression that he was both angry and upset.

'Any news?' Hackett asked.

Townley gave him a bleak smile. 'They say it looks worse than it actually is.' His eyes roved over the respirator tube, the drips and monitor wires, attached to the lean frame of the Irishman. 'Let's hope they're right.' He sighed. 'He's going to be so pissed off when he sees they've shaved off his hair.' Then, wincing at his own clumsy attempt at humour, he hurried on: 'They've sedated him because they're worried about him moving – the skull fracture could—' He stopped. 'I should never have allowed him to take on that bloody assignment!' His voice caught and he coughed. 'They say the next few days will be crucial.'

'His parents?'

'They'll be here by early evening.'

They listened to the click and hiss of the respirator for

some minutes without speaking and Hackett offered up a silent prayer.

'Did you come just to see the lad, or was there something you wanted to ask me?'

'You mentioned an assignment. Did you have reason to believe it could be dangerous?'

'Bloody Ellis!'

'We went to his flat,' Hackett started to explain.

'I know. It's my job to know. Overdose.' He shrugged. 'Doesn't help Dermot though, does it?' He glanced apologetically at Molyneux before saying, 'He'll hate me for betraying a trust, but—' He shrugged. 'To be honest I was more worried it'd be a waste of time. He'd had a tip from one of your lot.'

'Police?'

Townley nodded.

'Did he mention a name?'

'No, but I could check with the news team – see if he mentioned her to anyone.'

'Her?'

'He was quite specific about that. D'you want me to—?'

'I'd be grateful.' Hackett waited a few moments, then, registering Townley's hesitation and guessing its cause, he said, 'You go ahead. I'll watch him till you get back.' Townley had a cigarette in his mouth even before he had left the unit.

During his brief vigil Hackett had an opportunity to reflect on the events of the previous night. Something had been bothering him, some detail, teasing at the edges of consciousness and now, as he watched the steady rise and fall of the respirator and the fluctuating count of Dermot's pulse on the digital read-out, the feeling became more tangible and it framed itself as Nelson's question:

Why *would* Ellis take the trouble to try and cover up the sick prank on Dr Wilkinson? Presumably he had killed himself, as Ruth had suggested, because of his imminent exposure as a cheat and an incompetent, but hiding the fact that he had put the butchered animal in Helen's fridge would not have saved him from the humiliation of being dismissed from the university. In fact, it made more sense that he would *want* her to know who had left the box. Was this mendacity in the doctoral student force of habit, something that had become so much a part of his life that he didn't know when to stop? Or was it possible that someone had set Ellis up? After all, leaving the dissected mouse in Helen's fridge didn't make him a murderer. It did, however suggest a deeply unpleasant mind, and that might lead a plodding copper to think Ellis capable of more than this single, spiteful act.

He continued watching the rise and fall of Molyneux's chest, mechanically induced, an imitation of life and, in his depressed frame of mind, an intimation of impending death. Townley returned, breaking in on these morbid thoughts. His telephone conversation had proved unproductive. 'A woman, as I thought. A detective constable – that's all he'd said.'

Hackett groaned inwardly. Nelson would make of this an opportunity for griping about the unreliability of women detectives. 'We'll investigate from our end.' There weren't that many to choose from, so the task wouldn't be all that difficult.

He scuffed down the hospital corridors deep in thought. Where were Helen Wilkinson and Mick Tuttle between 11 p.m. and 12.30 the previous night? They said they had taken the scenic route back to Helen's house, but could just as easily have taken a taxi to Dermot's flat, hit him over the head, and torched the place. Had they been wrong to rule Helen out?

A blast of cold air and icy rain roused Hackett from his reverie. He found himself outside the hospital, with his car on the far side of the car park, and in it, his overcoat. He turned up his jacket collar and made a run for it. If Ellis really *had* left cakes, either Helen or Tuttle were perfectly capable of performing the dissection on the mouse and switching it for Ellis's offering – although he had to admit, Dr Wilkinson did look pretty sick afterwards . . . But why would she draw attention back to herself when pressure was just beginning to ease off? Of course she might've looked sick because she'd just got back from beating a man senseless and then setting his flat alight. In which case, the mouse was a suitable diversion. Made her seem the victim instead of the aggressor. There again, was it really feasible that Ellis had popped into Dr Wilkinson's with a box of cakes and then went off to top himself? And where had he got the keys from? None had been found in his flat, and yet he'd let himself into Helen's house. So, either he'd stolen and then dumped them, or he'd been loaned a set, which meant Helen, or someone close to her, was in on it.

He sat in the car for several minutes, gripping the steering wheel in concentration, and dripping rainwater. Why would Helen attack Dermot Molyneux in the first place? Why not let him use the photographs of Ellis in the next issue of the *Recorder*, alongside the bizarre story of the dissected mouse? Perhaps Dermot had got more than he bargained for – but who else had he photographed? Helen? Tuttle? Or both of them? And what the hell had they been up to?

And what about Clara Ainsley? They had an admission that she had seen Wilkinson at home, at around the time of the murder. Might she have gone back to the house to recover some evidence? What if Molyneux had photographed her? But this was pure speculation – Molyneux had computer–faxed two photographs, not three, and they had both been of Ellis. He fervently hoped Jem Tact would be able to work one of his miracles on Molyneux's computer.

Ruth picked at the chips on her plate. The refectory was noisy with lunch time traffic; the same disparate mixture of foreign visitors, lecturers, technicians and doctoral students as before although the students staying in halls this week were Japanese – they were quieter and more polite than the previous week's visitors, and Ruth looked on with amusement at the dismayed expression on some of the faces as they picked at the greasy mound of fish and chips on their plates. 'I tell you, the chef is a sadist,' she remarked.

'What?' Helen had managed soup and a roll and was feeling marginally pleased with herself.

Ruth looked down at her own plate and shoved it from her, disgusted. 'I just can't get that bloody animal out of my head. I mean is that how it is for you? Is that what it's like, constantly thinking of the blood and that poor mangled—'

'Don't do this, Ruth.' Helen was disturbed by the notion that Ruth was angry with her, punishing her for something.

'Well I can't look at food without seeing that damned mouse crucified on a board.'

'Ruth, shut up.'

Ruth stared, arched an eyebrow.

'I'm sorry, but you do go on at the worst of times and in the grossest detail.'

Ruth beat her breast in penitence, levelling a sardonic smile at her friend. 'I hope you know who you should thank for the sudden emergence of the new, forthright you,' she said.

In the pause, Helen wondered if she meant Mick.

'The angel of mercy who topped Edward,' Ruth said, attacking her chips with renewed appetite.

Sweet sounds, sweet, mellow scents. Daniel lay back on his bed and closed his eyes, imagining himself on the Andean mountains, visualizing the vast tracts of green and thin wisps of steamy condensation above the tree canopy. He took another drag from the inexpertly rolled spliff which he had made using a diagram a friend had drawn for him; three pieces, two end to end, and one to bind them together. He sucked deep, taking the smoke to the bottom of his lungs, like he'd been shown, and held his breath, waiting for the chemicals to find their way into his bloodstream. Simple diffusion, he thought, inadvertently allowing his biology revision to intrude on his thoughts. He giggled, expelling puffs of smoke. THCs in, stress *out!*

Terry Hackett pulled into the drive and sat for a minute or two, his eyes closed, trying to find the energy to get out of the car. An hour's sleep, then shower and back out, and find out who had leaked information to the Press, he told himself.

Daniel's bedroom window was open. 'How many times do I have to tell him that most burglaries are opportunistic?' he grumbled to himself as he found his key and let himself in. The bloody Yale wasn't double-locked, either.

Daniel was beginning to float. Some of his mates at school didn't rate Rocky, because they said it just made them feel dizzy, they preferred Skunk, but they didn't have dads with noses like bloody Pinocchio. Anyway, this . . . He sighed, smiling to himself. This was more than dizziness. This was special. He took another pull on his joint and relaxed to the South American music he had picked up on his last protest weekend. An Ecowarrior called Treecreeper had sold it to him. She was *gorgeous.* He listened to the breathy tones of the pan pipes, and pictured himself with Treecreeper on the platform of the tree she was protecting, smoking dope, listening to music, kissing . . .

She had two rings in her lower lip, and he tried to imagine how it would feel, tonguing the thin rim of gold, probing deeper into her mouth, his hand around her waist, straying under the rough edge of her woven waistcoat, beneath the coarse linen of her shirt, to flesh and bone. He groaned.

Hackett stamped upstairs, feeling increasingly irritated with

Daniel. He had no regard for their feelings. He sneered at their perfectly reasonable requests to switch off lights, or to close doors and windows, and yet he constantly lectured them about their exploitation of the environment with their use of two cars, and the washing machine and God knew what all else.

He opened Daniel's bedroom door.

Daniel leapt from his bed, yanking the radio-cassette, still attached to the headphones, from his bedside table. It fell with a clatter and the tape ejected. Daniel fastened his trousers, mortally embarrassed to have been caught in an erotic fantasy by his father.

Hackett strode over to his son and dragged the remains of the spliff from his hand, then pulled the headphones off. 'What the hell do you think you're doing?'

Daniel was too shaken to sneer.

'You should be in school. Why aren't you in school? Where did you get this?'

Daniel didn't know which question to answer first. He stood, blushing to his ears, wondering with agonizing distress if his father had seen him with his hand down his trousers.

'This is illegal, Daniel. Who's your supplier?'

Daniel regarded him in mute rebellion.

'Do you know what this stuff does to you? Do you know the lasting damage marijuana can cause?'

Daniel recovered enough to say, 'No one calls it *that* any more, Dad.'

'I don't give a *monkeys* what you call it,' Hackett yelled. 'Where's the rest?'

He started rummaging through Daniel's things.

'Dad!'

He turned on the boy. 'Empty your pockets,' he demanded. '*What?*'

'You'll bloody well do it here and now, or you'll do it down the nick.'

For a moment, neither moved. Daniel stared at him with absolute hatred, then he began emptying his pockets.

Hackett tried to contact Nelson at headquarters and at home. His mobile was out of action and he wasn't answering on his home number. No one had seen him or heard from him since they had split up after reporting in briefly that morning.

Hackett had taken a frightened and sullen Daniel to school, and had spoken to the headmaster, requesting that any and all absences be reported to him or his wife immediately. Sheila had gone to visit her sister in Leeds for the day, which was why Daniel had thought he wouldn't be disturbed. Hackett had arranged for his mother to be at home when school finished, and had left his mobile number so that she could let him know if Daniel was late. She had been delighted to be of use, and, mercifully, had not asked any awkward questions. He would talk to her and to Sheila that evening, and they would decide what sanctions to impose on Daniel.

In the meantime, he could not rest, and decided to drive around to his superior's house. He rang the bell and, turning his back to the door, cast a critical eye over the garden. Hackett helped Sheila with the garden when he could spare the time, actually enjoying it; he even knew the names of a few of the plants. Nelson's garden consisted of a square patch of lawn, well trimmed, a border ruthlessly weeded, but without a single flower or shrub. A barren suburban square.

He returned to headquarters and sought out Sergeant Brinckley. Jane had known Nelson a long time and Hackett had noticed that he tolerated her more easily than most.

'He got a call,' she said. 'Sounded urgent.' Hackett understood from her quick, frowning glance around the room that there was more to say, but not here under the eyes and within the hearing of people who, by profession and habit, were unashamed eavesdroppers.

He waited a couple of minutes, sifting through his memos to make it look like he had something to do other than track down his boss, and found the long-awaited search on Helen Wilkinson from Bolton. A rapid skim through the report increased his unease that they had been so quick to dismiss Helen as a suspect, and also prompted him to telephone his mother and tell her that Daniel was not to go to his room when he got in, but was to do his homework with her in the kitchen.

He followed the sergeant out of the open-plan office and into the corridor. She pushed through the door leading to the back stairs and waited for him.

'His son?' Hackett asked, saving her from the ignominy of betraying the inspector's trust so directly.

Jane nodded – a slight flicker of movement, no more.

Hackett considered asking – actually opened his mouth to speak – then decided against it: the sergeant had gone as far as she was prepared to.

'Thanks,' he said. 'If he gets in touch, tell him I've gone to question Wilkinson and Tuttle. Ask him to contact me urgently.'

She nodded, relieved that he had not asked for more.

'Jane—' Her expression grew pained. 'It's not about Nelson, but I do have a favour to ask.'

'You can ask,' she said, warily.

'Someone's been leaking info to the Press – about John Ellis. It's probably the reason we've got a photographer in hospital and a house burned out. For all I know, it triggered Ellis's suicide.'

'Messy.'

Hackett's forehead crinkled. 'Molyneux was shadowing Ellis,

hoping to be there at the arrest or something. His boss thinks Molyneux's source was a WDC.'

Jane Brinckley winced. 'You want me to find out who?'

'It'd be better coming from you than from me.'

Chapter Twenty-Two

Conor Smith had known Jack Nelson for ten years. In that time he had developed, perhaps even nurtured, a profound dislike of the man. Nelson's son, Ian, had been admitted as a patient during Dr Smith's first week at Wesley Hospital. Since that time, Ian had returned either as a voluntary patient or under a 'section' on scores of occasions. Nelson had refused to have anything to do with his son after he had reached sixteen, and so Care in the Community had meant, for Ian, a series of hostels, bedsits and, latterly, doorways and dosses. He had disappeared for a few weeks, living rough, returning to the hospital some nights earlier because his voices were whispering to him to kill someone, and his only source of pride, the only sense of achievement Ian had, was in knowing that he had never harmed anyone but himself.

Smith searched Nelson's face for some glimmer of compassion or regret or guilt – any hint that the man was reachable, any sign of emotion that would make him despise Nelson less and perhaps help him to understand a little.

'I'd only make him worse,' Nelson said, staring back at him.

'He's *asking* for you.'

'You saw what he was like last time.'

'He needs you,' Smith insisted. 'He's afraid of you, but he needs you. Let him know he doesn't need to be afraid.'

'I never laid a finger on him.' A slight flare of indignation in those curious marmalade-orange eyes.

Smith wanted to tell Nelson that his total rejection of his son, the literal fact that he 'never laid a finger' on Ian unless to perform some unavoidable act of care, perfunctorily and without affection, had wrought up the young man's psychosis, that he was convinced Ian would be a normal, sane twenty year old if Nelson had responded to him and loved him, instead of depriving him of human contact and parental approval and affection from the day of his birth.

Nelson shrugged. 'The boy is worse when I'm around.'

He can't even give him his name.

'Ian needs you,' Smith said calmly. Ten years of psychiatric work had trained him in the art of hiding his true feelings so effectively that sometimes he had trouble analysing what he truly felt. 'If you don't speak to him, I can't vouch for his safety.'

'I'm no good to him,' Nelson said, stubbornly, but would not meet his eye, and Smith knew he was making headway.

'Ian has a knife in there. I think he'll use it if you don't talk to him.'

For a fleeting instant Nelson looked up and Smith saw in his eyes an icy crystal of hope that all of this would finally end. It melted in the heat of shame and anger that followed. *Now* Smith began to understand. What Nelson desired most was what he was constitutionally incapable of achieving: he was one of the breed which longs for peace and creates only strife. Was it, Smith wondered, his wife's death that had set up this irreconcilable conflict, or had Nelson always been like this? Had Nelson driven his wife to despair with his endless struggle against his own discontent – and blamed Ian rather than face his own part in her suicide?

'Aren't you going to get a warrant, Sarge?' DC Wright was anxious: he didn't like taking action without DI Nelson's say-so.

'We don't need a warrant to ask a few questions, Constable.'

'Yeah, but—'

'The Super's approved this course of action, in DI Nelson's absence,' Hackett said, shrewdly striking at the heart of Wright's objections.

Wright had worked with Nelson long enough to know that he liked to be in control of things, long enough, also, to lose the imperative of working on initiative which had once been so important to him. He nodded. They'd have to wait a bit, anyway, if Hackett wanted to interview her at home. With a bit of luck, the boss would be back in time.

In the event, they waited until 5.30, acting on a message from the surveillance team that had been placed outside Helen Wilkinson's house. When Wright came through with the message, Hackett had been dozing pleasantly in Nelson's chair.

'Still no sign of the boss, then, Sarge?' Wright said, remembering with spiteful glee something Nelson had said about Hackett reminding him of a ginger tom his wife had once owned.

Hackett narrowed his eyes. Smiling, he stood and turned his back to the constable. 'D'you see any boot marks on my backside?'

Jerked out of his ill-will by the shock of having his mind read a second time, Wright muttered, 'No, Sarge,' then blushed at the stupidity of the answer. When he mustered the courage to meet Hackett's eye, the sergeant chuckled.

'Just remember the boot is on *my* foot, at least for the moment, eh, Wright?'

'I'll get my coat,' Wright answered. He wore an anorak of the type which Hackett's children described as 'sad'. Navy-blue, with a flimsy hood and a drawstring cord which tied under the chin. In other respects the constable showed reasonable taste: a good quality suit and a colourful range of silk ties, but the anorak, Hackett thought, was a mistake.

'What d'you expect to find, Sarge?' Wright asked, breaking a silence which in the confines of the car was too uncomfortable to sustain, even on the short ride from headquarters to the Wilkinsons' house. Wright was sensitive to atmosphere.

Hackett leaned across Wright and pressed the release button of the glove compartment. 'Take a look at those pictures.'

Wright slid the two photographs on to his lap. Ellis checking the roadway before nipping down the side entry. Ellis with a white box in his hand. His own personal version of Dunkin' Donuts.

'So?'

Hackett tapped the first picture. 'The car.' A gleaming silver-grey Nissan stood outside the Wilkinsons' house. 'It's not hers. I checked.'

'Well if you checked, you must know whose it is, then.'

Hackett grinned. 'Oh, I do. And I'd be interested to know if she does. 'Course, it'd be even more instructive if we knew what that poor bugger Molyneux had photographed – aside from Ellis with his confectionery delights, that is.' He turned down the corners of his mouth. 'But they've had plenty of time to clear up since last night, so I'll settle for a chance to sniff around—' He frowned, thinking of Helen Wilkinson, the thud overhead, finding her on the landing, the shock on her face, and the obvious lie that she had told about feeling faint and stumbling. 'Check the upstairs rooms, maybe,' he finished, somewhat distracted.

'Without a warrant?'

Hackett smiled. Wright was nothing if not dogged. 'It's surprising what people will agree to. After all, she is a grieving widow, isn't she? Surely a grieving widow would do anything to find her husband's murderer . . .'

Wright shrugged, unconvinced. 'D'you think someone's helping her?'

In answer to Hackett's quick, questioning look he went on, 'You said *they've* had chance to clear up. D'you reckon it's the gimp?'

Hackett shifted a little in his seat, the word offended his sensibilities. '*Doctor* Tuttle, or even her friend, Dr Marks.' He changed down, turning into the street which over the last week or so had become almost as familiar to him as his own. At this time of the day, the Wilkinsons' house was in deep shadow, while the other side of the street twinkled in sunshine after a shower. 'Dr Marks strikes me as the sort of woman who doesn't make affiliations, let alone friendships, lightly. But I should think she'd do a lot for someone she did like.'

'Pity you can't get them all together in the drawing room and sweat a confession out of them.' It was said with heavy sarcasm.

Hackett surprised him by laughing. 'It worked for Poirot, eh, Wright?' He drew in to the kerb and stilled the engine. 'I'm not sure she's got a drawing room – d'you think the kitchen will do?'

Wright got out of the car scowling. Hackett had managed to turn the tables again, making it look like it was *him* who was making all these bloody daft suggestions. Unsworth upset him further by strolling over from the surveillance car with his hands in his pockets and asking, 'What's up, Wrighty? Piles bothering you?'

Hackett laughed again. 'He's just feeling a bit *Hackett* off, eh, Wright?'

Unsworth raised his eyebrows at the pun and the sour look it elicited from Wright. Hackett seemed positively jaunty for someone who'd had no sleep for thirty-odd hours.

'She got here about twenty minutes ago. Arrived with Dr Marks,' he said.

Hackett nodded. 'I see the Press have made the connection between Molyneux and this lot.' Two sodden and rather sorry-looking journalists loitered outside the gate. 'If Tuttle arrives, make sure he doesn't leave until I've spoken to him.' Then, taking a deep breath of damp, grassy air, he walked, smiling, over to the journalists. Wright followed in bad humour.

Unsworth returned to the car. Sitting in it all afternoon, he had become inured to the combined smells of chips and stale farts and Wrigley's gum. He now wound down the window with a grimace of distaste.

'Hackett looks happy,' his partner commented.

'Wouldn't you? Not having to look over your shoulder for a change, see where Jack the Knife's going to stick the blade?'

Ruth Marks answered the door. 'All on your own, Sergeant?'

Hackett deliberately misunderstood the reference to Nelson's absence. 'I have DC Wright with me, Dr Marks.' Wright had his warrant card ready. Ruth took it from him, making a careful comparison of the photograph with the real thing.

'Doesn't do you justice.' A smile twitched at the corner of her mouth as she returned it to the blushing constable. 'But that's the British legal system for you. Come through.'

Hackett was once more struck by the way she moved. An easy stride, which emphasized the roll of her hips. It puzzled him, because instinctively he knew she wasn't interested in either him or Wright, she seemed to relish it as a game, this sexual teasing.

There was something different about the kitchen. He felt it as soon as he entered the room. It may have been in the brighter, more alert attention of Helen Wilkinson. Did she think the danger of discovery was past? Perhaps, but there was an alteration in the room itself, as though the furniture had been rearranged. He made a quick survey. All seemed neat, well ordered, unchanged from the previous night.

'How can I help you, Sergeant Hackett?' Helen asked.

'We've checked with the restaurant,' he replied. 'They've confirmed you left at eleven o'clock, but we haven't found anyone who saw you between that time and 12.30 when we were called to your house.'

'It was a wild night. There weren't many people about.'

Hackett grunted non-committally. Checks with local taxi firms had turned up nothing, but they had only Dr Wilkinson's word that she had left her car at home and walked into Chester. Hackett looked over at Wright. He fished in the inside pocket of his anorak for the photographs and placed them side by side on the kitchen table. Hackett took a step back and leaned against the sink unit. Helen cast a furtive glance at him, feeling herself colouring.

Ruth picked up the shot of Ellis outside the house and peered at it. She laughed suddenly. 'Isaac Smolder!'

'What?' Helen, grateful for the distraction from the thought of the knife – the murder weapon – being so close, moved nearer.

'Look—' Ruth held up the picture for Helen to see. 'That's Isaac's car. There doesn't seem to be anyone in it. I wonder where he was hiding. Jeez, Helen, you draw them like flies to shit!'

Helen looked, startled, into her friend's face.

'Manner of speech,' Ruth said. 'Bees to a honey pot, wasps to a picnic, butterflies to a buddleia. Whatever.'

'Is there any reason you can think of, why Dr Smolder would be outside your house?' Hackett asked.

Helen shuddered. Smolder with his papery skin and his cold, analytical scrutiny. He seemed to like watching her, always positioning himself in the refectory or the coffee bar where he could see and be seen. She heard the whisper of his

233

thumb against his forefinger as he carefully rubbed each tiny crumb of bread from his hands to his plate, an action so ritualistic she had half expected him to pick up the plate and wipe the crumbs into his glass – bread and wine. *Body and Blood*. The thought drew her eyes back to the sink unit, where Hackett stood.

'Dr Wilkinson?'

'Sorry? Oh, no. I can think of no earthly reason why he . . .' Her voice trailed off. It made her sick to think he had been outside her house, his unblinking eyes watching, watchful.

'You haven't had any other nasty surprises, Dr Wilkinson?'

Helen blanched, then recovered. 'No. Why do you ask?'

'It seems Ellis thought you had reported him to the Senate. Otherwise, why the rather crude attempt to shock you?'

'Not so crude,' Ruth said. She went to the kitchen unit and, having hustled the sergeant to one side, began rooting in the top drawer. Helen held her breath. 'There was a lot of blood,' she explained, 'which shows that he knew about Helen's previous research. Also' – she took out a teaspoon and slammed the drawer closed – 'in choosing a pregnant female, he demonstrated a knowledge of *why* she's unable to perform that particular aspect of her research now. I'd say brutal, rather than crude.'

Helen forced her attention from the set of drawers to Ruth, who was stirring large quantities of sugar into her coffee.

'You won't mind if we scout round and make sure he *didn't* leave anything else?' Hackett was already in the hallway when he heard a distinct and forceful:

'Yes, I *do* mind.' Helen jumped to her feet. She couldn't allow them to search the house. Not with the knife basking like a shark in the kitchen drawer.

He turned back.

'Why?'

'I don't have to give an explanation,' Helen said, trying to keep her voice steady, 'but I'll tell you anyway. I'm sick of the intrusion. My house doesn't seem like my own any more. If you want to search it, you'll have to get a warrant.'

Hackett saw that Helen's new-found confidence was a flimsy construct. He was about to push the point when Ruth Marks intervened for him.

'Helen! This is nice Sergeant Hackett. He's only trying to help.'

Helen stood her ground. 'I won't have them tramping through the house, prying—'

'Well, of course you are within your rights to refuse us permission to look around, but I *will* get a warrant, Dr Wilkinson, there's no question of that. You see we got notice today of a previous conviction. Assault, causing grievous bodily harm. That rather changes the complexion of things.'

Helen blinked. Staring out into the dimly lit hallway, she saw only the oily black night, a drizzle making a thousand pinpoints of light in the headlamp beams.

He's standing near a doorway, shuttered, as they all are against the vandals and the drug addicts. No shelter, but he doesn't need it; he can trade in broad daylight without fear of being caught. In the spotlight of the headlamps she sees something else – a quick movement, a flash of something silver, foil-wrapped. Sleight of hand: Now you see it, now you don't. Then he crosses the street, heading towards his own car.

She pulls out, anxious, the new driver, unsure of the acceleration, the power of her car. She needs to catch him before he gets to his car, to safety.

He turns, a casual look over his shoulder. He is handsome, young, convinced of his own immortality. An image comes unbidden, unwanted, of Robbie, grey, lifeless, already melting into a past she would give anything to be able to rewrite.

The pusher slows his pace, arrogant, daring her to sound her horn. Her foot presses heavily on the accelerator and the car slews a little to the left. Then she's moving forward, fast. She aims the car full at him and he turns again, smiling at first, but then alarmed. Terror strikes his features as they struck Robbie's. He tries to throw himself to one side, too late.

'What was it, Dr Wilkinson? Two years? It would have been a lot longer if he'd died, but you were lucky – that time.'

'Helen?' For the first time, Ruth seemed unsure of Helen. Uncertain how to react. Her cool cynicism failed her entirely.

Helen shrugged her off. Returning to the kitchen, she went to the sink and ran a glass of water. 'There was no luck in it,' she said. 'If I'd been *lucky*, my brother would be alive today.'

Hackett felt sickened by his own hypocrisy: he had wanted to beat seven bells out of the dealer who had sold Daniel the marijuana – he heard Daniel, exasperated, telling him *nobody* called it that any more. If he had been able to get a name out of his son, he probably would have gone looking for him. He might even have rammed the filthy stuff down his throat.

Chapter Twenty-Three

Nelson was surprisingly philosophical about the usurping of his authority. He even congratulated Hackett on his success. Nobody mentioned his unexplained absence – Nelson was not the sort of man whose health and well-being were enquired after: he had, over the years, cultivated in his subordinates a healthy respect for his privacy. The Super had called him into his office on his return, and he had gone without demur, another unusual occurrence.

Nelson had been with the Superintendent some thirty minutes, but he showed no signs of stress, nor even of annoyance. He was poker-faced, inscrutable.

Wright gained confidence with the return of his boss. It made him belligerent. 'I don't get it,' he said, suddenly heated, exasperated. 'We've got a confession from Clara Ainsley that she went to the professor's house just before he was killed. She admits she was pissed off with him – understatement – 'cos he was having it off with someone else. And you're not even interested.'

Nelson's eyes gleamed. 'Not interested, Hackett?'

'Let's say the focus of my interest has shifted.'

'Well,' Nelson growled. 'Let's hear it.'

Hackett explained that he had found the report on Helen Wilkinson on his desk that afternoon. She had deliberately run down the pusher who had supplied the E's that had killed her brother. He had survived, but she had been sent down for two years; the charge should have been attempted murder, but she had a sympathetic and extremely persuasive barrister. He recounted the details of their visit to Dr Wilkinson, her reaction to the news that Smolder's car had been parked outside her house, her refusal to let them search the house, all delivered in his usual, efficient, dispassionate manner, neither elaborating, nor offering his own interpretation, but sticking to reporting the plain facts.

'Missed anything, have I?'

Wright looked at his shoes and muttered 'No.'

Nelson thought for some time and Hackett left him to it.

'Have you applied for a warrant?' Nelson said at last. Hackett nodded.

'There's a few unanswered questions, as yet,'

Both Wright and Hackett answered 'Yes,' but somehow Wright felt his enthusiastic affirmative was the wrong answer.

Nelson and Hackett renewed eye contact. There was an exchange between them which Wright could not fully understand, because he had never before seen respect for another copper in Nelson's eyes.

'*Shershay le fem*,' Nelson said, elliptically.

Hackett dipped his head, self-deprecatingly. 'Have been, sir, but the prof's MO was to be extremely discreet in his early liaisons with a new lover. It was only when he got bored he got careless.'

'Clara Ainsley *invented* the other woman!' Wright said, heatedly. 'Why would he be seeing another woman when he'd got her all set up with a job as his secretary?'

'Last fling?' Hackett suggested.

'Couldn't help himself? One night stand? Or afternoon delight, to be more precise,' Nelson added.

'This is crazy!'

'You could be right, lad,' Nelson agreed. 'You could well be right.'

'But whichever way you look at it, Clara Ainsley is in the clear for the attack on Molyneux,' Hackett chipped in. 'Her mother came up from Swindon to stay with her yesterday. Apparently her husband has moved out, and the baby's driving her up the wall. She was with her the entire evening.'

'She's not in the clear for the murder, though, is she?' Wright said.

'No,' Nelson agreed. 'But it seems likely whoever did the murder, also attacked Molyneux.'

Hackett nodded.

'What about the husband?' Nelson asked.

'Ainsley was moving his stuff into his new flat. A Dr Rutherford was with him until nearly midnight, and the neighbours went up to complain at about one o'clock, when he was still moving furniture around.'

Jane Brinckley appeared and Hackett excused himself.

'Paula Jimson,' she said, coming straight to the point. 'What d'you want me to do about it?'

Hackett glanced at his watch. 'Can you administer a preliminary bollocking? The DI will want to speak to her when he's got a bit more time.'

'What about the Super?'

'See what Jack has to say first – no need to go bothering the Super just yet.'

Jane Brinckley relaxed visibly. 'Thanks, Terry.'

'It's like my daughter says – you can't have one rule for the lads and another for the lasses.'

'Where's Smolder now?' Nelson asked, on his return.

'At home, I should think.'

'Well, I hate to drag him from the warmth of his fireside on a night like this, but I'm sure he won't mind assisting us in our inquiries.'

Smolder did mind. He minded a great deal. So much, in fact, that he insisted on having his solicitor at the interview.

Nelson, playing up the emphasis on correct procedure, was assiduous in his identification for the tape of those present. They were: Dr Isaac Smolder; his solicitor, Mr Julian Farrell, of Midhurst, Farrell and Binks, Detective Inspector Nelson and Detective Sergeant Hackett.

'Now, can you explain what you were doing at Dr Wilkinson's house yesterday evening, sir?'

'No.' Smolder folded his hands in front of him, on the desk and gazed levelly at Nelson.

Nelson's eyes sparked. 'No?'

'No,' repeated Smolder. 'I *cannot*, since I was not there.'

'Sure of that, are you?' Nelson growled.

Smolder's solicitor, a small, balding man in a brown suit, tan shirt and brown woollen tie, leaned forward. 'My client has answered your question unequivocally, Inspector Nelson. Now, may we move on?'

Nelson smiled. He was enjoying this. He leaned back in his chair and casually assessed Smolder's appearance. Fussy-looking. A bit overdone with the yellow bow tie and matching silk hankie. A bit yellow round the irises an' all – still, we all enjoy a tipple once in a while, he conceded with a magnanimity born of recent suffering. Hackett, in his clear, factual presentation, had observed that Dr Wilkinson had shivered when she'd realized Smolder had been sat outside her house. Nelson saw nothing disgusting in the man. But then, he thought, You're not a woman, are you, Jack? His attention was drawn to the long, bony fingers of the academic. Something prissy, too particular in the way he neatly laced the fingers together, something creepy about the carefully manicured nails? He hardly knew what it was a woman looked for in a man, these days, it'd been so long since he'd taken an interest.

'I repeated the question to give Dr Smolder a chance to

correct himself,' he said, having finished his leisurely scrutiny of the man.

'I do not need to correct myself. I was not outside Dr Wilkinson's house.'

'You were seen,' Nelson purred, in confidential tone.

Smolder straightened up – a slight movement, checked part way. 'By whom?'

Nelson did not answer at first, but stared into Smolder's eyes. He saw something flutter there – guilt or fear. He raised one hand without looking away, and Hackett handed him the photograph of Ellis arriving at the house. Nelson identified the photograph for the tape with greater ostentation than was strictly necessary.

'This is your car, sir. The registration number is quite clear, as you can see. Parked outside Dr Wilkinson's house, last night.' He saw the faintest flush of colour in the stretched skin over Smolder's cheekbones. 'What were you doing there?'

For a moment, he thought Smolder would not respond, then, in a thin, dry voice, he began: 'I was concerned for Helen. I called to see how she was.'

'At the front door, then, were you? The car's empty,' he added as an aside to the solicitor, who was ill-placed to see the picture. 'Only it seems odd that Mr Ellis here – who, you have to admit, looks more than a bit shifty – would check the street and then nip round the back if you were stood on the doorstep in broad daylight.' Actually, it was twilight, but Nelson felt justified in stretching the point.

The patches of colour on Smolder's cheeks grew, so that he looked like an ageing thespian wearing too much rouge. 'I don't believe it's a crime to visit a bereaved colleague,' he said.

'No,' Nelson agreed, raising his eyebrows in a fair enough gesture. 'No, *that's* not a crime. But let me put this into perspective for you, Dr Smolder. Hours after this photograph was taken we had two serious incidents: John Ellis, found dead of a drugs overdose, and the lad who took this picture left for dead after a nasty attack,' he said, deliberately reversing the sequence of events. 'Now *that* puts you squarely in the frame.'

There was a rustle of concern from Smolder's solicitor, but Smolder waved one long-fingered hand to silence him.

'I – wasn't at the front door. I saw Helen leave earlier and tried to follow her – just to ensure that she was quite safe,' he added hastily. 'But she evidently did not want anyone to follow her, and I'm afraid she lost me. I returned to the house. I don't know what I intended to do – I suppose I was curious. I went down the side passage and tried the gate. It was secure. I was about to leave when I heard that wretched boy Ellis. I didn't know it was him, but I'd heard footsteps. I tried the gate of the adjacent house. It was unlocked. I hid in there for a few minutes and then the damned photographer arrived. He climbed over the gate – I was sure he would see me, but he was looking the other way. I waited a few minutes more. Then I left. I went home, had a large brandy and early night. That, gentlemen, is the truth.'

Chapter Twenty-Four

'You were rude to Sergeant Hackett,' Ruth said, smiling.

'I had good reason.'

Helen and Ruth sat next to each other on the garden bench. Helen could not stand the proximity of the knife any longer and had escaped into the garden as soon as the police had left. She did not know how to tell Ruth about the knife, and the difficulty had made her uncommunicative.

'Personally, I find it more satisfying to be rude without good reason.'

'Yes,' Helen said, distractedly, looking up, away from the house, at the neighbouring properties, where she imagined uncomplicated, tranquil lives were being conducted in placid, unvarying rhythms. The evening was still and cold. Iron-grey clouds clustered in the west and the remaining light gleamed dull and flat on the slate roofs.

'What are you thinking about?' Ruth demanded.

'Ellis and that poor boy – the photographer. He didn't deserve this. Neither of them did.'

'Who's to say what we deserve? And when did people ever get what they deserve?' She saw a shadow flit across Helen's face. 'You're thinking Edward did, am I right?'

'I was thinking about my brother, Robbie. And the bastard who sold him the E's.'

Ruth inhaled. Nodded. 'I must remember not to make assumptions about you any more. Who'd've thought that little Helen was such a dark horse?'

'It's not something you go shouting about. And please don't patronize me.'

Ruth pulled a face. 'Sorry.'

There was a silence which Ruth broke. 'People don't get what they deserve unless someone takes it upon themselves to make sure they do.'

'Well,' Helen said. 'I failed pretty miserably on that score.'

'The pusher? You tried, that's the main thing.'

Helen's eyes raked her friend's face. 'I'm not proud of it, Ruth.'

'But you don't regret it, either – the trying, I mean. You took your destiny into your own hands, meted out justice where the legal system failed.'

Helen's pulse quickened. 'Are you saying that's what happened to Edward? That he *deserved* to die?'

'He certainly didn't deserve to flourish.'

'I wish I had your conviction, your single-minded sense of purpose,' Helen said bitterly.

Ruth laughed. 'But you do! How else d'you think you've survived all of this? Edward, his petty cruelty, the miscarriage, the death of your brother, the indifference of your parents, and still managed to make your mark in this male-dominated arsehole of academe?'

'I put up with Edward's infidelity. I accepted his constant criticisms.'

'You wouldn't have for much longer. You'd been fantasizing about doing him in for months. It was only a matter of time.'

'I couldn't have killed him – at least I hope not. I might've left him.'

'Don't be so bloody wet, Helen! Left him! After what he did to you?'

'You meant it, didn't you?' Helen said, shivering in the cold, but unwilling to return to the house. 'When you said someone had done me a favour, getting rid of him. Do you really think the only fitting punishment for Edward was death?'

'Eye for an eye, life for a life. I can't help it, Helen, it's my Jewish upbringing.' Helen thought she was serious, at least in part. 'You should have some sympathy with that, being a good Catholic girl.'

Helen looked into Ruth's eyes and saw, for the first time in the blue irises, several shades lighter than her own, a cold, uncompromising venom. 'I'm an atheist,' she said, a little breathlessly. 'And anyway, Catholic teaching comes from the New Testament.'

'Turn the other cheek, all that bullshit? Spare me!' Ruth exclaimed. 'Accept that dishwater doctrine and you may as well go round with a "kick me" sign on your backside. That's your trouble, Helen. If a task is too unpalatable, you can't see it through to the end; it's a weakness that diseases every aspect of your life. Take your research – too bloody for you?' Her voice took on a whimpering, high-pitched, childish quaver. 'Let's use something innocuous and inoffensive, like nice, pale pink, agar jelly. What was it with the pusher? Did you feel sorry for him at the last moment? His poor upbringing, his lack of a good male role model? Did you ease off the accelerator a millisecond before impact? Too much *blood*, Helen? Edward did everything in his power to destroy you – your confidence, your reputation, your academic standing within the department, even your identity as a woman – and yet you couldn't find it in you to do something about it.'

Helen's heartbeat matched the noise in her head, imagined, yet real, the constant, insistent rhythm of Acid House music, the record that had been playing when she had heard the first screams and had run to find Robbie squirming on the floor, grotesque, his head swollen, his face distorted with pain and retained fluid. 120 beats per minute, the heartbeat of an infant.

'Come into the kitchen,' Helen said. 'I want to show you something.'

'You might be interested in this, sir.' DC Tact had interrupted the continuing discussion between Hackett and Nelson.

'Well, will I or won't I? Don't ponce about, lad.'

'Not for me to say, sir.'

Nelson sighed, heavily. Tact was another in the mould of Hackett. Said what he thought and remained impervious to criticism. He'd that dreamy, abstracted look on his face that said he'd been pratting about with computers. 'All right,' he said. 'Let's have it.'

'Best if I demonstrate.'

Nelson set his jaw and took a few deep breaths before slouching through to the main office with his hands in his pockets. Bits of cannibalized computer hardware had been tucked against the wall behind his desk, among the detritus Nelson recognized the dented outer casing of Molyneux's PC.

'There was a lot of damage,' Tact explained, his voice taking on an authoritative air that only ever seemed to surface when he was talking about computers. 'Blown chips, mostly. But the hard drive was intact, apart from a few damaged sectors. I've fitted it into a similar PC, so we can run the programs and data stored on it.' His eyes were fixed on the monitor. 'Actually, it was a good idea of yours, sir, to check it over.'

'We aim to please,' Nelson replied, heavy on the sarcasm.

Tact did not notice. 'I'm going into the folder where Molyneux stored the images of Ellis before transmitting them. As you can see, there's four images stored. The first two are of Ellis – I've checked them. But this one—' There was a delay, while the computer loaded the file. A blurred image, shadowy behind the window of Helen's study. 'I think he was working on it, trying to enhance the focus before downloading it to the *Recorder*.'

'Not much help, is it, bar the fact you can see it's a woman.'

'The next image,' Tact said, clicking on icons and waiting while the drive loaded the second file, 'is much clearer.'

'Oh aye,' Nelson said, taking his hands from his pockets and moving closer to the screen. 'You can see who that is, all right.'

'How does it feel to be a fugitive from justice, Helen?'

The two women sat at opposite sides of the kitchen table. Between them lay the tarnished knife, still wrapped in its plastic food bag. Helen was shivering more violently, but it wasn't from cold.

'You should know.'

'Fugitive implies on the run. I'm not running. What are you going to do about this? The police will be back soon, with their warrant.' She touched the corner of the bag, then withdrew her hand.

'I intend to give it to them.' Then: 'Someone killed Edward and kept the knife. I can't imagine why anyone would do that. A woman might kill out of jealousy, or because Edward was blackmailing her – there wasn't much Edward wouldn't do; a man, well, I suppose jealousy might be a motive there, too, but from a different viewpoint. Almost anyone in the various departments he had in a stranglehold might have killed him in a rage against his vicious treatment of them during the interviews.'

'So, you do understand.'

'I can understand the *motivation*, but not the hoarding of the knife, and I can't imagine what I did that so pissed them off that they planted the knife here, in my home.'

'Clara must be feeling fairly bruised. She's lost Ed and her husband,' Ruth suggested. 'She might blame you.'

'She may have a key, I suppose. Whoever it was had a key – there was no sign of break-in. But why would Clara blame me? And anyway, would she risk leaving the baby to come here and leave the knife, just to give me a scare?'

'Don't judge everyone by your own standards.'

Helen stared at Ruth. Her eyes seemed cold, wintry, bleak. 'That is a mistake I make, isn't it? For instance, when you concocted that story for the police about you and me being together most of the afternoon the day Edward was murdered. Were you my alibi, or was I yours?'

Ruth was astonished. 'Come on, Helen, there was a whole hour between 3 p.m., when we said we split up, and the time you got home. What advantage could that give me?'

Helen wasn't ready to discuss that as yet. She said: 'He *was* seeing someone else.'

'Clara. You knew that.'

'No. I mean other than Clara. I always knew when he'd found someone else, started a new affair. He was livelier. Jaunty. Never so alive as when he had a new lover.'

'Who do you think that was?' Ruth asked.

'I was hoping you'd tell me. You seem to know so much about everyone. We all confided in Ruth, didn't we? Reliable Ruth. Rational Ruth. Ruthless Ruth?'

'Nice alliteration,' Ruth smiled, uneasily.

'Did you want them to find it, Ruth? Did you want the police to arrest me? Why? I don't *understand*.'

'That makes two of us.' Ruth laughed. 'Look, why don't I pour us a drink and let's both calm down.'

'Sit down.' Helen picked up the knife and Ruth collapsed into her chair. 'The police knew he'd had sex before he was murdered – there's forensic evidence. Edward had a lot of failings, and believe me, I knew them all, but he wasn't a five-minute man. So, let's say, twenty minutes to get from the university to my house, time for a little foreplay, sex and murder, then enough leeway – another twenty minutes – for you to get back to your office – doesn't seem feasible.'

'You're bloody right it doesn't seem feasible—'

'Stop it, Ruth!' Helen begged. 'Please stop! Were you counting on the police thinking the same thing? That Edward's murder had been carefully planned and carried out – that it was unhurried, a precision job? With the alibi I gave you, how could they possibly suspect you?'

Ruth spread her hands. 'I really don't know what the hell you're talking about.'

'You put the knife in the cupboard upstairs. What was it? Some kind of game? You always did like your games, Ruth, didn't you?' She stopped, amazed she hadn't seen it before. 'You and Edward were so alike. Both supremely arrogant. Both feeding off control. Is that why you started seeing him? Because you had so much in common?'

'You bloody bitch! You've no idea, have you?'

'I know you had an affair with my husband while professing to loathe him, and all the while you let me believe that you were my friend.'

'Believe it,' Ruth said.

'I want an explanation—'

Ruth laughed, gently mocking, not without affection. 'I'm surprised you need one. And I'm not sure you deserve one. But for old time's sake . . . And do us both a favour – put down the knife. You know you're not going to use it.'

A few moments before, Helen had not been sure, but now she knew: she could not harm Ruth, no matter what she had done. She eased the knife on to the table. Ruth stared at it for some time.

'I did what you wanted, but couldn't do,' Ruth said.

'What?'

'You came up with the idea yourself. The fantasies. Killing him in bed, where he was at his most vulnerable, where he would least expect to be attacked. All I did was to act it out for you. It was the easiest thing in the world, persuading Edward I was infatuated with him. Narcissistic bastard! We had arranged to meet after he'd had a whole morning of humiliating his colleagues. He was horny as hell.' She smiled at Helen's revulsion. 'Yes I screwed him first. Just the once, to see what it was like. In a way, that's what all of this was about. Seeing what it was like. First encounters. New experiences. And, of course I knew I'd be helping you out.'

'I didn't ask for your help,' Helen said.

'Didn't you? Crossed wires, I suppose. Scrambled signals, but I took you at your word when you said you'd like to see the bastard dead.'

'I never saw you as an altruist.'

'You know, Nelson said almost the same thing, only he didn't use that particular word.'

'You underestimate people, Ruth.' There was open hostility between them now.

Ruth shook her head, her mouth curved down. 'Nah. I know, for instance that you won't turn me in. You see, you really did want him dead. You hated Edward, and I haven't heard you lamenting his passing – no one has. Also, you tried to kill someone before – and failed, admittedly, but the will was there. You understand it, Helen. Tell me you didn't enjoy the rush it gave you, seeing the look on his face.' She smiled. 'You can't, can you?'

'But I've disappointed you, haven't I, Ruth? What was it? The fact that I stopped acting like "poor little Helen", and started taking my own decisions? Did you disapprove of my independence? Or was it the loss of control that infuriated you? I wasn't following the sub-routines you'd carefully tapped into my programming – you'll have to get to grips with that little problem, Ruth. Neural Networks are *supposed* to develop minds of their own.'

Ruth felt a flare of heat on her face and for one brief fraction of time she was a scabby-kneed child, crouched in the hot dirt on a spring day, screaming at a beetle, wanting to make it notice her, finally *making* it take notice. Simultaneously, she felt the blade of the knife slip between Edward's ribs, as easily as the blackthorn into the thorax of the beetle.

'What is it?' Helen whispered, frightened by the expression on Ruth's face.

'Just reminiscing,' Ruth said.

'We *could* move in with the warrant and search the place,' Hackett suggested.

'And warn the other one we're on to her.' Nelson unwrapped the egg sandwich he had bought on the way to Helen Wilkinson's house. He'd parked with deliberate obtrusiveness directly outside her front gate.

'We both know it's got to be Ruth,' Hackett said. 'The picture's clear enough. Her going into the house shortly after Ellis left.'

'She's a friend of Helen's. She pops in and out all the time. Unless we can get confirmation from Molyneux that it was her who hit him over the head, we can't arrest her. Look, Hackett, I'm on your side. *We* know Ruth's done it, but what have we got? Bugger all's what we've got.'

Hackett muttered something about wasting their time freezing their arses outside an innocent woman's house.

'Tetchy today, aren't we?' Nelson said. He was feeling the kind of euphoria only experienced after the remission of a near-fatal hangover. 'Missed our beauty sleep, have we?' He sank his teeth into the egg sandwich, thinking with perverse satisfaction of the unsettling effect eggs invariably had on his digestion. 'Here.' He thrust a copy of the *Chester Recorder* in Hackett's lap. 'Have a squint at that, it'll take your mind off, make time pass.'

Hackett opened the paper. The front page headline read:

DON JUAN WIFE IN NEW ATTACK PUZZLE

Below it, a picture of Helen Wilkinson gazing up at the house. Next to it, a column on Dermot Molyneux – *Ace photographer* . . . 'Bloody hell,' Hackett grumbled. ' "Ace photographer." They're not serious, are they?' *Brought you the news as it happened* . . . He skimmed the rest. *Condition described as critical* . . . And a photograph. The tousled hair and disarming grin.

Beneath that, a shorter piece on John Ellis:

SECOND TRAGEDY STRIKES
JINXED COLLEGE

Hackett tilted the paper at Nelson. 'Yeah, really takes your mind off.'

Nelson found himself staring into the face of his son. He blinked, swallowed painfully, and the picture resolved into a bad passport photograph of Ellis. Hackett went back to reading the paper.

Nelson, who had never confided in a colleague, nor anyone else, as far as he could recall, since Beth had died, now felt the need to talk.

'You're a family man, aren't you?' he asked. Had he sensed a shift in attentiveness, had Hackett given him one of his cat's eye once-overs, Nelson would have clammed up immediately, but he didn't.

'Teenage kids don't constitute a family,' Hackett said. 'They constitute trouble.' He had spoken briefly with Sheila by telephone, to explain the situation. Daniel was not to leave the house. The rest would have to wait until later.

Nelson glanced across.

'Don't ask. You don't want to know.'

Nelson thought perhaps he did, which surprised him: he wasn't generally interested in the personal lives of his officers. He even thought he might understand. Of course, the boy's psychiatrist wouldn't agree: Dr Smith acted like *he* was the one with the problem and not the boy. 'Rejection, isolation, they're very damaging,' Smith had said.

'I told my boy's shrink today that I'd hated my son ever since my wife died.' Had he really said that, and to a shrink?

'Why?'

'Christ knows. I suppose I'm just so bloody knackered I was off my guard.'

'No, I meant, why do you hate him?'

Nelson realized belatedly that this was not something he wanted to discuss in detail. He had expected that he would say what he needed to say to unburden himself and that would be the end of it. He had not been prepared for this interest, even less for direct questions; however, since he had brought the subject up, he felt he had to say something aside from 'mind your own bloody business'.

'The shrink says it wasn't his fault.'

'Your wife's death?'

Nelson felt a shock like a physical blow. *Your wife's death.* Just like that. Out in the open, like any normal topic of conversation. Like: did you watch the match on the telly last night? or I wish this sodding rain'd stop, or how're the kids – and by the way, *how do you feel about your wife's death?*

'Maybe it wasn't his fault,' Hackett said.

'What do you know?' Nelson demanded. Hackett sighed and went back to reading the paper, leaving Nelson to his thoughts.

It was his fault. If he hadn't been born she'd've been fine. She was OK until she had Ian. They had given him his name when Beth was seven months pregnant; they had waited until then because Beth didn't want to invite bad luck. And they had loved him, made plans for him, for the three of them. They had loved and wanted their son until he was born, then, because Beth had rejected him, he found he no longer wanted the child, either.

'Christ!' he muttered. 'This bloody case is starting to get to me.' He threw the remains of the sandwich out of the window and stifled a belch.

Hackett grunted, distracted. He was poring over the article on Helen Wilkinson. 'This picture,' he said. 'Says here Molyneux took it.'

'So?'

'I've seen it somewhere else . . .' He thought back to the places he had been over the last ten days: Mallory's office, of course; the Wilkinsons' house; Professor Wilkinson's room at St Werburgh's – too neat – somewhere messy, somewhere cluttered, haphazard . . . Ellis's flat, mouldy dishes, unfinished work; his son's bedroom, sweet with the smell of marijuana. *No one calls it that any more, Dad!* Skim over that – no – backtrack – 'Ganjaaa!' He purred, affecting a West Indian accent.

'What?' Nelson, always on a short fuse, was experiencing the stirrings of irritation.

'There was a similar photo – not the same but very like. A different angle, I think. Softer focus. Not so much of the house showing in the background. It was in Ruth Marks's flat.'

Nelson frowned, running it through in his mind. Cluttered coffee table, steel shelves, coffee brewing to mask the smell of cannabis. Microscope on the table in the turret, mantelshelf a jumble of dusty postcards, wooden monkeys: *see no evil, hear no evil, speak no evil.* Behind them a photograph of Helen Wilkinson.

He shook his head, doubtful. 'Could be a copy from the *Recorder* photo. She could've ordered one.'

'Different picture. I'd swear to it. I think our Dr Marks likes to take mementoes. And if we can prove she got it from Molyneux's flat . . .'

'You know what it feels like to have that kind of power over someone else, Helen? The power to grant life or take it? It's godlike.' She closed her eyes and relived the moment: she had slipped downstairs in Helen's dressing gown, to fetch Ed a drink, and had returned with a tall glass of icy beer in one hand and the knife in the other.

'What have you got behind your back?'
'A surprise. Do you want it?'
'That depends. Will I like it?'
'You may not like it, but it's just what you need. And I promise you, I'll be quick.'

'And to get away with it. To watch the police chasing in little circles – even asking advice of the murderer! I tell you, Helen, it feels like I've fallen from a great height without so much as a bruise.'

'Is it some kind of revenge? Were you repaying the patronizing and the personal humiliations of a lifetime by killing the greatest chauvinist of all?'

'Spare me the psychobabble! I could have walked away, only I felt the need to help you out of the hole you'd dug for yourself.'

'And you wanted to see if you could do it.'

Ruth shrugged, a secret smile, a barely visible raising of her eyebrows.

'They were your keys, weren't they?' Helen said. 'How else could Ellis have got into the house?'

'Interesting choice, wasn't it – the mouse, I mean. "The mouse that roared", and all that. I gave him his chance to make his point to you – he bottled out of that, too.'

'He didn't *bottle out*, Ruth, he killed himself.' Helen was shouting. 'Don't you care? Doesn't it matter at all to you?'

Ruth sighed. 'It's not my job to care about every inadequate who takes on more than he can handle. I warned him he was pissing in the wind with his ludicrous research into Gaia. That's more than Mallory did for him' – she shot Helen a vicious look – 'or you, for that matter. You were wallowing so deep in self-pity over the miscarriage, it's a wonder you didn't drown in it.'

Helen nodded. 'I was too engrossed in my own misery to see Ellis's, but what's your excuse?'

'Marriage/miscarriage. I wonder if poets ever make use of that rhyme?' Ruth snapped to, sitting up and rapping the table with her knuckles. 'I don't need an excuse. I'm not sorry for anything, or ashamed of anything.'

'So is that really all this was?' Helen asked. 'An interesting experiment?'

'It was certainly that.'

'And what *did* I do that made you turn against me?'

Ruth smiled, but refused to answer.

'Is it Mick? Are you jealous of him?'

'Jealous? You replaced an emotional with a physical cripple,' Ruth said. 'I might feel nauseated, but jealous?'

'You know they'll find you,' Helen said. 'The police aren't stupid, Ruth.'

'Perhaps not, but they don't have any evidence, either. Here, look at this.' Ruth dipped into her jeans pocket and took out two fifty pence coins. She slapped them on to the table and looked up at Helen, triumphant. 'I've been walking around with those in my pocket ever since it happened.'

Helen glanced at the coins. 'You'll have to explain.'

Ruth picked up one coin between the thumb and forefinger of her right hand, the other in her left. She closed her eyes and carefully placed a coin on each eyelid. 'You did say his eyes had to be closed.'

'Christ, Ruth, you're sick.'

Ruth tipped forward, catching the coins in the palm of her hand.

'My only sickness was allowing your pitiful defencelessness to affect me, letting myself be taken in by you.'

'I wasn't trying to fool anyone, Ruth. I was being what I am: human. I'm sorry if you thought my vulnerability was all of me. That was how I felt at the time. I was being honest with you.'

'Well, then, you're best off without Ed, and I did the right thing.'

'Don't you regret the photographer? And John Ellis?' Helen asked, desperate to find some remnant of humanity in her old friend.

'Ellis would've been turned in by Ed, if he'd lived. Or he'd've pointed the great fat finger of accusation at himself with his flimsy data and his botched results. No. I don't feel sorry for him.'

'And the photographer – what about him?'

'I hadn't reckoned on the photographer. I don't even know him. Not really. Bit of a flirt, a ladies' man, no doubt, but that's hardly a capital offence. The problem is, when you act on someone else's behalf, there are complications. You have to look out for more than just yourself, and when you're looking out for someone else, sometimes things get by you. Like a photographer with a camera pointed right at you.'

Helen felt suddenly cold. 'What did he see?'

'Me at the window, I'd just put the knife in the bedside cabinet. Of course, he didn't have a shot of that, but he had me, on camera, where I wasn't supposed to be, at about the time a rather unpleasant package had been left in your fridge. If those pictures had been printed, you would have guessed—'

'I guessed anyway.'

Ruth smiled. 'Yes, you did, didn't you? But the problem was, with the photographic evidence, the police might have guessed, too.'

'So you tried to kill him.'

'Molyneux took a chance. People in his profession measure risks and weigh them against the potential glory. If he'd pulled it off and got that crisp, clear picture of me, then I'd be the one in deep shit, and he'd be in clover.'

'It *must've* been taken at the same time as this one,' Hackett said, holding the newspaper next to the photograph on the mantelshelf in Ruth's flat.

'You could well be right,' Nelson agreed, peering at it. He glanced over his shoulder, giving the SOCO the signal to get started.

'Is it enough?' Hackett asked.

'The *Recorder* haven't had any requests for that particular photograph from the public,' Nelson said. 'Where else would she get it, but from Molyneux's flat?'

'If we had the knife—'

'We'll search for it here, but I can't see her keeping it. She'd have chucked it by now, wouldn't she?'

Hackett shrugged. 'What about the forensic evidence from the bed? Could we do a match on the pubic hairs?' Hackett addressed this question to the SOCO who had just finished photographing the picture of Helen *in situ*, and was now lifting it with great care, into a sealable plastic bag, which he had already numbered and dated.

'Get us something to match them with—' he said.

'That's just what we're about to do,' Nelson said, grinning.

'You're already up to your neck,' Helen said. 'I know. Everything. I even know why, God help me.'

'You're my friend. Friends look after each other.' The bell rang out and Ruth twitched. 'Hackett, with his warrant to search. What are they going to make of all this?' she asked, indicating the knife and the coins, lying on the table.

Helen stared hard at her. 'My prints are on the knife. I expect yours are not. I don't suppose the coins can be traced back to you, or to Edward's body—' Helen stopped. At last she had got a reaction, but she didn't know why.

Ruth was thinking of the touching picture of Helen, very like the *House of Death* photograph in the paper, but by some trick Molyneux had harnessed compassion; there was a softness in the shadows, a kindness in the light – it seemed to understand her sadness. It must have affected Dermot, too, for he kept it, tacked up on his wall. 'I had to have it,' she said, closing her eyes against the dazzling stupidity of her actions. 'Another memento, another trophy in the game.

'However,' she said, brightening, ignoring Helen's confusion, 'when you analyse it, what exactly have the police got? A knife with Edward's blood and *your* fingerprints on it. A photographer with a fractured skull. His word would add weight to the argument if (if! Makes me breathless just thinking about it) he recovers. His fingerprints and mine on the portrait of you. Only Dermot knows I left him for dead. *Where there's life there's hope*, my mother used to say. Where there's life there's uncertainty, more like.'

'I know,' Helen repeated quietly, ignoring the continuous

ringing of the bell. 'I know you hit that poor man over the head and left him for dead.'

'Self-preservation, Helen.'

'I don't know if I'd've protected you if it was just Edward in the case; I think maybe I would. But there is Ellis's suicide. And, as I said before, Molyneux really didn't deserve this.'

Helen stared into Ruth's eyes, wondering if she had ever really known her, and Ruth stared back, wondering how she could have so misjudged the situation. The doorbell kept up its persistent ringing, an alarm, a warning of imminent disaster; footsteps could be heard in the passage to the side of the house. Between them, a knife, two coins and a chasm of difference.

Ruth reached and picked up the knife. Helen stood. Ruth was speaking, but all she could hear was the clatter of her chair as it fell and the sound of footsteps, rattling like stones in the side passage of the house. She backed into the hallway.

'You have been acting strangely,' Ruth said. 'You never really got over the miscarriage. But I couldn't believe it when you pulled the knife on me. I almost fainted with fright.'

Helen fumbled with the front door latch.

'It's on the mortise,' Ruth said. 'Of course I tried to get out, but you had locked the doors. I was terrified—'

Helen looked around, desperately trying to find some weapon, some route of escape.

'You came at me and I tried to grab the knife.' Ruth grasped the blade of the knife with her left hand and then pulled back with her right. She shuddered slightly, but did not take her eyes from Helen.

Helen watched, horrified, as fresh blood mingled with the old – with Edward's – on the blade. Blood dripped with the regular ticking sound of a clock on to the faded strip of carpet in the hall. Ruth paled and put her right hand against the wall to steady herself. The hammering at the back door grew louder, and Ruth turned slightly, distracted by the noise, and by the pain in her left hand.

Helen grabbed a walking stick from the stand next to the front door and swung it at Ruth, but Ruth ducked in time. Helen ran to the stairs, just a few steps, but she was weak, and she stumbled. Ruth caught her by the ankle, and she felt the blade of the knife graze her shin. She screamed, kicking, and made contact, heard Ruth's grunt of pain, did not stop to look, but carried on upstairs on her hands and knees.

She heard the crash of glass, followed by urgent shouts as Hackett ran into the kitchen. She collapsed on the top step, fear, exhaustion and lack of food finally depriving her of what little strength remained.

'Oh, my God,' she whispered.

Ruth lay on her back, her hands making small, involuntary movements, her mouth working soundlessly. The blade had glanced off her larynx and found the soft tissue between the rings of cartilage of the trachea. It was embedded up to the hilt, lodged between the third and fourth cervical vertebrae, and with each convulsive movement, it produced further damage to her spinal cord.

Helen screamed.

Ruth felt the flare of heat on her face once more: spring sunshine melting the dusty tarmac of the pot-holed road near her childhood home. She had made the beetle notice. She must have: she could hear its screams – not in her imagination – these were real, high-pitched screams, like a woman's. Simultaneously, she felt the blade of the knife slip sideways, and the screaming stopped. Everything stopped. And there was only silence.

Past Reason

by Margaret Murphy

Available in Macmillan hardback priced £16.99.

The opening scenes follow here.

Prologue

The boy stood uncertainly next to the car. He sucked in his lower lip – a habit only recently acquired – and chewed on it.

Never get into a strange car. How many times had he been told? At home, at school, at Beavers, and more recently at Cubs.

'Come *on*, for heaven's sake!'

But it wasn't like he was getting into a stranger's car. He wasn't daft.

'I can't wait all day.'

The boy darted a look over his shoulder, unconsciously twisting one foot behind the other.

'I'm getting cross now . . .'

He didn't like to be naughty, but if he *didn't* get in the car he was being disobedient, and if he *did*—

'Stop pratting about and get in!'

The boy jumped, nearly fell over, just disentangling one leg from the other in time to save himself. 'Mummy said—' he ventured.

'Mummy said. Mummy said. Where's Mummy now?'

The boy frowned. He loved his mummy, and he wanted Mummy to love him, but she shouted at him all the time and made fun of him when he cried. He looked back towards the house again, hoping she would magically appear and take the decision out of his hands, but she didn't come. She never did.

'Come *on*! . . . Look, if you're so worried, we'll telephone your mother from— We'll telephone your mother later, so she doesn't worry. All right?'

The boy edged forward, scraping the toes of his shoes on the gravel.

The kitchen was pristine; its surfaces wiped and disinfected and its stainless steel buffed to a dull gleam. A tap dripped with measured solemnity into a solitary cup, steadily filling with water. A bumble bee passed through the open door, explored with absent-minded disinterest, butting into the glass fronts of the display cupboards, moving on to the brightly coloured picture tiles dotted about the walls, and bumbling out the way it came, ignoring the still form of a woman lying on the floor.

For a while – perhaps an hour – after she had first fallen, bleeding, to the floor, she had heard the tick-tick-tick of the tap, and had mistaken it for her own blood pulsing in her throat, pooling on the floor beneath her. As the dripping of the tap slowed, she had felt her pulse diminish and falter, fluttering as if her heart had forgotten the rhythm, but she could not find the strength to save herself: she had used it all in saving him.

A sudden rapid, shallow clamour of systolic contractions, quickening as if to finish the job, to end her suffering. It ceased. The pool around her head and neck stopped growing and began to congeal, and the tick-tick of dripping of water gradually changed tone, becoming a deeper, viscous splosh.

Chapter One

They ran, laughing like lunatics, screaming through the night, their shoes echoing in the empty streets like the clamouring footsteps of killers in a 1940s film. A few muffled barks went up – half-hearted yelps mostly – the dogs' fury tempered by the physical barriers of locked doors and high garden walls of the wealthy.

Lobo saw a light go on and yelled up at the window, 'What're you lookin' at, nosy 'ole?'

Lee-Anne grabbed his arm, still laughing, gasping for air. 'You'll get us done, you mad-arsed bastard!' She bent, both hands on her knees, trying to catch her breath. Which gave Lobo an idea.

He pulled at his trouser belt and dropped his pants, mooning at the alarmed house owner.

They ran all the way down to Aigburth Road and flagged a taxi. Fell into it, still giggling.

'I couldn't believe it when you dropped your kecks! I thought the old biddy'd have a heart attack!'

'Give her somethin' to look at, didn't I? Nosy fucking bitch!'

Lee-Anne hiccuped. 'God, Lobo, I think I'm gonna spew.'

''Ey! 'ey!' The taxi driver had been watching them in his lower mirror, but hadn't yet spoken. 'Don't go pukin' in my cab.'

'Why?' Lobo said. 'Isn't her puke good enough for yer?' He'd seen that on Harry Enfield – *The Scousers*. He was boss, him.

Lee-Anne made retching sounds and the driver went "Ey, 'ey,' again.

They imitated him, then cracked up. It was ace how they had the same sense of humour.

Lee-Anne looked up, tears running down her face with laughing. 'Don't worry, mate,' she said. 'I'm not gonna spew any more. I think I'm gonna piss meself instead!'

Pure comic genius, that. She should be on the telly, Lobo thought. Suddenly, he wanted her. "Ey, come on, mate,' he said. 'Stop arsin' about. We want to get 'ome tonight, you know.'

'It might help if you told me where you wanna go,' the driver said.

Lobo gave an address a quarter of a mile from their flat and fumbled at the door of someone else's house until the cab driver disappeared – they didn't want the police tracing them to the right place, did they? And Lobo was easily remembered: dark, almost black, hair that spiked aggressively, uncontrollably in all directions from his scalp, a wide, red mouth and a mad-eyed stare that he had been working on since his school days. Lee-Anne was small, red-haired – hard-looking, but still easy on the eye. Put the two of them together and people were bound to recall the mad, bad lad and the skinny girl.

As the taxi clattered around the corner, Lobo stuck his hands in his pockets and started the trudge home, then stopped when he realized Lee-Anne wasn't following. She was leaning on the wall of the house the taxi had dropped them at.

'I really am gonna spew,' she said, miserably.

She did look green. Lobo tugged at her shirt, and glanced over his shoulder. 'Come on,' he said. 'It's done now.'

'The state of her, Lobo. You should've never took me there.

I wish we never – I never wanna see nothin' like that again. Never.' Instead of throwing up, she surprised him by bursting into tears.

'Come 'ead,' he said. 'We'll go the cash till. See if any of them numbers work. That'll cheer you up.'

She kept on bawling and he started getting rattled: anyone who saw her like that would make connections when they saw it on the news. He could see that talking would do no good, so he grabbed her by the scruff of the neck and dragged her down the street, crying. The barking in this part of town had a sharper edge, like the dogs really could get out of their backyards, given a plank of rotten timber and a bit of luck, and this gave Lobo an acid tingle of excitement in the pit of his stomach.

MARGARET MURPHY

Goodnight, My Angel

Pan Books   £5.99

'Kate felt a chill creep over her. It's not Melanie, she told herself. This isn't my child. It's just some kind of sadistic game . . .'

Kate Pearson is just coming to terms with the unsolved murder of her daughter Melanie when a sinister message appears on her computer screen:

WHY DID YOU LET HIM HURT ME, MUMMY?

As the messages escalate in number and menace Kate realizes there is only one person who could be doing this to her – Melanie's murderer. He is intent on destroying her completely.

But Kate has already lost the one thing that gave her life meaning. So instead she will turn his evil back on itself and unmask the killer . . .

MARGARET MURPHY

The Desire of the Moth

Pan Books £5.99

'Ann had known him immediately. Even in the dark. Even with the ski mask covering his face. More importantly, she had known why.'

Dorothy Hardy and Ann Lee have two things in common. Both are social workers with connections to the scandal-hit Calderbank children's home. And both have been abducted . . .

But there is another link between the two women – their former colleague Dr Christine Radcliffe, a sophisticated, self-possessed consultant psychologist. Detective Chief Inspector Alan Jameson, in a race to find the women alive and well, cannot ignore this connection.

Especially when their prime suspect, Philip Greer, is Christine's foster brother.

And when Christine herself is clearly nursing a dark, violent secret from her past . . .